the universes await ...

Discover all of the Balky Point Adventures!

The Universes Inside the Lighthouse
The Secret of the Dark Galaxy Stone
The Planet of the Memory Thieves

the Secret *of the* Dark Galaxy Stone

a Balky Point adventure

Books by Pam Stucky

FICTION

The Balky Point Adventures (Middle Grade/YA sci-fi)
The Universes Inside the Lighthouse
The Secret of the Dark Galaxy Stone
The Planet of the Memory Thieves

Mystery
Death at Glacier Lake
Final Chapter (A Megan Montaigne Mystery)

The Wishing Rock series (contemporary fiction) (novels with recipes)
Letters from Wishing Rock
The Wishing Rock Theory of Life
The Tides of Wishing Rock

NONFICTION

the Pam on the Map travel series
Iceland
Seattle Day Trips
Retrospective: Switzerland
Retrospective: Ireland

From the Wishing Rock Kitchens: Recipes from the Series

www.pamstucky.com
twitter.com/pamstucky
facebook.com/pamstuckyauthor
pinterest.com/pamstucky

The
Secret
of the
Dark Galaxy
Stone

a Balky Point adventure

Pam Stucky

Published in the United States by Wishing Rock Press.

Cover design and artwork by Jim Tierney jimtierneyart.com

ISBN: 1-940800-09-9 (print)
ISBN-13: 978-1-940800-09-7 (print)
eBook ISBN-13: 978-1-940800-10-3
eBook ISBN: 1-940800-10-2

www.wishingrockpress.com

for you, dear reader,
and for all the aliens from outer space secretly living on Earth

perhaps the two groups overlap
everything is possible

"We are made of starstuff."
"We are a way for the cosmos to know itself."

~ Carl Sagan, *Cosmos*

chapter one

"I think Rupert needs a friend." Emma Nelson stared at the two-dimensional life-sized elephant off in the distance, in a space called "the Hub" that stood undefined between "inside" and "outside." Emma picked subconsciously at the edges of a fresh bandage on her left upper arm and tucked her legs underneath her on the lush cushion of the sunshine-yellow chair she was sitting on. "I don't want him to be lonely."

"A friend?" said Eve. Her long blond hair swayed as she sat down on a midnight-blue couch across from Emma. After months apart, they were together again, enjoying a small but comfortable lounge area they'd created earlier that day in the Hub.

The Hub, a place where all the universes converged, was both a part of every universe, and apart from every universe. Inside the Hub, everything was possible—including the ability to create things with the power of one's mind, like a couch, or a two-dimensional elephant.

Eve followed Emma's gaze to study Rupert. "He doesn't seem lonely?" she said, her words more a question than a statement. She settled a plate of carrots into her lap and picked one up. A wide bracelet, set with several small rocks of various types, slipped down her arm as she brought her hand up to her mouth.

"It's hard to say," said Emma, still watching as the paper-thin pachyderm swung his trunk and munched, in his own way, on the tall grass. "I was reading up on elephants last semester. They like company. The girl elephants especially like to be part of a herd. But the boy elephants like to travel alone sometimes. So I'm not sure, since Rupert is a boy. Maybe he likes being alone. Still, I think he needs a friend." She rubbed the area around her bandage again and frowned at the slightly bruised feeling. The scientist who had drawn blood had told her it wouldn't hurt. The scientist had lied.

Emma's twin brother, Charlie, overheard this conversation as he and their friend Ben Stewart joined Emma and Eve in the lounge. Charlie rolled his eyes and punched his sister lightly in the shoulder as he squeezed himself next to her in her chair. "Dork. Point One: Rupert is not a real elephant. Point Two: there's really not room for a herd here, don't you think?"

Emma punched her brother back with slightly more force. Charlie and Ben had gone off to the Hub's new Experimental Building without her, while she was left behind to be tested and prodded. "Dork. Point One: who's to say whether Rupert is 'real' or not? Just because he doesn't fit your definition of 'real' doesn't mean he's not completely and totally real. I mean, he exists, right? That's real. And Point Two: we are in the Hub. The Hub is infinite. By definition, there is plenty of room here for pretty much anything. And in the Hub everything is possible. Therefore, if we want to give Rupert a herd, we can. Hmph." She would forgive her twin soon enough; she always did, and besides, he had meant no harm. Still, she wished they would have waited for her. All those tests had been disconcerting and a bit scary, and had put her on edge.

Ben sat down next to Eve and grabbed a carrot from her plate. "Emma has a point there, Charlie. It's the Hub. We can do pretty much anything. Within reason." He looked at the bandage Emma was still picking at and frowned sympathetically. "More tests today?"

The young girl twisted her neck to peer down at her shoulder. "Yeah. Dr. Waldo wanted blood drawn. He also wanted to know if I just happened to have some blood saved from before I traveled through the universe. Like I keep vials of blood around! What they drew today will just be a control, I guess. Something to compare my future blood to if I ever travel like that again." *Which I sort of hope I don't,* she thought. She glanced at Ben and thought she saw a quick look of concern pass over his face, but when she looked again, it was gone.

Twins Charlie and Emma had returned to Dogwinkle Island for their two-week winter break of their senior year of high school, having spent the previous summer on the island. The previous summer had brought them far more adventure than they'd ever imagined—discovering a portal to other universes just a few miles from their vacation cabin, and subsequently traveling with Eve, who was not from Earth, and Ben, who was, to other planets and universes. Among the many incredible places they'd discovered was this Hub. Dr. Waldo, a man from Eve's planet Lero who led scientific operations in the Hub, had explained to them that anything that was possible anywhere, was also possible in the Hub. With each universe being infinite, and the number of universes being infinite, that meant pretty much everything was possible somewhere. And, by extension, within the Hub, everything was possible.

Their adventures had opened up their minds in more ways than they could have imagined—especially Emma's. The scientists had discovered methods to travel through space and time with the aid of portals such as the one at the island's Balky Point Lighthouse (called "elevators"), or with devices they'd invented. Emma, however, had discovered the ability to travel through space and time using nothing but her own mind and energy.

And it had nearly broken her.

When the summer had ended, the twins had gone back home. Ben, who lived on the island, had stayed on as an apprentice to Dr. Waldo, commuting to the Hub from his home at the south end of the island, in the town of Wishing Rock. Each day he drove up to Balky Point and walked through the lobby of the lighthouse into what looked for all the world like a storage closet, and then walked out the other side … into the Hub.

Since leaving the island, Emma and Charlie had spent most of their time thinking about getting back. They'd given their parents almost no choice but to return for the winter vacation, and had just gotten in the day before. Immediately on Emma's return, she had been scuttled away for testing. MRIs, CAT scans, Emma had no idea what all the tests were. All she knew was that the scientists in the Hub were intensely interested in her ability to transport herself and others anywhere in the universes.

But she just wanted to visit with her friends.

Well, visit with her friends … and explore.

While Emma had been whisked away to be prodded and scanned, Ben had taken Charlie to see the new Experimental Building. Last Emma and Charlie had seen it, the building—and everything else in the Hub—had been completely destroyed by a man who was under the influence of The Void, a dark entity that was spreading throughout the universes. Over the last few months, Dr. Waldo and his colleagues had undertaken the enormous task of recreating the science lab, the housing cabins, the lawn, everything, right down to Dr. Waldo's favorite "elephant in the room," Rupert. Ben, as Dr. Waldo's apprentice, had been allowed to help, and Emma was beyond jealous. To know that Charlie had seen the new Experimental Building before she had—a building where Dr. Waldo played with ideas, creating rooms such as a maze of thought and a garden of secrets—had put her into quite a mood. Ben and Charlie were lucky Eve was there now, to help ease the tension.

Emma bit her tongue and reminded herself it was no one's fault that she and Charlie had been forced to go back to school. They were here now, after all. But come next summer, Emma was determined to return and work at the Hub for good.

"Did Dr. Waldo find anything in all those tests?" Eve asked. Sensing how much it had bothered Emma that Charlie and Ben had gone off without her, Eve had stayed behind. She spent most of her time at the Hub, anyway, and had already seen its marvels. Eve patted her own shoulder in sympathy with Emma's. "Your poor arm."

"No, I don't think so," Emma lied, averting her eyes. "Not yet." She looked across at Ben, who was still chomping away on carrots from Eve's plate, and changed the subject. "So what's it like working here? Do you love it? I'm so jealous." She smiled.

"It's amazing, Em," said Ben, enthusiasm beaming out of him. He spread his arms wide and looked up at the sky. "All of this. I watched them create all of this, just from the power of intention. It's trickier than you'd think. So easy to get it wrong and mess up. Took me a while to figure it out, but I'm starting to get the hang of it. The Experimental Building is great for that. Dr. Waldo gave me a whole wing of the building. It's mine to just try things out and practice and learn. When I'm not inputting data and logging information, that is." He laughed. "It's not all exciting and glamorous. I mean, the creating stuff and the travel to other planets and stuff, that's incredible. But sometimes, it's just computer work."

Emma's heart jumped to her throat. "Travel to other planets? You've done more of that?" she said, trying to sound nonchalant. She finally noticed that Ben was wearing a bracelet that matched Eve's—bracelets that she knew were much more than met the eye. The stones embedded in their bands enabled their wearers to camouflage themselves amongst aliens, breathe in foreign atmospheres, translate other languages, and much more. She subconsciously rubbed her wrist where she, too, once wore a bracelet.

Ben noticed the subtle movement. "I'm sure Dr. Waldo will let you have your bracelet back," he said. "And yeah, just a few planets, mostly to stand there and take down information while the scientists do their work. I'm just an apprentice. But it's been pretty cool." He couldn't help but smile.

"That's awesome, Ben," said Emma. "I mean, I'm totally jealous, but, you know, we had to go to school. So." She turned to Eve. "What about you and your dad? Any luck? Any more clues leading to your mom?"

Eve and her father, Milo, had originally come to Earth with a mission: to find the man who was threatening to destroy the universes, and stop him. With the help of Emma and the others, that task had been completed. However, in the course of events, it came out that they had another goal, as well: to find Eve's mother. She had disappeared without a trace more than a year before. Searching all the ever-expanding universes was an impossible task; still, Eve was determined. After Emma and Charlie returned to school, Eve hadn't taken on a full-time role at the Hub as Ben had; after all, she was a year or two younger. (The difference in their ages was difficult to say, exactly, given the tricky nature of time, and the fact that they were from different planets with different-length years.) But she'd spent plenty of time in the Hub, as well.

Eve sighed heavily. "Not really." She hesitated. "There's one thing, but we can't really figure it out."

Charlie leaned forward. "One thing? What's that? Maybe we can help! We're the smartest people we know!"

Eve laughed. "I'm sure it's nothing," she said, digging through the red-and-yellow-striped oversized bag next to her feet. "She just left us some notes, is all. The weird thing is that it seems like some notes are missing."

"What do you mean?" asked Emma. She squeezed herself out of the chair she was sharing with Charlie and re-situated herself on the arm of the couch, peering over Eve's shoulder.

"Well," said Eve. She pulled some envelopes out of her bag and handed one to Ben and one to Emma. "Look at the top of the notes. Mine says 'Read this second,' and Dad's says 'Read this third.' But we can't find the first note. And that's got to be the key. We're supposed to read it first." She scrunched her face in a look of frustration and shook her head. "We've looked everywhere." Finishing the last of the carrots, she moved the plate to a low table beside the couch.

Emma quickly scanned the envelope Eve had given her. She read out loud the words written along the back of the envelope, just a few words per line:

> *Remember:*
> *Your mother*
> *will always love*
> *her girl*
> *and nothing*
> *can EVER*
> *change that.*

She looked at Eve, whose eyes were glistening. After pulling out the note, Emma handed the envelope to Charlie for his inspection.

"*READ THIS SECOND*," Emma read from the note. "That's what it says at the top, in all caps." She paused. "Wait a minute. I can read this. I don't have a bracelet on, with the translating rock. Why can I read this? Isn't it written in your language? Is my brain ..." she trailed off. Was her brain starting to change somehow? Had traveling through space knocked loose something inside her head, making her now capable of translating alien languages? Could she …

"Dork," Charlie said to Emma, reading the envelope she'd handed him. "It's written in English." He looked at Eve. "I'm right, right? It's written in English? My brain hasn't changed, and I can read this. But why is it written in English?"

"You're right, it is. And that's a good question," said Eve. "I know Mom visited Earth at least a few times. She worked with Dr. Waldo a lot, and your Earth is his favorite planet along this elevator's track. I'm sure she picked up on his enthusiasm for your planet. But why would she write the notes in your language instead of ours? We don't know. We hadn't found these letters the first time we visited Earth. But now that we have, I'm all the more convinced there's some connection. We just have to find it."

Mildly disappointed but also a little relieved that her brain had not changed into an automatic translator, Emma continued reading the note. She began again.

READ THIS SECOND
My darling,
You are always on my mind. I'm so sorry I've been gone. When we
are reunited, I will explain everything. I miss you, but
I know you are smart and clever and will be all right. You have such
a good mind. I smile when I think of you, as a child, solving puzzles.
We'd all watch as your mind whirred, putting pieces together.
I loved watching you. Seeing you grow into a brilliant young woman has

been a blessing. I will see you again soon. In the meantime,
   may the
Planet Xylia shine on you at night.
Ever yours,
Mom

Emma looked at Eve for her reaction. Eve's face was woven with resolve: she would not cry. Emma looked away out of courtesy.

"Huh," said Charlie. "It doesn't say a whole lot, does it? But she's thinking of you, that's good?"

Eve nodded.

"What is the planet Xylia?" asked Ben. "Is that a clue?"

"It's just a really bright planet in the sky. I used to ask Mom to help me find it at night when I couldn't sleep," explained Eve. "We made wishes on it. Seeing that it was still there made me feel safe. But it's not a clue, I don't think."

"What does that note say?" Emma said, nodding at the note in Ben's hands.

"It's short," Ben said. "Nothing written on the envelope." He put the envelope down next to him on the couch, and read from the letter.

READ THIS THIRD.
Milo, remember when we met?
Our trust and our love were so strong. I hope we can
return to that trust and love. You and Eve
are my everything. I shouldn't be gone long.
When I return, I hope we can talk. I still love you.
Kata

"Kata, that's your mom's name?" Emma asked softly.

Eve's face was hidden behind the waterfall of her hair. She nodded. Ben reached over and gave her a silent hug.

"That's deep stuff there," said Charlie.

"Mr. Obvious," said Emma, rolling her eyes.

Eve wiped her tears and pushed her hair back. "We *have* to find her."

"We will," said Ben, gently rocking side to side with Eve on the couch.

"That's right," said Emma. "We will." She took a deep breath. "You're right, though, we need to find that first letter. These tell us next to nothing. She must have said something in the first letter that tells you where to look. It doesn't seem like she's trying to keep it secret, does it? The way she talks about how good you are with puzzles, she's telling you to figure this out. She's left a clue, for sure." Emma hoped her voice sounded more certain than she felt.

"Yes," said Eve, her voice tinged with despair, "but where is it? We've looked all over. I'm almost out of hope."

"Never lose hope!" said Charlie. "Not while we're here."

"I think a trip to Lero is in order," said Emma, delighted to help her friend, but also to have an excuse to take the elevator again to another world. "Don't you?"

Charlie and Ben nodded vigorously. "To Lero!" said Charlie.

"To Lero!" cheered Ben.

Eve smiled through her tear-stained face, her hope renewed, her heart bursting with gratitude. "Thanks, guys. I'm so lucky to have met you." She looked up at the Hub's infinite sky. "May the planet Xylia shine on us all. Mom, we are going to find you. To Lero!"

chapter two

Ben quickly gathered travel packs for Charlie and Emma that contained everything they needed to travel the universes, including their own stone-embedded bracelets and a pendant with a rock that served as a master key to the elevator and the Hub. Once they'd double-checked the contents of the packs to make sure nothing was missing, the foursome piled into what they called the "elevator." It was really nothing more than a tiny room, but through science or the magic of space and time it somehow connected infinite universes. Eve's father, Milo, had explained it this way:

"Dogwinkle is a thin spot. Think of a quilt. You know those simple quilts some people make, just layer upon layer of cotton batting, tied together every few inches with pieces of yarn? Imagine that each layer of cotton is a universe. And those points where everything is tied together, those are thin spots. At thin spots, the universes are right on top of each other, almost intermingling. At thin spots, everything is possible."

And, he'd gone on to explain, elevators such as this one existed at many of these thin spots—portals that were fixed, in a sense, into one place within a stack of universes. The elevator the teens were entering would always return to the Balky Point Lighthouse, and would always go to the same spots in the same other universes. On

Earth (or at least on this Earth, seeing as there were infinite parallel Earths), all elevators were in lighthouses. Not every lighthouse contained an elevator, but every elevator was in a lighthouse.

This elevator would also take the teens to their current destination: a location on Eve's planet, Lero, in another universe.

As the doors slid shut behind them and fused into a seamless wall, Ben leaned in to whisper in Emma's ear. "Have you seen Dr. Waldo today?" he asked. "When you had your tests done? Was he around?"

Holding Ben's arm for balance, Emma sat down on the floor. "I haven't done this for a while," she explained. "I don't want to fall over." She laughed. "No, Dr. Waldo wasn't there today. Another scientist had instructions from him, but he didn't show up himself."

"Did the other scientist mention where Dr. Waldo was?" Ben asked. He was trying to sound casual, but his brows were slightly furrowed.

"No, why? I saw him yesterday. He didn't mention going anywhere," she said. "The only non-work thing he mentioned was that we're coming up on the anniversary of his wife's death. He looked pretty sad about it so I didn't push."

"He's … he's been gone a lot lately," said Ben. "I'm sure it's no big deal. Maybe he's just taking some time off."

From the look on Ben's face, though, Emma knew he was concerned. Dr. Waldo was a bit of a mystery. As gregarious and outgoing as he was, he didn't talk much about himself. Emma remembered that he'd shown them his Secret Garden in the Experimental Building that summer. In it, he'd planted a secret that apparently was so overwhelming he couldn't hold it inside himself. Emma had wondered then what the secret might be, and she wondered now whether his recent absences had anything to do it.

"Maybe he has an appointment somewhere?" Eve suggested as

she tapped coordinates into a panel on the wall, targeting the elevator to take them to Lero. "Sorry, didn't mean to eavesdrop. We're in a close, confined space, though. Generally other scientists come to him—people rarely turn down a chance to visit the Hub—but it's not impossible that he went somewhere for a meeting." She wrinkled her nose skeptically.

"He doesn't say where he's been going?" asked Charlie, who had plunked himself down next to his sister. "He just disappears?"

Ben shook his head. "He just sort of mumbles that he'll be back 'soon'—if he says anything at all. He was gone for a whole day once. And," Ben continued, "I'm not convinced he hasn't been gone longer. I think maybe he's time traveling, too, to get himself back before we start to get suspicious. Sometimes when he's only been gone a few hours, his beard looks like it's been growing for days. Something's up." He shrugged his shoulders.

"Hmm," said Charlie.

"Very insightful, there, Charles," said Emma.

Eve finished entering numbers into the control panel. "Ready, everyone? Hang on!"

"So long as we're not going to a ghost universe, I'm ready!" said Emma. Despite her excitement, her stomach leaped with a bit of nausea when the elevator started whirring through universes. "I'd forgotten this," she laughed. The elevator did not shake or make noise, but nonetheless the teens felt its movement deep within their cells. There was a jolt, a flickering of lights. The sound and vacuum-like sensation of a boot being sucked out of mud. Finally, the scent in the air that, while rather unidentifiable, was best described as a combination of metal, and smoke, and the slightest sweetness of honey.

No one had yet figured out exactly how the elevators worked. It wasn't as though anyone could stand outside it and watch. Everything happened, somehow, within the elevator's walls. One moment they were on Earth, and the next, Lero.

When the elevator settled again and the panel on the wall indicated they'd reached their destination, Eve tapped another button. The wall opposite the one through which they'd entered from the Hub opened up, revealing a dim room with rough clay walls.

"Where are we?" said Charlie, his jaw wide with wonder. They walked out of the small room. The doors sealed behind them, and the elevator disappeared. "Are we inside a cave?"

"Oh, that's right!" said Eve. "You haven't been here before! It was the other Charlie who was here, your parallel self. Yes, we're in the side of a hill."

Ben, the only non-Leroian of this group who had been to Lero before, led the group outside to the fresh air, into a pastoral scene of green fields and a bright sky.

"This is Lero!" said Eve, beaming as she spread her arms wide to embrace her home planet. "Welcome home!"

They stepped out into the grassy field, shimmering under the dazzling sun. Leaves glistened with drops from a recent rain, and the air was rich with the clean smell of wet dirt.

"Definitely not a ghost universe," said Emma, with relief. Her eyes soaked up Lero's verdant beauty. The hillside from which they'd exited was one of the tallest of dozens of small rolling hills, a landscape of fields and low hills as far as they could see, lushly covered with a carpet of moss, short grass, and scattered wildflowers.

"I know Dr. Waldo says it's dangerous to go to the ghost planets," said Ben, who had been here before and was less absorbed in the newness. "But I gotta admit, I wish I could have gone with you guys."

"It was interesting, for sure," said Emma, "but I didn't like getting stuck there. And I sneezed something awful. Who knew you could be allergic to ghosts? Did Dr. Waldo ever look into that any more, the ghost vaccine the other Charlie told us about?"

Ben frowned. "Yeah, actually, he did. I came in to the Hub last Monday, and there was a note for me from the other Charlie, just saying hi, we should meet up sometime. He and the other Emma had been to the Hub. I asked Dr. Waldo about it, and he said Charlie brought a sample of the vaccine. I don't know if he's done anything with it, though."

"The other Emma was here too?" said Charlie. "Dang it, I wish I could have seen her. We should go visit them sometime. Last time was a little chaotic." He smiled at Emma, but she was frowning, and wouldn't meet his eyes.

"Okay, you guys lead the way!" Charlie said to Ben and Eve. He put a hand on Emma's shoulder and held her back, waiting for the other two to start walking. When they were several steps away, he turned to his sister. "You're not telling me something. What did Dr. Waldo find in the tests?"

Emma started walking, following slowly behind Ben and Eve. Charlie kept step. "It's … nothing for sure, I guess," she said. "Dr. Waldo wasn't there today, so he didn't tell me anything, obviously."

"Don't play, Em. This is serious. Did one of the other scientists say something?"

Exhaling heavily, Emma nodded. "It's part of why the other Charlie and Emma were at the Hub," she said. "Dr. Waldo didn't have blood samples or DNA or anything for me from before our travel, so he wanted to compare it to theirs. He tested their DNA, and yours too, against mine. The scientist told me there's these things called telomeres, sort of like end caps on our DNA. They shorten with age, or with stress. Yours and the other Charlie's and Emma's, yours are all sort of about the same length. Mine, though …" she paused.

"Yours … are shorter?" Charlie finished.

"Mine are shorter. A 'small but significant' difference." Emma looked at her brother. "I'm not sure what it means. I need to talk to Dr. Waldo." She turned her head at the sound of a bird chirping nearby, but couldn't find its source.

"But what did the other scientist think it means?" Charlie asked, ignoring the bird.

"She wasn't sure, but … well, they think that there could be a relationship between shortened telomeres and shortened life span."

Charlie stopped in his tracks to take in this news. "But we all traveled through space. You only traveled alone that once, out of the ghost universe. All the other times, someone was with you. Why are your telomeres shorter if ours aren't?" He frowned.

"I don't know," said Emma, grabbing his arm and pulling to get him moving again. Ben and Eve were getting farther ahead, and Emma didn't want to lose them. To her unaccustomed eyes, all these hills and fields looked a lot alike. "That's what I want to talk to Dr. Waldo about."

Emma hadn't told everyone everything about her experiences after her interuniversal travel: how she'd felt weak for weeks afterward; how sometimes she felt she could almost see through herself, like she wasn't completely there. Her brain got muddled somehow, she was sure of that. Not all the pieces fell back where they were meant to, she thought. Or maybe it was because of her time at the ghost planet. She wasn't sure. She didn't tell anyone, but she did not feel completely right just yet. In science class this semester, her teacher had told the students that an atom is about 99.999999999 percent empty space; that if you removed all the empty space from all the atoms of all the people on Earth, the entire human race could fit into the volume of a sugar cube. That seemed rather unbelievable, Emma thought, but nonetheless she felt that something had gone wrong with her own empty space, and she didn't know what.

"So when you traveled without elevators, using your mind, you shortened your life?" Charlie shook his head. "That can't be right. You saved the universes, from Vik, and from The Void. That can't be your reward." He kicked the ground. "I don't accept that."

"I don't know, Charlie," said Emma. "I need to find out more. Dr. Waldo needs to find out more."

"But traveling with the elevators, or with those other things, the pigeons and the Dark MATTER, those devices Dr. Waldo made, that's harmless?"

"I think so. I don't know. I don't want to talk about it anymore," said Emma. Leaving Charlie and the discussion behind, she ran to catch up with Eve and Ben, slipping between them and linking arms with each of them on either side. "So where are we going?" she asked with forced ease, as though she didn't have a care in the world.

Eve squeezed Emma's arm. "We're going to where my mom used to live," she said. "After they separated." She frowned.

"Who lives there now?" asked Emma. She checked over her shoulder to make sure Charlie was still in sight.

"No one," said Eve. "It's empty. Dad ... my dad kept up the house after she disappeared."

The foursome had been walking along a well-worn dirt path, but now came to what appeared to be a road, though there were no vehicles on it. Charlie, who had been trailing behind the group, lost in thought, finally caught up to the others. He gazed down the long, paved road. "Do you guys have cars?"

Eve reached for Charlie's hand. "We do, but not a lot. Most people travel by foot or our version of a bicycle, or on the underground subway. The people who came to Lero after leaving our mother planet of Napori were tired of seeing so much construction above ground. The houses are built into the hillsides, and a lot of the transportation is underground."

"You're like ants," said Ben. "Or moles. Living and traveling in the ground."

"So cool," said Charlie, surveying the scene. Sure enough, in the hills alongside the road, spaced far apart and almost hidden, embedded doorways were framed by stone or wood, leading into the hillside and whatever lay beyond. "Good thing there are enough hills for everyone," he said.

"Some of the hills are man-made," Eve explained. "But they're just as good as the real ones. They're cozy. It's home. I like it. Your houses feel so exposed to me. We were on Earth in a windstorm once, and I thought the whole house was going to blow over. Our homes feel sturdy and secure. I'm glad our founders built this way."

Just as they reached a fork in the road, a vehicle whipped by, its driver honking and waving at the group.

"Friendly," said Ben, jumping to the side of the road, though he'd been in no danger.

Eve laughed as she turned to wave enthusiastically at the car that had passed. "Leroians are the best," she said. She turned back and pointed down a road to the left. "That way," she said, her excitement subconsciously causing her to pick up her pace.

"Is it far?" Emma asked. "Your mom's home?"

"Not much farther at all," said Eve, her smile growing. "We're almost there."

Eve pranced ahead, spinning and walking backwards to face the others. "I'm so glad you guys are all here. I didn't have a chance to show Ben and the other Charlie much of Lero last time. I can't wait for you to see it." She turned back around and ran ahead, stopping at a doorway tucked into the side of the hill. The door, made of wide wooden slabs, was painted red. It was surrounded on all sides by large stones, carefully interlaced so as to leave no large gaps. A dust-colored mortar filled the spaces between the rocks. On one side of the door, a thick glass window was set into the stones at approximately face level.

Eve reached into her pocket and pulled out a large, decorative copper key.

"It's not digitized?" said Charlie. "I thought you guys would have keypads and robots and stuff."

Eve smiled. "Just a key," she said. "Some people have keypads. Mom liked keys." She turned the key in the lock, and swung the door inward. "No robots. Well, some robots, but not here."

She stood at the door, not entering. "Mom?" she whispered. "Are you here? It's me, Evella."

The interior of the house remained silent.

Eve stepped inside, and the others followed. Ben, the tallest of the group, was only about half a foot shorter than the entrance. "Are people on Lero shorter than people on Earth?" he asked, measuring the space between the top of his head and the top of the door frame with his hands.

"I think we just have shorter doorways," said Eve. She felt along a wall until she found a light switch. She flipped it on, illuminating the inside space.

"It's like a hobbit house!" said Charlie.

"That's what the other Charlie said when he was here," said Ben, smiling at the coincidence. "Totally like a hobbit house." He paused. "I wish I'd met the other Ben. There must be another Ben on that other Earth, right? Maybe I can meet him sometime. The other Charlie should bring the other Ben to the Hub."

Charlie tilted his head. "It's still so weird. The other Charlie is me, but he's not me. But we have so much in common. But not everything. Some of the same life experiences, but not all. I know how he thinks, but I don't know what he's thinking. Weird. Like, is he having this same conversation right now? Weird."

"He's not having this conversation because they're not on Lero, dork," said Emma, barely paying attention to the boys' conversation. She moved slowly through the home, not wanting to disturb the sacred space of a missing person.

The house was not large. The front door led through a short entryway into what appeared to be a living room, with a light beige couch and two cozy chairs. Off to the side a space had been set up as a small office, with a desk and file cabinet, and shelves heavy with books and papers in neat piles. A doorway led off into what looked like a kitchen; a hallway on the other side led down to more rooms. Boxes—closed, taped shut, and labeled—were stacked and scattered around the rooms. "What exactly are we looking for?" Emma asked.

"I don't know, really," said Eve, absently opening and closing drawers in the desk as she'd done dozens of times before. "Clues."

"Well, that clarifies it," said Charlie. "Clues. But we Earthlings don't know what's supposed to be here and what's not, so how can we find anything?"

Emma saw a look of distress cross Eve's face. "Don't worry, Eve," she said. "We'll help you look. Something will show up somewhere."

But even after what felt like hours, something did not show up. They searched the whole house, kitchen to bedrooms to bathroom to living spaces. Emma, Charlie and Ben were fascinated to get a thorough look at a Leroian home, but as far as the whereabouts of Eve's mother, they came up empty-handed.

"Well, it makes sense, I guess," said Ben. "You searched her house before, right? Nothing new's going to magically appear."

"That's just the thing, though," said Eve, "it's weird. Those letters I showed you back at the Hub, they *did* magically appear. I don't know when she left them, but neither Dad nor I remember getting them in the mail, and we both swear they weren't here when we first packed things up. But when I went through her desk again a couple of months ago, I found them. I *know* they weren't there before. I guess we just didn't see them." She shook her head and shrugged, unconvinced. Her eyes looked just a tiny bit wet.

"That's not the strangest thing that's ever happened, but it's strange," said Ben. "Maybe I missed something the first time. Can I look at those letters again?"

Eve sighed. "I've looked at them a million times. We need to find the first one. I'm sure that's the one with the answers. But you can look again if you want to," she said. She reached into her bag and handed the letters to Ben.

Ben tested a large box for sturdiness and sat down on it. Elbows on his knees, he read the first letter to himself, the one to Eve, studying it intensely for any clue Kata might have left.

"Wait," said Charlie suddenly, staring at a wall. "That window." He looked around the room suspiciously, then walked purposefully to the front door. He stepped outside, disappearing from sight, then returned a few moments later. "That window," he said, pointing, his voice full of accusation. "This house is built into a hill. That is not a window."

Eve laughed. "Good eye, Charlie! No, it's not a window. It's a video screen. It's set to show the outside world directly above ground. They're all video screens," she said, indicating other windows around the home. "That one," she said, pointing at what seemed to be a skylight directly overhead in the peak of the ceiling, "that one's real. During the day it's a window." A wispy cloud floated past the skylight as if to prove her words. "It collects energy during the day, and at night it can be turned on as a light."

"Solar power?" asked Emma, craning her neck to look out the

overhead panel at the bright Leroian sky.

"Basically," said Eve. "I think." She smiled.

"What if it's not sunny enough?" said Charlie. "Is it just dark at night?"

"Well, it's pretty efficient," said Eve. "Right now it probably has about a month's worth of energy stored up in it. Maybe more, since no one's been using it." Her smile turned to a frown.

"Okay, what else should we do here?" said Charlie, sensing Eve's mood and returning to the task at hand. "Is there another home we could search? Your house? Or her work place or something?"

"There's Dad's storage unit, I suppose," said Eve, staring off at the video panel Charlie had first noticed. "I think Dad looked through it a bit, but there's really no reason there'd be anything helpful there." She sighed. "But where would that first letter be? It's ridiculous. These two letters show up one day, but not the one we need."

Ben looked up. "Hey, does anyone have paper and a pen? Something I can write on?"

Emma, a list maker at heart who was always prepared to write down any list, pulled writing instruments out of her bag and handed them to the young man. Eve rushed to Ben's side. "Did you find something? What is it?" She sat down on an edge of the box next to him and peered eagerly at the papers she'd read so often they'd become dog-eared.

"I'm not sure," Ben mumbled. "I just want to test something." With the others watching on in anxious anticipation, he scribbled words on the paper. After a minute, he frowned. "Darling, are, reunited …. No, that doesn't make sense." His shoulders drooped.

Eve sighed heavily and turned away, trying to hide her disappointment.

Charlie put a comforting arm around Eve. "We'll figure it out, Eve. Don't worry. We will. Should we go to the storage place? I mean, it can't hurt, right?"

"Wait!" said Ben. With another burst of excitement, he scribbled more notes on the paper. His face broke out into a hopeful grin. "Does 'dark galaxy' mean anything to you?" he asked Eve.

The color washed from Eve's face. "Dark galaxy? Why?"

Ben held up the letter he'd been looking at, the one Kata had written to Eve. "I was thinking, maybe the 'read this second' was actually a clue. I've seen codes where you're supposed to read the second or fourth word, or some other specific word of each paragraph or line. I tried that, and it didn't make sense."

The others crowded around him to look at the letter once again, this time paying attention to the words written on each line.

"The line breaks, they are sort of weird," said Emma. "I hadn't noticed that before."

Ben smiled.

The letter read:

> *My darling,*
> *You are always on my mind. I'm so sorry I've been gone.*
> *When we*
> *are reunited, I will explain everything. I miss you, but*
> *I know you are smart and clever and will be all right. You*
> *have such*
> *a good mind. I smile when I think of you, as a child, solv-*
> *ing puzzles.*
> *We'd all watch as your mind whirred, putting pieces to-*
> *gether.*
> *I loved watching you. Seeing you grow into a brilliant*
> *young woman has*
> *been a blessing. I will see you again soon. In the meantime,*
> *may the*

Planet Xylia shine on you at night.
Ever yours,
Mom

"If you read the second word in each line," said Ben, "it says 'Darling are reunited know good all loved a Xylia yours.' The last line doesn't have a second word so I ignored it. Either way, it's total nonsense. But, if you read just the first *letter* of each of those words," he said, pointing the tip of the pen at the first letter of the second word on each line, "it spells out 'dark galaxy.' The 'd' in 'Darling,' the 'a' in 'are,' the 'r' in 'reunited,' and so on." He looked at Eve expectantly.

"Does 'dark galaxy' mean anything to you, Eve?" Emma asked, repeating Ben's question.

"No," said Eve, "but that seems like an awful big coincidence that it would spell out real words like that." She took a deep breath. "Oh my gosh, my heart is beating so fast. What about the other letter, the one to Dad?" Eve grabbed the other envelope from Ben's lap and pulled out the letter it contained. "Read this third," she read breathlessly.

"So we're looking at the third words this time," said Emma.

Eve nodded, and read the letter out loud:

Milo, remember when we met?
Our trust and our love were so strong. I hope we can
return to that trust and love. You and Eve
are my everything. I shouldn't be gone long.
When I return, I hope we can talk. I still love you.
Kata

"The third words are when, and, that, everything, return," said

Charlie. He listed out the first letters of the third words: "W–A–T–E–R. Water? That's a horrible clue. Water? Water is everywhere. What good is 'water'?"

Emma saw the consternation cross Eve's face. "It's a clue. We'll work on it. It's more than we had before, right? Hey, didn't the other envelope have writing on the outside, too? What does that one say?"

The envelope of the letter to Eve was still in Ben's lap. He turned it over to the side with the writing:

Remember:
Your mother
will always love
· her girl
and nothing
can EVER
change that.

"But it doesn't say which word to read," said Charlie."

"It must be the same as the letter that was inside, 'read this second,'" said Ben. "The first line only has one word, so we skip that. Then it's M–A–G–N–E–T. Magnet."

Emma stared at Ben. "It can't be a coincidence that these spell out real words. Dark galaxy, water, magnet. Does that mean anything to you, Eve? Think: anything at all. Anything?"

The teens from Earth all stared at Eve intensely, willing her to make the connection. Eve shook her head in frustration. "I feel like I should know 'dark galaxy,' but I can't remember. I need to remember! What is it?" She thumped her fist against her head.

"Would your dad know?" asked Charlie.

"Of course! Dad would know!" She pulled out her cell phone,

a special device Dr. Waldo had fabricated that would reach across universes to wherever her father might be. She called Milo's number, set the phone to speakerphone so everyone could hear, and waited impatiently as the phone rang once, twice, three times.

On the fourth ring, Eve's father answered. "Hello?" Milo's voice crackled across space and time.

"Dad?" said Eve. "Dad, it's Eve. Where are you?"

"I'm in the Hub," said Milo. "Where are you?"

"We're at Mom's house," she said. "I'm here with Ben, Emma, and Charlie. Dad, does 'dark galaxy' mean anything to you?" She put a hand to her chest to hold her pounding heart.

Milo was silent on the other end of the line.

"Dad?" said Eve. "Are you still there?"

"Where did you hear 'dark galaxy'?" Milo said, the tension in his voice clear.

"Ben decoded Mom's letters," said Eve. "Does it mean something?"

Milo paused again. "It might," he said, finally. "Go to my storage unit. I'll meet you there as soon as I can."

chapter three

"I'm glad it's not raining," Charlie said, gazing up at the clear cerulean sky as the teens walked briskly along the quiet Leroian road. Eve took the lead as the group sped toward her father's storage unit. Tall trees lined the edges of the road, but these were not the evergreen or deciduous trees the Earthlings were used to. Like Earth trees, these trees each had a solid trunk as a foundation. However, about three feet above the ground, the trees' smooth, barkless trunks changed color from dark brown to a rich grassy green. At that point, the trunks branched into multiple limbs, all of them growing in a tangle of thick curls. The trees had no leaves or needles; just a swirling mass of smooth, bright-green boughs.

"Does it rain here? Do you have seasons?" Emma asked, taking in the surroundings.

"It rains a lot, but usually at night," said Eve. "Technically we have six seasons, though really it's more like three. Basically a summer, fall, and winter. There are transitional seasons in between, but they're short."

"That's a lot of seasons to fit into a year," said Charlie. Seeing a small fallen branch by the side of the road, he picked it up to inspect it. The green curls of the limb had dried to a lighter shade, somewhere between green and beige. "It's like a giant, pointy curly fry," he said, poking the stick at Emma.

"Stop it, Charles," said Emma. She reached out to feel the branch's smooth casing. "Silky," she said.

Eve nodded, and returned to Charlie's comment. "It's a lot of seasons, but one of our years is longer than one of yours. That's why I'm only ten years old in Lero years, ten and a half, really, but you guys and I are all somewhere around the same age. It's hard to compare exactly because of time travel and passing through universes and so on. But one day when I was bored, Dad helped me figure out the Earth-to-Lero age calculations. Multiply your age by .6, and that's about how old you'd be here."

"Nineteen times .6 … what is that?" asked Ben. "Anyone have a calculator?"

"Nineteen?" said Emma. "I thought you were eighteen?"

"I had a birthday since you guys were last here. One every year!" Ben said with a wink and a smile.

Emma blushed. "Happy birthday! Sorry we missed it." She wished they could have joined in the celebrations. *Stupid school*, she thought.

"We should have cake," said Charlie, who never passed up an opportunity for cake. He tossed the stick back onto the side of the road, and scanned the landscape with its scattered hills of various heights, some with doors embedded into their sides, and a few with Leroian words written in signs over the doorways. "Say, Eve," he continued, "very serious inquiry, highly important. Do you guys have pizza here?"

Eve laughed at the unexpected question. "No pizza, sorry! Maybe you could move here and open a restaurant! Start a new trend!"

A slow glow spread over Charlie's face. "I could be the Pizza *KING*. Can you imagine? The first time on the whole planet that anyone tastes pizza? It'd be a miracle!" He slapped Ben on the back.

"Ben, we should totally do this. You and me. Ben and Charlie's Pizza. Charlie and Ben's, maybe. We'd become famous. Famous in another universe! People would bow down and celebrate us. They'd probably create a national holiday in our honor. I mean, come on!"

"What about me?" said Emma. "Aren't I included?" Truthfully, she had no desire to start a pizza business. But she did want to be included.

"You and Eve will be too busy doing science," said Charlie. "We'll be here doing the important work, perfecting the cheese-to-sauce ratio, and so on. This might save the universes, frankly," he said with feigned seriousness. "I wouldn't be surprised."

"They'll probably have to invent some sort of Nobel prize," said Ben, "except everyone in the multiverse will be eligible, not just Earthlings."

"So you're in?" said Charlie. "Lero Pizza? Charlie and Ben's Pizza Inside the Hill?"

Ben laughed. "It sounds like a can't-fail idea, but I'm out. I like working in the Hub."

Emma blushed again and looked away. She was relieved. She didn't believe Charlie would actually start a pizza restaurant on Lero, but she didn't like to even imagine that Ben might leave the Hub. When she graduated high school in the spring, she was hoping to move to the island and work in the Hub herself. She loved the science of the universes, the possibilities in the Hub, the travel through the multiverse, discovering new worlds and mysteries … but she had to admit, the chance to work alongside Ben was not without appeal.

"Here we are!" Eve said, interrupting Emma's thoughts. She stopped in front of a bright turquoise door tucked cozily into yet another grassy hillside.

"Is every single building on Lero built into a hill?" said Charlie, not even trying to hide his amazement. "I was expecting a row of big-box rooms. Even your storage units are in the hills?"

"What do you do when you run out of hills?" asked Emma, continuing Charlie's line of thinking. "I know the planet's population is pretty small now ... what did you tell me, like a hundred thousand or something? But at some point, don't you need to build up? Buildings with several floors?"

It was true. When Eve and Emma had been stuck in a cave the previous summer, Eve had explained to Emma all about Lero's history: people from the planet Napori had overbuilt their own planet to the point where there was almost no nature left. As a last-ditch effort to save themselves, a small group of Naporians many generations earlier had picked up and moved to Lero. The founding pioneers had very consciously chosen to create a world on which the planet's natural resources were respected and preserved, but even so, growth was inevitable.

"That's something I'm interested in studying, actually," said Eve. "Figuring out how to keep our planet looking like this, rather than Napori. It's a challenge. But," she said, "that's for another time. We're here at the storage unit now, and that's first priority. Let's go in."

She pulled out a bundle of keys from her pocket. Finding the one she wanted, she slipped it into the lock of the turquoise door. It turned easily. A motion-sensitive light inside the room turned itself on, and the teens entered the cool interior.

Ahead of them stretched a long hallway, which branched off left and right with more hallways after about a dozen feet. Another twenty feet or so down the corridor more hallways led both left and right again, creating an underground mini-maze. Eve led them down to the end of the first hallway and turned right. The rock walls were carved with supreme craftsmanship, chiseled smooth and in some places painted with beautiful airy scenes from the outside world: bright blue skies, vivid flowers, bucolic rivers meandering through grassy plains.

Eve walked past the murals to the last door on the left, which was painted a bright buttercup yellow. This door opened with a keypad rather than a lock and key. Eve tapped a code into the keypad and opened the door.

"I hope Dad gets here soon," she said, as another motion-sensitive light flickered on, illuminating the unit. "I have absolutely no idea what we're looking for. Dark galaxy." She shook her head. "I know I've heard that phrase. But when I try to remember, it just won't come. Dark galaxy, dark galaxy, dark galaxy…"

"Dark galaxy!" A voice boomed from behind them in the hallway. "You know this, Eve!" A tall man with thick blond hair, interspersed with gray, appeared in the doorway. A giant smile bloomed on his face upon seeing his daughter.

"Hi, Dad!" said Eve, greeting her father with a tight hug.

The wrinkles at the corners of Milo's eyes were borne of a combination of a light-hearted personality, quick to smile, and years spent squinting into the sun on archaeological digs on his own planet. He returned his daughter's hug with vigor, then released her, looking her intently in the eyes. "Eve! Dark galaxy! Do you remember?" He shifted his gaze to scan boxes on a shelf in the storage unit, running his fingers along their exteriors as he read their labels. "No, not here; no, not this," he murmured under his breath, moving to the next set of shelves.

"Can we help look? What are we looking for?" asked Ben, his eyes sweeping over the contents of the room. Boxes of all sizes filled the shelves, and shelves filled half the room. The open area of the storage unit was strewn with a random assortment of furniture: a couple of tables, some wooden chairs, and several strange-looking instruments Ben guessed might be related to Milo's work.

"An archaeological dig I did long ago here on Lero," said Milo distractedly. "It was from a place so old ..." He lost his train of thought as he searched more and more boxes, methodically taking off lids, scanning the contents quickly, and returning everything to its place with the care of a man whose work depended on the ability to be meticulous.

"A dig?" said Eve, a look of deep thought on her face, as she struggled to remember what it was her father was sure she couldn't have forgotten. She scoured the boxes for clues, but her gaze remained blank.

"Aha!" cried Milo, pulling a dusty file box off its metal shelf. He set the box on a small table and took off the lid. Inside the box were more boxes, labeled in Leroian with scrawled handwriting. Milo started rummaging through them, finally pulling out individual boxes so he could reach the others underneath.

When he got to a small charcoal-black box, about the size of a fist, he stopped.

"Dark galaxy," he said triumphantly but reverently. His eyes were shadowed with a look of the long-lost past. He gently pulled the box out of the larger file box. "From one of my early digs. We'd only been married a couple years, your mother and I. You were not more than one."

"That would be about ... oh, twenty months, on Earth," Eve quickly calculated for the others. "A toddler."

"Your mother would come out to the dig all the time; it wasn't too far from home. She'd bring you and a picnic, come for lunch or the evening on those long summer nights. This was from a dig of one the early settlements on Lero, from millennia before the people of Napori moved here. An ancient civilization; the oldest we've found yet." He smiled, lost in the memory. "Mostly we found the usual things. Pottery, weaponry, bones. But at one home, we found some unusual items—items we'd never seen anywhere else, before or since. Including an unusual stone. It was your mother's favorite. She called it the 'dark galaxy' stone. She thought it looked like a galaxy had been trapped inside of it. You played with it all the time," Milo continued. "I told your mother it was too precious to be a toy, but she said nothing was more precious than you."

Eve warmed with her father's words, memories flooding her mind and tears filling her eyes.

Milo opened the top of the box with a flourish. The others stood by, holding their breaths in anticipation. Milo solemnly lifted the top layer of tissue paper and peered underneath.

"What?" he gasped. His dismay growing, he rummaged through all the layers of tissue, dingy with time and dust. Whatever treasure had once nestled inside the tissue paper was gone. Milo's face fell. "It's gone!"

"No!" said Eve, taking the box from her father's hands. She removed the layers of paper one by one, shaking each to ensure she didn't miss anything, but her search was fruitless.

Deflated, Eve sat down on a dusty chair. "Where could it be?"

"What made you think about 'dark galaxy' anyway?" asked Milo. One by one, he pulled out the other boxes within the file box, checking within each to make sure the stone hadn't somehow been misplaced.

"I remembered a code I'd once seen," said Ben, and then he explained the rest: the "read this second" code; the clues they'd found of "dark galaxy," "water," and "magnet."

"Do any of those other words mean anything to you?" asked Emma, helping Milo put the contents of the file box back into its careful order. "'Water' and 'magnet' are so vague; they could mean almost anything. We were really hoping 'dark galaxy' would help."

"Well, just because the rock isn't here doesn't mean the clue doesn't help," said Charlie. "Maybe Kata took it herself? Who else would have access to this storage unit?"

Milo found another chair and moved it to sit next to his daughter, resting an elbow on the table and his chin in his hand. "Me, and Kata, I guess. She still knew the code. I didn't know she had the key to the whole building, but she might have. Lots of people do. It had to be her. No one else knew it was here."

"So that's a clue then, too. Maybe she wanted you to know she took it," said Emma. "Do you have any pictures of the stone? Maybe that would help?"

Milo nodded. He reached for a file folder tucked into the side of the box they'd been looking through. Inside the folder, an envelope bulged with photos and papers. Milo flipped through the images until he found the one he was looking for.

"I give you the dark galaxy stone," he said, handing the photograph over to Emma with a flourish. "The only one we've ever seen on Lero, that I know of."

This time, it was Emma who gasped. "I know this stone!" she said. "It's a black opal! They come from Australia! I'm sure that's it!"

Charlie leaned over his sister's shoulder to look at the picture. "How do you know that, Em? It's pretty, I'll give you that. But you haven't been to Australia. Where did you see this?"

A pink tinge flushed up Emma's neck. "Well, what with all the rocks we dealt with last time we were here—the wishing rocks that open the elevator, and all these stones on our bracelets—" she said, running a finger over the tiny but life-giving and life-saving rocks embedded in the bracelet around her left wrist, "I just got curious. I read up on rocks on the internet. I saw the black opal stones, and I remember them because they're so beautiful and so rare. I thought the same thing your mother did," she said to Eve, "that some of them look like they have galaxies or nebulas trapped inside. They come in all sorts of colors, some more red, some more blue and green, but all with that dark background, all with the sparkles of light and color and fire inside. I know that's what it is. I'm sure of it." She handed the picture to Eve.

"Black opals? From Australia? That's on Earth, right?" Eve said, forgetting that with rare exception, most places Emma knew were, in fact, on Earth.

"Southern hemisphere," Ben offered. "Near the bottom of the planet. From our perspective that is, I guess. From their perspective they might say their side is up and ours is down."

"Pretty far away from Dogwinkle Island," said Charlie, "but maybe worth a visit! Do you think your mom was trying to tell us to find her in Australia? It's a big country, isn't it, Emma? How would we even start to look for her?"

"It's a huge country," said Emma. "About as big as the United States. But, lucky for us, the black opals are pretty rare. There's really just one main place you can find them, and that's about it. A little town called Lightning Ridge."

"Lightning Ridge? That's our destination, then! But …" Charlie hesitated. "Australia is a long way away." He looked at Ben. "Does Dr. Waldo have something that will get us there fast? Not the pigeons, I know those just take you to a pre-designated spot." The last time they'd visited, many of the teens had had the opportunity to try out the device Dr. Waldo called a "pigeon," named after a homing pigeon, because it would only take you to one place—usually home. "That Dark MATTER thing we tried blew up when we used it. Does he have something else? Something that won't blow up or spread our atoms all over the universe?"

"Maybe Emma can get us there?" Eve said with a laugh, not knowing anything about Dr. Waldo's findings about Emma's telomeres.

Charlie quickly spoke before Emma had to explain anything

about how the travel may have shortened her life. "Not again! That was crazy. Let's check with Dr. Waldo first."

Ben, Dr. Waldo's acolyte, called Dr. Waldo's number and put the phone into speaker mode. As the call rang through, he smiled. "Interuniversal phone calls. Who would have ever thought? Craziest thing of all of things."

The phone rang and rang. Dr. Waldo had not set up any sort of voice mail just yet, being busy with other tasks. The ringing continued. Finally, a raspy voice answered.

"… Hello?" Dr. Waldo's voice carried across the millions of miles in barely more than a thin whisper. "Hello? Are you there? Help me!"

The phone went dead.

chapter four

"Did he...?" said Charlie. "Was that Dr. Waldo?" His brow furrowed in concern.

"I think it was," said Emma. "But that didn't sound good. Try calling back, Ben. He seems to be in trouble!"

Ben was already redialing Dr. Waldo's number as the others spoke. The scientist's phone rang a dozen times without answer.

"We have to help him!" said Eve. She pulled out her own phone and speed-dialed Dr. Waldo. Again there was no answer. "This isn't good," she said, shaking her head. "Can we ... I don't know, trace the call?"

"He didn't call us, we called him," said Charlie. "Can we reverse trace? Figure out where he answered from? Ben? Do you know?"

Ben had been staring at the phone, as if it would somehow give him answers. "We can try," he said, uncertainly. "But I think it'll only work—or even have a chance of working—if he was on a planet or in a universe we've already catalogued at the Hub. We've catalogued a lot, but, you know, infinite universes and all. We haven't catalogued all of them."

"Well, we have to try," said Milo, who was quickly packing up all the boxes and replacing everything back where it belonged on the shelves. He took one last look around the storage unit with resolve in his eyes, and not just for Dr. Waldo. "Let's get back to the Hub."

They retraced their path out of the maze of storage units and piled into Milo's car outside. He zipped the vehicle along Lero's empty roads back to the hillside in which the elevator was hidden.

When they arrived, Ben jumped out of the car before the others even had their seat belts off, and ran ahead into the hillside. He had the elevator door open and waiting when the rest of the group arrived. They huddled inside the small space, all of them mentally willing the door to close faster. When it did, Ben immediately opened the door on the other side that led into the Hub.

"Is Dr. Waldo here?" he called out to anyone within hearing distance as he rushed into the space in which everything was possible. "Has anyone seen Dr. Waldo?" Ben and Milo both ran off to talk to any scientists they could find.

"What did Dr. Waldo say again?" asked Emma as she, Charlie, and Eve raced to Dr. Waldo's work area. As scattered as Dr. Waldo was, his work space was surprisingly organized. The long, black lab table was more functional than fashionable, with various instruments neatly aligned at crisp right angles. Dr. Waldo's dark computer desk (designed to look as though stars were embedded within its depths) was clean but for his computer, a jar holding a few pens, a note pad, and a neatly stacked set of black mesh desk trays, each filled with an assortment of papers.

Once again, as at Eve's mother's house, they had no idea what they were looking for, but they felt they had to try. "What were his exact words?" Emma poked tentatively at papers in the desk trays, not wanting to disturb anything private but also not wanting to abandon the scientist in his time of need, wherever he might be.

"'Help me,'" replied Charlie, flipping through the note pad to see if anything was written on any pages further down. "I know he said 'help me.'" Charlie awakened Dr. Waldo's sleeping computer. An on-screen version of Rupert, the two-dimensional elephant, swept the computer screen with its trunk, indicating a field where a password must be entered to continue. Charlie sighed.

"Something like, 'Are you there? Help me,' is what I remember," said Eve. She randomly opened and closed drawers, but it seemed most of Dr. Waldo's work was locked safely inside his computer, protected by the digital pachyderm.

Emma was deeply disturbed. Not only did she want to find Dr. Waldo for his own sake, but she had big questions about her mind and her travel for which she needed answers ... or at the very least, someone to whom she could talk about it. She knew she could talk to Charlie, but for some reason she felt the need to shield him from her fears. She wasn't sure he could handle the truth. He was so protective of his sister; she didn't want to scare him unnecessarily. And Ben, she could talk to him; after all, he'd been studying and working in the Hub for months. But she wasn't quite ready to let him know how scared she was. No, she needed Dr. Waldo back, for her own selfish reasons. The realization of her own self-absorption embarrassed her, but it was a fact.

"We have to find him," said Charlie, watching Emma's mind whir and guessing at the thoughts within. Emma only nodded.

Ben trotted up to the group, out of breath from running all over the Hub. "No one has seen him since yesterday," he said. "He hasn't checked in, and no one knows where he went." He sat on the edge of Dr. Waldo's desk.

"Same thing I heard," said Milo, who had rejoined the group just after Ben. "No one knows. Okay, Ben, let's see if we can trace him somehow. You know how to do that?"

"Like I said, it'll only work if it's somewhere we've catalogued. But we can give it a try," said Ben.

"Let's try," said Emma. "We have to at least try."

They followed Ben to his work station. When Ben had first started working at the Hub, Dr. Waldo had designated an empty, open space as Ben's work area. Ben's first task had been to "build" his own desk, chairs, and other furniture, all through the power of his intention. It took Ben three tries before he had a usable desk and a chair that didn't collapse under his own weight, but he was as proud of what he'd created as if he'd built it with his own hands. The desk was about eight feet long and three feet deep, made of a dark mahogany wood. Stylish but simple brushed-metal handles adorned well-crafted drawers that flanked the desk on either side. The chair was made of the same wood, in a complementary style.

"Is that real wood?" asked Emma, running her hand over the smooth surface.

"I don't know, to be honest," said Ben. "I don't know if I killed a tree to make this. I hope not. What I like to believe is that somehow I called together molecules that wanted to be a tree, or maybe used to be a tree, and they came together to form this masterpiece." He smiled, and tapped a button on his computer keyboard to awaken the computer from its slumber.

As Ben opened programs and rapidly entered information into the computer, Charlie studied the desk more closely. "These drawer pulls," he said. "They look like our bracelets." Mirroring the bracelets they each wore, several small stones were embedded in the brushed metal of the drawer pulls. "There's the amber one, that helps us breathe," said Charlie, pointing at the stones in turn, "and the translating stone, the clear one … you have all of them! I love it!"

Ben beamed. "Exactly the idea," he said. "Different stones on different drawer pulls, but they're all there. I figure if they help us in the universes, they might help me in my work, too. At least I hope so."

As the young man spoke, a whirlwind of numbers flashed across his screen. The computer searched within its own files to see if some connection could be made between where Dr. Waldo was when he answered his phone, and anywhere the scientists had been before. After only a few seconds, the whirring stopped. Coordinates appeared in a new window on the screen.

"Did it find him?" asked Emma. "Where's Dr. Waldo?"

A pallor fell over Ben's face. "It looks like ... he's in the ghost universe."

"The ghost universe!" said Charlie. "You mean where Eve and Emma went? With the other Charlie?"

"Same universe," said Ben, his fingers racing over the keyboard as he gathered more information from the depths of the Hub's computer network. "Same universe, that is, but a different planet. Not the same one they went to, I don't think."

"You don't think?" said Eve. "But you're not sure?"

"No, I'm sure. Not the same planet. I'd know if it were the same planet. It's the same universe, but it's a planet we haven't catalogued before. Somehow ... the computer already knows this planet, though. I don't get it." Ben said.

Emma recalled her own trip to the ghost universe, to a planet where she'd nearly gotten lost, or worse. "We have to try to find him," she said, but the idea of going back made her throat tighten and her heart rush. She could vividly recall how Dr. Waldo had once warned them of the dangers of going to the ghost universe, and they had not gone there intentionally. Why was he there now? He, who had told them in no uncertain terms that spending too much time there could lead to their not being able to return? Why had he gone there, and was he stuck now?

"He must be stuck there," said Ben, echoing Emma's thoughts. "Thus the call for help. He needs us to get him out of there."

"I don't know if Emma should go back," said Charlie. "Wasn't she allergic to the ghosts? She should stay here. I'll go."

"If I'm allergic, you probably are, too," said Emma defiantly. "You aren't going without me. I got myself out of there before, and if I have to I can do it again."

Charlie shook his head at Emma. "No, Em. It's too dangerous."

"Wait," said Eve. "What about the vaccine from the parallel Earth? Ben, you said that the other Charlie had brought a sample of it? But you didn't know if Dr. Waldo had done anything with it yet?"

Before she could say anything else, Ben rushed off again, this time to Dr. Waldo's secondary lab area—one farther away from other people, where he performed the more dangerous experiments. As the others caught up to him, Ben was quickly but carefully rummaging through all the vials on one of the desks. "If it's here, it would be in this tray, I'm sure of it," he said under his breath. "Dr. Waldo can seem scatterbrained, but when it comes to his science, he's meticulously organized." One by one, he pulled each vial from the wire mesh cage that held them, read its label, and returned it to its holder.

"Did he say what he planned to do with the vaccine?" asked Eve.

"I assumed he was going to study it, maybe recreate it," said Ben, "but I never asked."

"Maybe he was going to vaccinate himself before going to the ghost universe?" suggested Charlie. "I mean, if he knew he was going, he might have wanted to take precautions? Or maybe he wanted to test the vaccine, using himself as a test subject?"

"That's possible," said Eve. "He wouldn't have wanted to make someone else do it. That's probably what he did, Charlie." Charlie nodded proudly at Eve's acceptance of his brilliant deduction.

While Ben continued his task, Emma wandered around the large lab area. Something inside a small metal bin caught her eye.

"What's that?" she said, half to herself. Peering inside the bin, she saw a broken glass pipette. A white label scrawled with smudged ink clung to one piece of glass; the glass itself was covered in a mysterious liquid. Knowing how unwise it would be to pick up the broken pieces with her fingers, Emma looked around for gloves or tongs. She found some metal tongs in a caddy on the desk. Carefully, Emma lifted the piece of glass with the label, angling it so she could read the words.

"Ghost vaccine," she read out loud. "Ghost vaccine!" She called out to the others. "Guys, I don't think Dr. Waldo injected himself with the vaccine!"

"Why do you say that?" said Charlie, coming to her side.

Emma showed him the broken tube. "He must have dropped it or something. It looks like the liquid spilled out."

Ben stopped his search. "But if he didn't take the vaccine, why would he go to the ghost universe?"

Emma shook her head. "I don't know, but we still need to go help him, regardless."

"Not without the vaccine," insisted Charlie. "I don't want to risk losing you again."

"Likewise, dork," said Emma, punching Charlie in the arm. He punched her back. "Let's call the other Charlie. Maybe he can bring more vaccine?"

"Excellent idea, Emma," said Eve. "I just hope he can bring it quickly!"

The door from the elevator to the Hub opened. All eyes turned to see who was entering. "Vaccine delivery, at your service!" Charlie from the parallel Earth, Parallel Charlie, stepped out into the Hub with a bag in his hand and a Cheshire-cat smile on his face. "You guys! You guys! I've missed you!" He spread his arms wide, awaiting the warm greetings he knew would follow.

"Charlie!" squealed Emma, jumping to give her parallel-Earth twin a giant hug. They'd shared quite an adventure over the summer, and while he wasn't her Charlie, he had become special to her, too.

"Hold on, there, Em!" said her own twin. "Don't bump him and make him drop the bag!" Charlie took the bag from Parallel Charlie and set it down carefully on a nearby table.

"No worries," said Parallel Charlie, wrapping his arms around Emma and picking her up off her feet. "It's injections in plastic syringes. Nothing breakable in there. Normally you get a full vaccine every five years, but you can get over-the-counter boosters that last one year. It's for people whose ghost allergies pick up after a funeral or something. I brought extra. I figured you all could get vaccinated while you're at it." He smiled his very Charlie smile—the smile both Charlies shared; a smile that could disarm the unhappiest of souls, or raise up the lowest of spirits.

Eve returned his smile joyfully. "Oh, Charlie, what a great idea. Good thinking. We definitely should all vaccinate, just to be safe."

The fact that people on Parallel Charlie's parallel Earth—an Earth that was so similar to her own Earth, in most ways, at least up to the time they all met—could actually see ghosts, still amazed Emma. "Ghost allergies picking up after a funeral," she said, shaking her head. "So bizarre. Your Earth is a strange place. But it has some pretty fabulous people." She released Parallel Charlie from her hug but kept one arm around his waist. "Where's Emma? I'd hoped to see her, too."

Parallel Charlie shrugged. "She doesn't know you guys as well, and she's more shy to start with. She stayed home. But you guys can come visit anytime, you know," he said, winking. "On our Earth, our family moved to the island after the summer holiday. Mom and

Dad just wanted to stay, and of course we did, too."

"You didn't go back home after the summer?" said Charlie.

"Just to get our stuff. We packed up and moved here—well, to the other side of that door—" he said, nodding at the elevator, "before school started. Been here—there—ever since."

"I don't mean to interrupt this reunion," said Ben, "but we have to find Dr. Waldo!" He looked in the bag, counting quickly. "Great, you brought what, a dozen doses? Perfect, Charlie, thank you." Parallel Charlie nodded. "Now, who is going?" said Ben.

Emma could feel her brother's eyes burning into her. He'd made it clear that he didn't want her to go, but she knew she had to. "I'm going," she said firmly, not looking at him. "We know I can get out if all else fails. The rest of you stay here, in case something happens. I'm going."

"You can't go again, Em," said Charlie. "I'll go. There's no reason for me not to go."

"There's every reason for you not to go, Charlie. You haven't been there. It's the ghost universe. It's mesmerizing. It sucks you in. I can't risk your going," said Emma.

"*You* can't risk *my* going?" Charlie's face was red with heat. "Why is it your decision? Just because you're the mental space traveler, suddenly you're in charge?"

Emma squirmed. She was determined to hold her ground, but fighting with Charlie made her uncomfortable. Still, she knew, she *knew* in her gut, that she needed to be the one to go.

Luckily for Emma, Milo broke in. "Charlie, I completely understand your wanting to watch out for your sister, and Emma, same with you, wanting to protect Charlie. I'm afraid I'm going to have to agree with Emma on this one, though. She's been there. We need every advantage we can get. I think Emma should go. And—"

"—and me," said Ben. "I've been studying and working with Dr.

Waldo for months. I'm more familiar with the travel and how Dr. Waldo thinks. Emma and me. We'll go."

"You can't!" said Emma. "We can't endanger more people than necessary. Just me."

"What happens if you have to carry Dr. Waldo?" said Ben. "You're amazing, but I'm physically stronger than you. And if something happens to you, someone needs to be there to help. I'm going."

Emma blushed at Ben's casual compliment: "You're amazing." She nodded. "Fine. We don't have time to argue. You can come."

Charlie looked from Emma to Ben. His sister wouldn't let him come, but Ben was allowed to go? The air was thick with tension. Charlie walked away briskly and sat down on a couch in the lounge.

"That's perfect," said Eve, trying to lighten the mood. "I trust Emma and Ben, and this way I get to stay here with the Charlies and catch up. It's been too long since I saw either of them." She grabbed Parallel Charlie's hand and pulled him over to sit with Charlie.

Seeing that Eve was going to keep him company while his sister went off to save Dr. Waldo eased Charlie's pain a little bit, but not a lot. Mostly, he hated being at odds with his twin. He sat and sulked while Milo injected Ben and Emma with the ghost vaccines. Then, Charlie realized that if something happened to Emma and she didn't return, he'd never forgive himself for letting her leave while they were angry with each other. Without apologizing or commenting on their squabble, he got up to help her pack for whatever lay ahead.

"Do you have everything?" he said, handing Emma a bottle of water.

"I think so," said Emma, smiling with gratitude at Charlie's reconciliation and packing the water into her bag. She briefly reached out to squeeze Charlie's hand, then looked into her backpack. "Test me."

"Food?" said Charlie.

Emma double-checked her pack. "Protein bars, check."

"Water?"

"Three water bottles, check. Water filter in case we run out of water, check."

"Extra vaccine?"

"Syringe to use on Dr. Waldo, and three back-up syringes just in case. Check." They had agreed they were not going to take the risk of giving themselves only one chance.

"Swiss army knife?"

Emma held up her Swiss army knife, identical to the one she knew Charlie was carrying; their father had given them the knives as gifts on their last birthday. "Check. Nothing I can't do with this."

"Positive attitude?" Charlie smiled.

"Dork," Emma said, punching him lightly on the shoulder.

Charlie went to punch Emma back, but then swept her into a bear hug. "Stay safe," he whispered into her ear.

"I will," she said. She didn't know why she felt such a foreboding. Ben would be with her, and hadn't she faced worse before? Still, she tried not to let on how scared she was. If Dr. Waldo was missing, it could not portend anything good.

"I'll be here if you need me," said Charlie. "Phone?"

Emma patted a pocket of her bag. "Phone: check," she said.

"I'm here if you need me, too," said Parallel Charlie. "Say the word, we're there."

"I know," said Emma. "Love you guys." Eyes on the verge of tears, she turned to Ben, who had gotten himself packed up with Eve and Milo's help. "So how are we getting there, Mr. Science Lab?" she said, blinking hard. "Will the elevator get us there?"

"Dark MATTER," said Ben. He held up a small black sphere. "Our old friend, the Dark Multiverse And Time Travel Energy Redistributer. Dr. Waldo has been working on it. We've used them several times, and they haven't imploded again for a while," he said with a smirk.

Emma shook her head with a small laugh. It was a dysfunctional Dark MATTER sphere that had gotten them stuck in the ghost universe the last time. "Are you sure?"

"As Dr. Waldo likes to say, 'The greatest and most challenging element of the pursuit of truth is learning to embrace uncertainty.' No, I'm not sure. But it's our best choice right now. And Dr. Waldo needs us."

Emma nodded. "Okay then." She looked Charlie in the eye and the twins exchanged an unspoken vow: *Everything will be okay.*

Ben handed Emma a sphere identical to the one he was holding. "A backup. In case something goes wrong with this one. And I have another one in my bag, too. No mistakes this time."

Emma took the sphere and zipped it securely into an interior pocket in her bag. "Right," she said under her breath. "What could go wrong?"

chapter five

Travel by Dark MATTER was different from travel in the elevator. For one thing, as with the pigeons, a person didn't have to enter any sort of portal or special room, but could travel from anywhere— even from inside the Hub. After checking his computer carefully to ensure he didn't make any errors, Ben entered the ghost planet's coordinates into the small sphere. Tightly linking elbows with Emma, who also grasped his arm with both her hands for good measure, Ben swiped a finger across the sphere's face.

The effect was instantaneous. Ben and Emma felt themselves disappearing, disintegrating, disassembling from the outside in. Their consciousness remained, but as their molecules dispersed and mingled with those of the universes, so did their awareness. They became the multiverse, and the multiverse became them, and only that precious consciousness of self kept them from completely integrating with all of existence, past, present, and future. Before they had a chance to contemplate this, however, their cells started to reunite, reconvene, reassemble, and all at once they were again separate entities, individuals, Ben and Emma, human beings on another planet in another universe so very far from home.

"I'd say this is the definition of discombobulated," said Ben, shaking his head and taking several deep breaths. "I can't believe it happens that quickly."

"I remember this," said Emma, blinking hard as she tried to focus. "It's like it takes a few minutes for all your cells to settle back where they're supposed to be. Including brain cells." She concentrated on breathing normally, pleased as always to learn that, whether due to compatibility with the planet's atmosphere or the influence of the rock on her bracelet that enabled her to breathe, her lungs were still satisfied with the air she was taking in.

"All right, let's figure this out," said Ben once he started to feel realigned and human again. "Where are we?" He looked around. They had not landed outside, but rather inside, in a dim, rustic room. There were no lights, but the wooden slats of the walls did not all meet, and several long slivers of bright light sliced through the shadows. It was daytime: small windows high up on the walls let in some sunshine as well, which illuminated the tiny dust motes floating in the air. The floor was nothing more than dirt, leveled and swept even. In one corner, a dirty lump of rags was piled on the floor.

"Do you see a door?" said Emma, squinting as her eyes adjusted to the dim. She cautiously reached out an arm to touch the wall, then traced her fingertips along the slats as she walked the edges of the room.

When she got to the lump on the floor, it shuddered.

"Aaaiieeeee!!!" Emma jumped and screamed, running to Ben. "What is that?" she cried, pointing at the lump of rags. "It moved!"

Even as she spoke, it was still moving, the amorphous shape unfolding, the rags taking form: human form. An arm reached out slowly from the rags to shield an emerging face from the light streaming in from the windows.

Ben cautiously stepped closer to the lump of cloth, looking closely. "It's ... No! Dr. Waldo? Is that you?"

"Ben … help me …" gasped Dr. Waldo, and he collapsed again.

Emma ran to the scientist's side, her fear gone. "Dr. Waldo! Dr. Waldo! Wake up!" She frantically rummaged in her bag to find food and water. "Help me," she said to Ben. "Hold him up so I can get some water in him."

Ben sat down and scooped the weak man's torso into a more upright position, holding him tight. Carefully, slowly, Emma let drops of water trickle into Dr. Waldo's mouth. The older man's survival instincts kicked in, and he swallowed the water greedily. Each swallow brought him closer to consciousness. After several minutes, he started to come to.

"Ben … and Emma," he said, each word an effort. "You found me." Despite his weakness, he smiled widely. "I knew you would. Good … good children."

"Dr. Waldo," said Emma, "We have to get you home! What are you doing here on a ghost planet? And why are you here in this dirty room?"

"When did you get here? How did you find me?" said Dr. Waldo weakly. It was unclear whether he hadn't heard Emma's questions, or was ignoring her. "Did you use the Dark MATTER?"

"We did," said Ben, still holding his mentor upright. "Worked like a charm."

Dr. Waldo grinned, his eyes barely open. "I didn't see or hear you arrive. It worked, then. I put a little trick into it. When you arrive somewhere, it blasts out a disorienting vibration that disrupts the memories of anything that could have a memory, enough that it will be confused. The confusion will be transferred to the person's own mind to stop them wondering how you appeared suddenly out of nowhere. If you pretend you're confused too, you'll fit right in." The effort of so many words wore him out. He breathed heavily and reached for the water bottle Emma was still holding. She helped him drink more of the life-giving fluid, drop by slow drop.

Emma looked at Ben. "We need to get him back, but I'm afraid of him traveling in this condition," she said in barely a whisper, hoping Dr. Waldo wouldn't hear.

Ben nodded. There was so much they didn't know about traveling the universes. "Soon, though," he said.

After a bit, the scientist pulled himself into a seated position on the floor, his back supported by the wall. Ben shifted, pulling his knees to his chest.

"Do you think you could eat something?" Emma asked, searching her backpack for a protein bar.

Dr. Waldo nodded. "A bit. Some food would be nice."

Emma unwrapped the bar and handed it to the older man. She wondered again how long he had been there. Though she knew he'd only been missing from the Hub for a day, his grizzled beard suggested several days of growth. He neither looked, nor, frankly, smelled, like he'd been anywhere near a shower for a while. Some time travel seemed likely.

"You avoided Emma's questions," said Ben. "What are you doing here? And why did you need help? Can't you leave?"

The scientist nibbled at the protein bar, sighing with pleasure. "Delicious. Haven't eaten in quite a while, I'd say. Time is tricky. How long have I been gone by your measure?"

"Not too long," replied Emma. "A day maybe. Time is tricky." Seeing that Dr. Waldo had almost emptied the water bottle, she handed him another. "Now. No more evading us. Are we on a ghost planet?"

Dr. Waldo nodded, lifting his head up and down just once. "Indeed." His demeanor changed, and he was suddenly alert. "We must be quiet. I don't know when he'll be back."

"He who?" said Ben. "Are you locked in here?" Across the dim room from where Dr. Waldo was sitting, the outline of a door was barely visible. Ben walked to it and felt the sides for a doorknob. "How does this open?" he asked.

"From the outside only," said Dr. Waldo wryly. "No way out from the inside."

"I don't understand," said Emma. "Someone's keeping you here? Who else is here? Surely not a ghost?"

"Yes, a ghost," said Dr. Waldo. "The man who's trying to take my life."

"Take your life!" said Emma. "He's trying to kill you? Why would he do that?" She watched him carefully. His labored breathing concerned her, and she could tell he was struggling to stay awake.

"No, he's not trying to kill me," said Dr. Waldo. He paused for another drink of water. "He's literally trying to *take* my life. He wants it for himself. He wants to be alive again."

Ben returned to where Emma and Dr. Waldo were sitting and found a place on the floor for himself. "You're going to have to back up, Dr. Waldo. I'm not understanding."

"Yes," said Emma, "I'm curious too, but we should get out of here first. I know you're weak, but we need to get you home. We brought extra Dark MATTER devices, and the one we used didn't seem to burn out this time. Looks like your upgrades worked!" She forced a smile and reached into her bag to find the device that would return them to the safety of the Hub.

But Dr. Waldo was shaking his head. "You can try," he said, "but I don't think it'll work here. I'm surprised you were even able to get in. There's a force field around this building. The man who built it used to be quite a scientist himself." He laughed softly. "The madness of a mad scientist doesn't go away after he dies, it seems."

Emma was distraught. The fact that the Dark MATTER might not work here was one thing, but what disturbed her more was Dr.

Waldo's demeanor. He seemed completely different from the man she'd met before; he'd lost his vigor and his irrepressible joy. Her own confidence waned with Dr. Waldo's hollowed presence.

"Has the man taken some of your life already?" she asked cautiously.

Dr. Waldo nodded weakly. "He has."

Emma pulled the Dark MATTER sphere out of her bag. "Well, we're going to try this anyway," she said firmly. "Never hurts to try." She entered the coordinates for the Hub into the black sphere, then linked one arm through Ben's, and held Dr. Waldo's hand. Focusing all her energy on taking the trio back where they belonged, with her other hand, she activated the sphere.

The air in the room shimmered ever so slightly. Then, silence.

They had not moved.

"I didn't think it would work," said Dr. Waldo, both pleased with the accuracy of his prediction and disappointed.

"Once more," said Emma, swiping across the sphere's surface again, not ready to give up after just one try. This time she thought she heard the slightest high-pitched hum, but they remained quite definitely inside the dim room on the ghost planet.

"I am going to get this to work!" she said, mostly to herself. Then, "Ben, did you happen to bring a pigeon? Maybe that will work."

As Ben searched his own backpack for a pigeon, Dr. Waldo looked on with hopeful resignation; he was more than happy to let Emma try her best, but in his heart he knew her efforts were futile.

With a look of confusion on his face, Ben pulled one of the devices called a pigeon from the depths of his bag. "Didn't know that was in there," he said. "Okay, let's give it a try!" They all linked arms again, and Ben activated the small machine. This time, not even a shimmer or a hum disturbed the air.

"Nothing," said Emma, the edges of fear starting to grow inside her. She looked at the scientist, weak by her side. The food and water had briefly revived him, but he seemed to be fading again. Would he even survive the trip back? If the Dark MATTER and the pigeon wouldn't take them home, her own ability to transport herself and others through space and time with her mind might be their only hope. And yet …

She took the third bottle of water from her bag, wishing she'd brought more, and handed it and another protein bar to the scientist. "Dr. Waldo," she said, "did you … before you left, did you have a chance to look over the results from any of my tests?"

The older man took the sustenance with gratitude, and nodded solemnly. "I did."

"Do you still think every time I move through the multiverse without a pigeon or a Dark MATTER or something, my life gets shorter? 'Small but significant' differences, your notes said?" Emma's words came out in a rush, as if speaking them quickly could lessen the impact.

The scientist hesitated, blinked. Nodded slowly. "That is what I think, at this point, yes."

Emma took in a deep breath, letting it out in a long exhale. It seemed unavoidable: she was going to have to make that sacrifice once again, and deal with the consequences later.

"No! There's got to be another way," said Ben sharply, following Emma's train of thought. Emma looked at him in surprise. "I … I know what's going on. I overheard some scientists talking about your telomeres," he explained. "I did some research on the telomeres when I first heard about them. It didn't sound good." He paused. "Dr. Waldo, I know your notes said there was a 'small but significant' difference in Emma's telomeres, but the scientists were saying it's not so small." He looked sternly at Dr. Waldo, waiting for an answer.

Dr. Waldo said nothing for a long time. Emma looked from Ben to the elderly scientist. "Well, Dr. Waldo?" she said. "Is it true?"

"Those scientists should not have been gossiping," said Dr. Waldo with an uncharacteristic hint of anger. "It's not necessarily true. We need to do further studies."

"But it's possible?" asked Emma.

The older man looked at her kindly. "Everything is possible."

Emma exhaled deeply.

"Your … skills … are a last resort," said Ben. "I won't let you subject yourself to that kind of mind travel any more than necessary."

Emma raised her eyes to his. "I appreciate your concern, Ben," she said, "but that's my choice, not yours."

Ben looked surprised, then smiled begrudgingly. "You're right, exactly, of course. I just … don't want you to get hurt. But it's your choice, not mine."

Emma smiled from the inside out. "Still, let's see if we can think of something else first."

The young man stood up and started feeling his way around the walls, testing their sturdiness and looking for weaknesses in the gaps. "Next time, remind me to bring a crowbar," he said. The windows in the room were high on the walls, too high to even see anything but the light-blue-gray sky high above. Ben jumped to try to catch the ledge, but his fingers slipped from the narrow surface every time. "Crowbar and a ladder, that is," he said.

"Has anyone ever tried to make things out of intention in a ghost universe, like you do in the Hub?" asked Emma.

Ben frowned. "I have no idea," he said. He paused, quiet in intense concentration, trying to conjure up a crowbar or a ladder like he'd learned to do back at the lab. His face grew red with exertion, but nothing materialized. He shrugged. "I don't think it works here."

Emma squinted up at the windows. "Maybe if you boost me up I can reach?" she suggested.

"Worth a try," said Ben. He interwove his fingers to form a cradle.

Emma gingerly stepped one foot into Ben's hands, leaning against the rough wall for balance. "Okay," she said, "ready." Ben lifted her carefully, but she lost her balance and tumbled to the ground.

"Ouch," said Emma, holding one elbow. She looked up at the window again, assessing its height. The idea of shortening her telomeres was looking more and more appealing. "Maybe if I stand on your shoulders?" she said, brushing the dirt off her clothes as she picked herself up off the floor.

Ben squatted, enabling Emma to sit on his shoulders. He grasped Emma's hands, and slowly stood up. "Ha," he said, smiling as he staggered slightly with the unfamiliar and off-balance weight. "Never done that before. Easier than I thought!"

Emma held her breath and tried to avoid any sudden movements. The window sill was now at her chin level, giving her a view of the strange outside world on which they'd landed. Compared to the first ghost planet she'd been to, this one was lush and almost green, though even the green of the multitudes of trees and plants outside the window was muted with a gray translucence. The building they were in was built on a gently sloping hill that led down to a calm, gray-blue lake, surrounded by gray-green trees that looked a bit like pine trees, tall with branches filled out with dark, foot-long needles. As far as Emma could see, there were no other buildings between them and the lake. She pressed her face against the glass to try to see more of the landscape around them, and to look for other buildings or for people—ghosts—in the vicinity, but her view was severely restricted.

Emma took her right hand out of Ben's, still holding tight with her left. She felt around the edge of the window, searching with both her eyes and her fingers for some way out. There was no way to open the window, she quickly determined; it had no latch she could release to push it out, nor would it slide in any direction.

"It's closed and sealed tight," she said. Cautiously, she tapped her knuckles against the glass. "I suppose I could try to break it?" Off in the distance she thought she saw movement. A ghost? A ghost animal in the forest? The trees, blowing in the wind? Was there wind on this ghost planet? On the other ghost planet, a warm, gentle breeze had blown softly but incessantly. Was the weather on all ghost planets alike? Was it even really weather? Or some other force, brought on by the ghostly inhabitants?

"Breaking the window wouldn't do any good," said Ben, bringing Emma's thoughts back to reality. "It'd be dangerous, all that broken glass, and I don't know how we'd get all of us up there and out the window, anyway."

Emma nodded. "No, you're right," she said. "Turn around so I can see the rest of the room. Maybe I can see something from up here that we missed. Carefully."

Ben did as Emma asked, turning slowly, but Emma saw nothing.

"Okay, let me down," she said, once she was satisfied with her search.

Ben lowered to a squat again, and Emma hopped off his shoulders with more grace than she could have hoped. Ben rubbed his neck.

"Sorry, did I hurt you?" said Emma.

"No, I just twisted funny when I lifted you, I think. I'm fine."

The teens sat again by Dr. Waldo, who had watched their efforts in silence.

"Worth a try," he said. "Always worth a try."

"Why are you here, Dr. Waldo?" asked Emma, finally broaching the subject she and Ben had been curious about since the moment they arrived. "Why are you on this ghost planet? Did you get here accidentally?" Her own visit to a ghost planet had been unplanned; maybe this one was too.

For a moment, Dr. Waldo seemed not to have heard. He stared off into a distance beyond the walls of the small room, seeing something that was not there. Finally, he said, "My wife is here."

"Your wife?" Emma said, recalling her conversation with Eve, in which the girl from Lero had told Emma that Dr. Waldo's wife was dead. "She's here?"

"She was, anyway," said Dr. Waldo. His eyes glassed over with memory and the glimmer of oncoming tears. "She's gone." He shook his head and looked away, off into the distance, into the past.

Emma shifted her legs on the ground, trying to find a more comfortable position on the hard floor. "I'm so sorry, Dr. Waldo. I'm confused, though. She was here but she's gone? When was she here? Where did she go?" she said.

"My wife," Dr. Waldo began, "died many years ago. She had a disease unknown on Lero, which she contracted from my lab in the Hub. We didn't know...." Memories flooded his thoughts. "It was my fault. It was my fault she got the disease, and it was my fault she died from it. I should have found a cure."

"I'm sure it wasn't your fault," said Emma. "You can't cure everything. You didn't know, right? You can't solve every problem." But to herself, she wondered: how did Dr. Waldo's wife get a disease in the Hub? Were diseases just lying around in there? She might have to be more careful, if they ever got back.

"I was in the Hub," said Dr. Waldo, shaking his head, unwilling to forgive himself. "Everything is possible in the Hub. I should have found a way beyond my own limitations. I should have found the cure for her. There had to be one. I just didn't find it in time." He paused, lost in his shame and his sorrow. He looked up at the light streaming through the high windows, watching the dust motes on their slow dance in the indifferent sunbeam. "I loved her so much," he continued at last. "She was my soul mate, you see." He laughed mirthlessly. "In all the universes, she was the one. And that's a lot of people to pick from. Somehow, we found each other. We always imagined retiring to a little cottage on the lake. A lake just like the one outside this building. Just Lora and me, a little garden, maybe, for fresh produce and for flowers. Fresh air. Peace. After a lifetime of looking to the stars, the idea of seeing the world right before me for once seemed like a nice idea.

"After Lora died, I was distraught. I worked endless hours in the Hub, trying to forget. But of course you never forget. You just push the thoughts aside and hope they don't push back. But I knew, I knew without knowing but still I was sure, that Lora was somewhere, thinking of me, too. I knew she hadn't passed to nothingness. My thoughts met with her thoughts and they wouldn't let each other go.

"One day at work, I found out about the ghost universe. This universe. I was traveling, doing research on another planet, one far more advanced than Lero. Their scientists had been traveling through the universes and doing scientific research far longer than we had. A gentleman there told me about the ghost universe, and the different ghost planets. He said there was a ghost planet for people who, for one reason or another, hadn't yet moved on; for people who had died but were still emotionally tied to loved ones back at home.

"I knew instantly I would find Lora on that planet. Without telling him why I wanted to know—he'd already warned me of the dangers of traveling to ghost planets while still alive—I asked for more information on this planet, for its coordinates. I went back to our elevator and entered the coordinates into it, holding my breath, hoping. As you may recall, not all elevators stop at the ghost universe; it's like the thirteenth floor on elevators on your Earth. By some stroke of luck, some miracle, some coincidence—or maybe, no coincidence at all—our elevator did connect to this planet. It took me directly here. I opened the elevator door and saw what you saw from that window up there, Emma, this beautiful, if muted, land. In the distance I could see a lake, the lake you saw, Emma. I started walking toward it, and before long, I saw someone walking toward me." His face glowed at the memory. "It was my wife, looking like she did before she got sick, so beautiful, more beautiful, even, than I remembered. We reunited and talked for hours, so long, I don't even remember. I had to go back to the Hub only because I foolishly hadn't brought any food or water with me, and I wasn't so sure about drinking from a ghost lake." He laughed. "Visiting a ghost universe didn't phase me, but drinking the water, now that's where I drew the line. But I'd been gone so long that I almost wasn't able to wrench myself away. In the end, to be honest, my wife had to take me to the elevator and stuff me in. Once the door closed I came back to my senses. But it wasn't enough. I wanted to see her again.

"I came back the next day, and we talked again for hours. She had to force me to go home again. When I came the next day, she told me we could not go on like that." The scientist sighed deeply. "She wouldn't move on, but she wouldn't let me stay. She told me to come back on our anniversary. And so I did. The first year I came, she led me here. You probably couldn't see it from that window," he said, "but there's a little cottage just a few meters behind this building. Lora enlisted the help of some other ghosts, and together they built the house she and I had dreamed of. By the next year, she had started a garden. Of course I couldn't eat the food from it … it's ghost food, not food for Leroians. Still, it kept her happy.

And we went on like that for years. For eleven years I visited her on our anniversary, and each time I had to devise a way to make sure I didn't get stuck here. As you are well aware, Emma, it is all too easy to get stuck on a ghost planet, to forget that you want to leave. Lucky for me, Lora never forgot.

"Our anniversary was three days ago," he continued. "I showed up like usual, but something was different. Lora didn't meet me at the elevator, for one thing. I walked here by myself. When I got here, I saw this building."

"It wasn't here before?" asked Ben.

"No, this was new. And the garden, I noticed without thinking about it that the garden was overgrown. It wasn't until afterward, when I was stuck here, that it dawned on me. My brain saw it but I didn't think about it; that happens, you know."

He coughed briefly and drank some water. "When I got here, the door to this room was open. My stupidity, assuming I could come to no harm on a ghost planet," he laughed wryly. "As I poked my head into the room, someone came up behind me and knocked me out cold. When I came to, I was tied up in here, with a ghost I'd never seen before looking me over. He never told me his name. He explained that shortly after my last visit, he'd arrived on this planet himself and befriended my wife. On hearing that I visited every year, he devised a plan. He convinced my wife to move on, and then built this shed. He's a scientist, too, from Lero, but not one I'd met before. He's insane. Perhaps he was in life, as well. He built this shed, created a force field around it, calculated the date I'd arrive next, and waited. Every day I've been here he's come in several times to do a blood transfusion, my blood into him. He thinks if he can take enough of my life, he can jump-start his own."

Emma sat, mesmerized by Dr. Waldo's impossible tale. "Do you think it would work?" she asked. "Can the blood from one person revive a ghost? One that's been dead for almost a year, even?"

Dr. Waldo shook his head. "I don't think so," he said, "but I don't know everything. I haven't seen his lab, his tools, his plans. All I know is that he's been taking my blood. And a lot of it. I'm feeling a bit dizzy, you see. He has given me water, but not much, and nothing to eat. Do you have any more food in that bag of yours?"

Emma pulled out another protein bar and handed it to Dr. Waldo. He unwrapped the bar and broke off a small piece, which he popped into his mouth and savored like chocolate.

"Dr. Waldo," Emma said, "did you use any ghost vaccine on yourself before you came here?" Though the water and food were reviving him a bit, his face seemed to have grown more pale even in the short time they'd been there.

The scientist shook his head. "No, the other Charles brought me some, but I put it in a pipette, and then proceeded to drop it. Getting old, I guess." His look of disappointment in himself stung Emma straight through the heart.

She pulled one of the vaccine syringes from her bag. "I think we should give you a dose," she said. "We had the other Charlie bring us more. I think this might help." She tried to sound confident, but in fact had no idea. However, Dr. Waldo nodded his agreement and reached out his arm, pulling up his sleeve.

Emma stared at the instrument in her hand. "How do I do this?" she asked Ben.

Ben twisted his mouth. "I don't know?" he said. "Stick the needle in him and plunge the plunger, I guess?"

Dr. Waldo shook his head again, this time in amusement. "It is not difficult, children," he said, reaching for the syringe. Pointing the needle toward the ceiling, he pushed the plunger just enough that the slightest bit of vaccine spurted out the top, forcing out any air bubbles. Then, wincing only slightly, he stabbed his upper left arm with the sharp needle and pressed the plunger again, releasing the liquid vaccine into his body.

Emma watched him closely. How long would the vaccine take to work, and how would they know, anyway? She decided they couldn't afford to wait. "Okay, then," she said. Resolved, she slapped the ground on either side of her. "We have to get out of here, and soon. I guess it's me." The seventeen-year-old brushed her dark auburn hair behind her ears, cleared her throat, and closed her eyes. *Wait: how did I do this last time?* she thought. In a sudden panic, Emma realized that although it had only been a few months since she last traveled through the multiverse, it felt like a lifetime ago. *I already have everything I need,* she thought, echoing the words Eve's great aunt Doethine had told her when Emma, Eve, and the other Charlie had been stuck on another ghost planet. Thoughts of shortened telomeres—a shortened life—danced through her mind. She shook her head to make the thoughts go away. Taking a slow, deep breath, Emma thought, *I can do this.*

I already have everything I need. The Hub, Emma thought. *Take us back to the Hub. Me, Ben, and Dr. Waldo. The Hub, with Rupert, the elephant in the room, and where the Charlies are, and where Eve is. The Hub, with the new Experimental Building, where Ben made his own wing and is learning all about the universes. The Hub ...*

She tried with all her might to focus her thoughts and energy. She waited for the feeling she remembered so well, the feeling of all the breath being squeezed out of her, to be replaced by all the oxygen in the multiverse. The vibration of all her cells, the complete emptiness and fullness of eternity and infinity.

None of it came.

Emma opened one eye to see Dr. Waldo and Ben watching her, expectantly.

"It's not working," she said. She squeezed her eyes tight and tried to focus again, to focus like she'd never focused before. *The Hub*, she thought. *The Hub, the Hub, the Hub! We need to get back to the Hub.*

"Stop," said Ben, who had been wracking his mind for an alternative. He didn't want to watch Emma sacrifice herself for him. Maybe there was another way. "Stop. I might have another idea."

Emma exhaled a sigh of relief and opened her eyes. "What's your idea?" she asked.

"We still have some ghost vaccine, right?" said Ben. Emma nodded. The extra syringes were packed safely in her bag. "What if we use it on this guy—this ghost—who is trying to take Dr. Waldo's life?"

Dr. Waldo's eyes lit up as he quickly caught Ben's meaning, revealing the vaguest hint of his former ebullient self. "Yes, yes! Ben, I think you may have something there ..." But then the light went out and he slouched, listless, against the wall.

"Dr. Waldo!" cried Emma. "Dr. Waldo, are you okay?" The older man was completely unresponsive. Emma checked his wrist for a pulse. "He's still alive," she said. She picked up the half-empty water bottle next to the elderly scientist, and clumsily poured a few drops of water into Dr. Waldo's mouth. In a daze, the man swallowed instinctively. He opened his eyes briefly, then closed them again. Emma took slow breaths to counter her racing heart.

Worry crossed over Ben's face. "Emma, we have to get him out of here."

"I agree," she said. "What's your plan?" She drizzled a little more water into Dr. Waldo's mouth, hoping to revive him again.

"Those vaccines," said Ben, as he helped hold Dr. Waldo's head back to allow the liquid to trickle down his throat. "If they vaccinate against ghosts, and that guy is a ghost, maybe it'll sort of stun him temporarily. I mean, it probably can't kill him, right?"

"Seeing as the guy's already dead and all," agreed Emma. But she wondered: had administering the vaccine to Dr. Waldo killed him? Was he too weak for the vaccine? Was there something wrong with the vaccine? Or was it coincidence, or something else?

Ben continued. "The man has some of Dr. Waldo's life in him. With that, and with the ghost part of him, maybe the vaccine will debilitate him. For a while, anyway."

"It's worth a try," said Emma, thinking that there had been many things that day that they'd deemed "worth a try" … and yet none of them had worked. She hoped this time, their efforts would be successful.

"Should we … try to wake him up?" Ben said, looking anxiously at Dr. Waldo. "I can carry him if we have to, but …"

Emma looked at Dr. Waldo, slumped helplessly against the wall. Seeing him so weak made her anxious. *Be strong,* she told herself. *You can do this.* "I think you're right," she said. "I just have a bit more water; hopefully that will do." Mentally she berated herself for not bringing more bottles. *A lesson for next time,* she thought.

Carefully, Emma held Dr. Waldo's head as she once again tried to trickle water into his mouth. The older man sputtered slightly but didn't open his eyes. "Come on, Dr. Waldo," Emma said gently, "we need you alert for this." *Wake up, wake up, wake up,* she thought. *Universes, help me! Wake him up!*

Whether of his own accord or with the help of the universes, Dr. Waldo finally opened his eyes. He was not at peak performance, but he was alert. Alert enough. Emma almost shook with relief that the vaccine hadn't killed their friend.

"We have a plan, Dr. Waldo," said Ben softly but urgently, and he and Emma proceeded to tell the scientist their idea.

The tiniest sparkle of joy lit up Dr. Waldo's previously lifeless face. "Excellent, children," he said weakly. "Excellent idea. I think

... it may work." His speaking and breathing were labored. They would have to act fast.

"Now," continued Dr. Waldo, "Emma, my dear ...." He paused, breathing heavily. "Be ready with the Dark MATTER as soon as we are out of here. If that doesn't work, we will have to run to the elevator as fast as we can."

Emma and Ben exchanged looks. "As fast as we can" was a very different speed for them than for their dear mentor, in his current state of being.

"Which way is the elevator?" Emma asked. "In case we have to go there." She very much hoped they would not have to. Aside from the fact she and Ben would most likely have to carry the scientist, she also knew every minute on a ghost planet put them at greater risk of never escaping.

Dr. Waldo lifted his head. "About a fifteen-minute walk ... that way." He pointed to the left of the door. "There's a trail. You can't miss it."

"The Dark MATTER will work," Ben said sternly. He looked at Emma. "It has to."

"Dr. Waldo," said Emma, "If the ghost follows us, could he out-run us?"

He looked at her and paused before nodding weakly. "Most definitely," he said. "The ghosts are basically weightless here, whereas we mortals are not."

Emma nodded. They would simply have to escape another way.

Having no idea when the ghost might reappear, they swiftly started to put their plan into action. On Dr. Waldo's suggestion, Emma and Ben tied him up again, loosely, just a suggestion of knots to the unsuspecting eye, so that the ghost man wouldn't become suspicious immediately upon entering the building. Then, the teens took up positions on either side of the door, Ben with one syringe of vaccine held firmly in his hand, Emma with the other two.

"As soon as we stick the needles in him, I'll grab him," Ben said with more confidence than he felt.

Emma nodded, but could not help but have her doubts about the whole plan. The ghost man was … well, a ghost. Could needles even be stuck into his body? Or would they float right through him?

"I'm hoping he has enough of my life in him by now that he's closer to flesh and blood than he might have been," Dr. Waldo had said before taking up his too-convincing lifeless pose in the corner. Emma hoped he was right.

They crouched and waited in the dimly lit room. The ghost planet was eerily silent. No cars whipped by on nearby streets, but even more noticeable than that was the complete absence of the sounds of life. No birds chirped, no squirrels scuttled by carrying their treasures. Even the wind seemed muted.

Emma shifted several times, trying to decide from which position she could best pounce. A cramp in her left hamstring almost caused her to shout out in pain. Careful not to stab herself with a syringe, she gently kneaded her muscle to make the cramp go away.

"What if he doesn't come back?" she whispered to Ben.

"He will," whispered Ben, shifting his weight once more and bouncing lightly on his toes. "He has to." But he didn't sound sure either.

And they waited.

After a while, Emma whispered, "Should we check to make sure Dr. Waldo is still alive?"

"I am still alive, my dear, not at my best, but still alive," came a soft reply from the lump in the corner.

"Stay that way," said Ben.

"I'm trying," said Dr. Waldo.

They waited some more. Emma's legs screamed with pain from crouching so long. "Ben," she finally said, "wouldn't it make more sense for us to stand, anyway? Why are we crouching?"

Ben looked at her, puzzled. "I don't know? I guess it seemed sneakier?"

Emma laughed quietly. "I think we might have a better chance of attacking him if we're at his level," she said. She painfully drew herself up to a standing position. "Ohhhh, so much better," she whispered with a sigh of relief.

Following suit, Ben rose to standing position. "You're a good thinker, Emma Nelson," he said.

Much to her surprise, Emma found herself winking at him. She blushed immediately.

"A ghost planet," said Ben, oblivious to both wink and blush. "I would never have imagined any of this a year ago. I mean, think about it. If everything is possible somewhere ... that's a lot of possibility. If we can imagine it, it could exist. A world where animals can talk."

"A world where trees are made of chocolate," said Emma. "Like chocolate bar chocolate, not just cacao beans."

"A world where there are multiple forms of intelligent life, all living together on the same planet," said Ben.

"A world where people are always kind," said Emma.

"A world where no one is ever sad," said Ben.

"'Everything is possible' is not the same as 'Everything is,'" came a voice from the lump in the corner. Emma had almost forgotten Dr. Waldo, had almost forgotten that they were there with a purpose, that they were not there simply to stand, endlessly, waiting.

"Do you think ghosts have good hearing?" Ben asked.

"I hope not," said Emma. "I guess we should be careful."

They stood in silence. Emma continued pondering all the possibilities contained in the idea that "everything is possible." Worlds made of diamonds? Worlds with intelligent life as small as ants? Worlds where people lived under water? Worlds where time moved backwards? Surely not *everything* was possible. Finally, she decided that, as Dr. Waldo had pointed out, "everything is possible" was different from "everything is."

Suddenly, they heard a rustling outside. The hair on Emma's skin stood straight up. Everything depended on their quick action, their good aim … and luck. Emma looked at Ben. Ben nodded. They were ready.

A scraping sound at the door indicated whatever lock the ghost man had created was being lifted. The door swung inward, slowly.

The ghost man appeared.

Before they even had a chance to assess the man, Emma and Ben were on him. Emma jabbed both syringes into whatever body parts were nearest, and Ben did the same with his, a flurry of arms and vaccine.

The ghost man never had a chance.

He fell, not like a brick but a little like a brick with some helium inside: slower than expected, but still decidedly succumbing to the laws of gravity.

"Well," said Emma, looking down on the ghost on the ground. He did indeed look like a cross between a ghost and a live being: slightly more solid, but still with a transparent, ethereal, timeless look to him. Somewhere between alive and dead.

"That worked!" said Ben, jumping up and down with excitement. He high-fived Emma with a burst of joy. "Yes! Yes!!"

Meanwhile, Dr. Waldo had worked himself free from the loose knots. "No time for that! OUT!" he said, running faster than Emma or Ben would have imagined, grabbing their hands and spinning them and their attention toward the door. He swung the door open wide and ran free.

With a last look at the ghost man, Emma and Ben ran after him. Emma started to close and lock the door behind her, but Dr. Waldo stopped her.

"We can't stoop to his level," the scientist said. "Having been imprisoned does not justify imprisoning someone else. We must always strive to be the better person, even when we are wronged."

"But what if—" Emma began.

"Emma, use the Dark MATTER *now*," said Dr. Waldo, interrupting her. "If it doesn't work, we'll worry then."

They linked arms, and Emma quickly set the Dark MATTER to the Hub coordinates. A movement inside the dark building spurred her on. She swiped the front of the black sphere, closed her eyes, and hoped.

chapter six

Back at the Hub, Eve, Charlie, and Parallel Charlie were happily chatting and enjoying a snack in the lounge. Charlie had been hungry, and had asked Eve if she could create a little food for them out of nothing.

"What do you want?" Eve had asked.

"Something unique and international," Charlie had said.

And so Eve had intentioned up some English Breakfast tea with cream, and a plate overflowing with spiced pumpkin scones.

"That's hardly unique and international," Charlie had complained.

Eve had just winked. "It's unique to me, Charles," she had said. "I'm an alien, remember?"

Not one to argue long over food, Charlie had taken a bite of a tender, delicious scone and decided it was sufficient.

Now, the three were sitting on the couch, wondering what to do with themselves while the others were away.

"This lounge needs a name," said Parallel Charlie, scarfing down his third scone. "You can't just call it 'the lounge we made.' That doesn't have a ring to it." He took another bite. "Mmmmmm. Eve. You're a good cook."

"Cheerio, I agree, old chap," said Charlie, raising his teacup and affecting his idea of a British accent. "Whatnot and tally ho! You guys have a Great Britain on your Earth, too, right?" He took a sip of his tea.

"We do indeed, my good man," said Parallel Charlie, mimicking Charlie's accent. "Or, we did. Of course it broke up into separate countries a long time ago. There's England, Scotland, Wales, and New Ireland. Ireland and Northern Ireland used to be separate but they blended into New Ireland decades ago. That is, if I remember my history right. It's been ages, right-o!" He spread some more butter on his scone and took another bite. "Mmmm. Just like old King George used to make!"

Eve, for her part, was giggling helplessly on the couch and wondering if Parallel Charlie's stomach was bottomless. The entertainment of one Charlie was wonderful enough for a girl who had spent so much of her life without friends her age, but two Charlies was almost too much. Almost. Rupert must have agreed, as the normally rather solitary pachyderm had meandered ever so slightly closer to the lounge area, and was watching the goings-on with one little two-dimensional eye. Eve could have sworn she saw the tiniest grin creep up from under his trunk.

Charlie was pouring a fresh cup of tea for Eve when suddenly the air split and crackled as though hit by lightning. Startled, he spilled the hot liquid all over the table just as Emma, Ben, and Dr. Waldo tumbled right into the center of the sophisticated scene, scattering tea and scones everywhere.

"What in the—" said Charlie, in whose lap Ben had landed. "Ben! If you wanted some tea, all you had to do was ask!" He quickly checked to make sure his sister was among the returning group. "Emma!" he said in relief. Then: "Dr. Waldo! They found you!"

But the exertion and stress of the excursion had left Dr. Waldo clinging tenuously to life. With hardly a "hello" to her brother, parallel brother, and friend, Emma quickly took action. "He needs help! Charlie, can you lift him? Ben, is there a … I don't know, a Hub hospital? A medical doctor?"

As Emma frantically scanned the Hub trying to figure out where they might take him, the Charlies and Ben scrambled to lift the scientist.

"Over there!" said Ben, looking to other scientists who had seen the commotion and were running toward the lounge. The Charlies each took a side of Dr. Waldo, lifting him under shoulder and knee, and followed Ben to the quickly assembled rescue team.

Emma stood, watching them, panting. Eve stepped up, wrapped an arm around Emma's waist and lay her head on the exhausted girl's shoulder.

"He'll be okay now, don't worry," said Eve. "What happened?"

But Emma was overcome and couldn't answer. She looked at her blond alien friend and suddenly the emotions all rushed in. She collapsed on the couch, crying.

Eve sat next to her, stroking Emma's hair. "You're safe now," she said. "It's okay. These doctors will get Dr. Waldo all back to normal, don't worry."

Wiping her tears, Emma sat up and looked at Eve. "I know he'll be fine. It's just everything at once. It's a lot."

"I know it is," said Eve. "It takes some getting used to. But it's not always dangerous, believe me. Sometimes it's fun." She smiled encouragingly at Emma. "Right? Sometimes you have fun?"

In their distress, neither Emma nor Eve had seen Rupert softly galumph right into the lounge. Feeling her hair being lifted rather clumsily, Emma looked up to see the elephant peering down on her with what she was certain was concern.

"Rupert!" she said, almost in awe. The Hub's "elephant in the room" had been there as long as she'd known about the Hub, but somehow, she'd never been so close to the enormous, flat creature. She stared into his eye—as he was two-dimensional, there was no way to look at both eyes at once—and was sure she saw recognition there. "You know me, don't you?" she said softly.

In reply, Rupert stroked her face with his trunk.

"Ouch!" laughed Emma. "Rupert, you have to be careful or you'll give me a paper cut!" She gently stroked the side of Rupert's trunk, then stood and reached high to scritch behind his ear. "Yes, sometimes it's fabulous," she said to Eve, answering her earlier question.

Having left Dr. Waldo in the care of the doctors and the Charlies (who were not "helping" in Dr. Waldo's care so much as they were clowning around and trying to lift his spirits), Ben rejoined the young women in the lounge.

"This one is a lot more social than the first Rupert," he said, watching with a mix of awe and fondness as Rupert continued to carefully stroke Emma's hair. Emma winced occasionally; Rupert's edges were surprisingly sharp. But she would not stop him.

The first Rupert, of course, was the one Emma had met that summer, when she and Charlie initially discovered the Hub. That Rupert had been destroyed—killed—along with everything else in the Hub. Dr Waldo, Ben, and the other scientists had worked hard to rebuild the space after the annihilation. Many things were the same, but they'd taken the opportunity to improve on some objects where they could see a way.

"I guess it's not really the same Rupert," said Emma, frowning as she rubbed Rupert's side. "Should he have his own name? Rupert 2.0? Is it wrong to call him Rupert?"

"Nah," said Ben, rubbing Rupert at the top side of his trunk. Rupert delighted in the attention, wagging his tail and trunk and flapping his ears with joy. "He's like the Dalai Lama or a vampire slayer. When one dies, another rises. He's Rupert. It's not just a name, it's a title. 'Rupert, the Elephant in the Room.'"

Emma smiled and leaned into the elephant, cuddling him as best a person can cuddle with a two-dimensional object. *Yes,* she thought, *travel through space and time is not so bad after all.*

With the magical efficiency of the Hub and the expert skills of its scientists and doctors, Dr. Waldo was feeling better in no time. He wasn't immediately back to his former self, but he felt well enough to sit with the teens in the lounge. Everyone who had not gone to the ghost planet was filled in on what happened. There was an unspoken agreement to leave alone Dr. Waldo's motives for visiting the planet, for him to sort out in his own time.

"My goodness," said Dr. Waldo, resting in a recliner chair with an IV drip topping off his fluids, and a tank of oxygen by his side to be used if needed. "Look at you all. Just look at you! Emma, Charlie, Charlie, so good to have you back. We've been having great fun exploring the mysteries of the universes while you've been gone, haven't we, Ben and Eve? So much fun. I tell you, that Ben, he's got scientist blood. Science in his genes. It was he who suggested some of the ideas to improve the Dark MATTER globe, did he tell you? Such a humble young man, he probably didn't tell you, but you see, you see, it worked, so much better than before!"

"Almost anything—" Emma started to say that almost anything would be "better than before," but stopped herself in time. She didn't want to hurt Dr. Waldo's feelings.

"Yes," said Charlie with an amused smile, "Ben, your targeting was amazing! Landed you all literally right in our laps! Maybe next time aim for a few feet away?" He and Parallel Charlie had cleaned up all the spilled snacks, and Eve had brought forth from the air some new treats for everyone: more tea and scones, but also some chocolate, which everyone knew was full of healing powers.

"We wanted a soft landing," said Ben, with a laugh. "How was I to know you lazy bums would still be on the couch?"

"Are you sure you're feeling up to being up?" Emma asked Dr. Waldo. She looked him over carefully, studying him for signs of weakness. "I know the medical treatments here are advanced, but …"

"To be sure, to be sure," said Dr. Waldo, "Not a problem at all, I am well, blood and water and oxygen and a bit of a pumpkin scone and some tea, that's all I needed, fit as a fiddle again, fit as a fiddle!"

"Is a fiddle fit?" asked Eve, raising an eyebrow and popping a small piece of chocolate into her mouth. "Isn't a fiddle a string instrument? That doesn't make sense to me."

"Ah, all the idioms make sense if you just trace them back to their roots," said Charlie.

"Like, 'keep your eyes peeled,'" said Parallel Charlie. "Makes no sense, right? But if you trace it back, it has to do with peeling potatoes. You know, peeling the eyes of the potatoes."

Eve looked skeptically from the Charlies to Emma, who was rolling her eyes. "Is that true?"

Emma shook her head. "I have no idea, but somehow I doubt it."

Charlie and Parallel Charlie fist-bumped at their collective cleverness.

"Well, don't keep me in suspense, now, young intelligent life forms, what have you been up to whilst I was … away?" said Dr. Waldo. "Charlie said something about a note you deciphered?" He looked at Ben.

"I mean, we all worked on it," said Ben humbly.

"No, it was you," said Emma. "You figured it out. We might not have unraveled that riddle without you."

A blush creeped up Ben's neck. "Group effort. Anyway, we figured out that the notes Kata left for Eve and Milo had clues in them. Long story short, the clues spell out 'dark galaxy,' 'water,' and 'magnet.'"

Eve looked at Dr. Waldo with hope in her eyes. "Do those mean anything to you? Dad believes the 'dark galaxy' is reference to a stone he found a long time ago on Lero. Emma thinks it's what they call a 'black opal' on her Earth, from the country of Australia. But we don't know what 'water' and 'magnet' mean. They're so vague. They could mean anything. Originally we thought there was a missing note, since the other two notes said 'read this second' and 'read this third,' but now we know that was just a clue to deciphering the message."

Stroking his chin—he had not yet taken time to shave since he returned, and a grizzly gray fuzz covered the lower half of his face—Dr. Waldo nodded, humming softly. "Yes, yes. Kata did like Australia," he said, half to himself. "Kangaroos and quokkas and pademelons and echidnas, all the animal life, and the dry red earth, the ancient monoliths, the endless Outback, yes, she talked about it enthusiastically every time she returned. Yes, yes, she did like Australia."

"She did?" asked Eve. "How come she didn't tell me?"

Dr. Waldo looked at the girl with a mix of sympathy and sadness. "You and your father were gone a lot, you know."

Heat rose up Eve's face. "Are you saying it was my fault?" she sputtered.

"Oh, no, no, my dear! No, no, not at all. I'm just saying, adults, we aren't perfect. We may want you kids to think we have it all figured out, but we don't. At any rate, it's not for me to debate. The fact remains, your mother loved Australia. Do you know where you might find the black opal rocks? Australia is a big country."

Hoping to diffuse the tension, Emma spoke up brightly. "Lightning Ridge!" she said with forced enthusiasm. "The black opals are mostly found in Lightning Ridge."

"Aha!" said Dr. Waldo, pointing his finger to the air. "Then that is where you should start!" He coughed lightly.

Parallel Charlie, who had been watching with delight and fascination, jumped in. "Hey, I have a cool idea. I should come, too. Can I come, too?" He looked at Emma. "Last time was amazing. Except for all the parts where we were nearly killed, but other than that, off the hook."

Emma laughed and rolled her eyes. "Dork," she said to Parallel Charlie, with a wink to her own Charlie.

"Do we even know where we're going?" said Ben. "I mean, Lightning Ridge, sure, but ... beyond that?"

"We've had less to go on before," said Emma, warming to the idea of another adventure. After all, Ben and Eve had had their share of travel the last few months, but she and Charlie had been stuck in school, dreaming of life back in the Hub. "We figured out the clues, even if we still don't know what they mean. We can't just give up. It's Eve's mom. We have to at least try."

Ben nodded. "Of course." He reached over and gave Eve a hug. "For Eve, and her mom, anything."

Tears filled Eve's eyes and she looked away, but the cascade of hair that hid her face couldn't fully cover her smile. "Thanks, guys," she said.

When Ben released her from his hug, the Charlies looked at each other and, without a word, quickly ran to surround Eve in their collective arms. "Charlie sandwich!" said Charlie.

Eve squealed and laughed, half squirming to escape and half reveling in the love. "You guys!" she said with delight. "Okay, okay! Enough!" She tucked her hair behind her ear and wiped away her tears. "Okay. We need a plan."

"Well, first," said Emma to Parallel Charlie, "if you're going with us, we need to call you something other than 'Charlie.' It gets too confusing."

"Can't we both be Charlie?" asked Charlie, looking at Parallel Charlie. He knew instinctively that Parallel Charlie would not want to give up his name any more than he would himself.

"No," said Emma. "This is all weird enough. Other Charlie, what do you want to be called?"

"Why do I have to be the one to change my name?" asked Parallel Charlie, pouting.

"Because you're tagging along with us, not the other way around."

"So does that mean I get to come?" Parallel Charlie hopped with joy. Charlie joined him, and the two do-si-doed around the rest of the group.

"Oh stop!" said Emma, tired and alternating between crankiness and laughter. "Other Charlie. Can we call you Chuck?"

"Hmmmm," said Parallel Charlie. "Not quite sure on that one."

"We could call you by your middle name," said Charlie. "Rainier? Is that it?"

"Rainier!" beamed Parallel Charlie. "That's it! Named after the mountain?"

"Named after the mountain!" Charlie high-fived his parallel Earth twin.

"But I think I'd rather be called Chuck," said Parallel Charlie. "For now. Until I change my mind."

"Chuck for now it is," said Emma. "Now. On to the important things. Dr. Waldo, the elevator won't take us to Australia. And that is a really long flight. Do you have another method we could try?" Emma realized she was starting to get spoiled by time and space travel. Six months prior she wouldn't have imagined it possible to travel to another universe, and here she was, trying to shave off a few hours of travel time on Earth.

"Ah, yes, my dear! Yes! Your Ben, didn't he tell you? That was one of the projects we had him helping us with, working on the Dark

MATTER sphere to enable more precise travel."

"Thus the landing targeted straight in the middle of the lounge," grinned Ben.

"So we can just use the Dark MATTER to get from here to Lightning Ridge?" asked Eve, her enthusiasm bubbling over.

"Well ..." said Ben.

"We've not perfected it just yet," said Dr. Waldo. "The fact we got back here in one piece from the ghost planet, was, well ... let's just say if it hadn't been an emergency I'm not sure I would have recommended it." He coughed.

Emma rolled her eyes. "Dr. Waldo! Are you kidding me?"

But Dr. Waldo was laughing. "I'm joking, my dear! Joking indeed! Would I let you use something dangerous?"

At this, everyone laughed. "Other than everything we've ever used to travel?" said Emma. "The pigeons? The first time we used the Dark MATTER?"

Dr. Waldo shook his head. "Well, well, my dear! Those were special circumstances, special indeed, would not have sent you off with an untested sphere if it weren't for Vik being here to destroy the multiverse. I think, in retrospect, it was not the worst idea I ever had?"

Emma responded by shaking her head and laughing.

"It's true, though," said Ben. "We did work on the Dark MATTER, and it's pretty precise. Still, though ... well, if we're just traveling just from one point on Earth to another point on the same Earth ... I'm just going to suggest we start outside, on Earth."

"Why?" asked Charlie.

"Uh ..." said Ben, "... you know, no reason. Not that it's relevant to this conversation or anything, but I just want to say that if I ever killed anything—accidentally, of course—it was a robot. No living creatures have been harmed in my experiments."

"...Yet," said Parallel Charlie, now known as Chuck, to Charlie, though his spirits and enthusiasm were not dimmed at all.

"You don't have to tell me twice! Let's go!" said Charlie, racing Chuck to the elevator. "Australia, here we come!"

chapter seven

Having been convinced that rushing off to Australia with no preparation at all might not be the best idea, the Charlies were lured back into the Hub long enough for everyone to pack and plan. With great delight, a much-improved Dr. Waldo danced a quick jig as he distributed to everyone some newly fabricated, extremely lightweight jackets, shirts, pants, and shoes, the molecules of which would self-adjust to compensate for heat or cold.

"I call it WaldoWear," he said. "The clothes ... well, one might say they rather melted in early tests, leaving our mannequins naked, but I am fairly sure we have fixed that."

"Fairly sure?" asked Chuck, holding up his WaldoWear pants and looking skeptically at Ben.

Ben laughed. "They fixed it. Don't worry. I wouldn't wear these if they didn't!" he said. He pointed at the shirt he was wearing. "This is WaldoWear. I've had it for weeks. I have a whole Waldrobe full of WaldoWear. Nothing has melted yet!"

Concerned about running out of water again, Emma packed plenty of extra water, as well as a powerful filter and several water purification tablets. She made everyone else do the same.

They then used Dr. Waldo's sophisticated computers to get an aerial view of Lightning Ridge, and Ben plotted a point for them to land—not directly in town, in hopes no one else would be around when they landed, but not too far out of town, so they wouldn't have to walk too far. Australia, being in the southern hemisphere, was at the peak of its summer.

Charlie brought up a weather report for Lightning Ridge. "It's ninety-three degrees there?" he said, flabbergasted. "Maybe we don't even need clothes."

"Actually," said Eve, "it's not ninety-three degrees there right now. That'll be the middle of the day. Lightning Ridge time is seventeen hours ahead of Balky Point time. So it's about … 10:00 tomorrow morning there. But it'll heat up soon, I'm sure, don't worry." She filled another bottle with water, just in case, and swallowed a swig of the liquid for good measure. The water added extra weight to her bag, but she didn't want to take any risks. "Dr. Waldo, weren't you working on something that could capture water from the air?"

"Good memory, young lady, good memory!" said Dr. Waldo. "Yes, yes, that is in the works, should be quite helpful to you all when you travel, assuming you travel to places with hydrogen and oxygen molecules in the air. Hmm. It's a conundrum! But we are working on it! We are very, very close, you will see, one day and one day very soon, perhaps before you get back, one never knows, you will not worry about water at all! Yes, we are working on it!"

Indeed, Dr. Waldo and his fellow scientists at the Hub had been working on many projects. Earlier that year, they'd figured out how to create a phone that would make interuniversal calls—from any place in any universe to any other place in any universe, any and all hubs included. Once they had that figured out, a special team worked on perfecting it, adding in specialized technologies and instruments used for interuniversal travel and within the Hub itself. With much glee, Dr. Waldo had dubbed these units "iPerts."

"iPert?" Charlie asked. "Why iPert?"

Near bursting with self-satisfaction over the name, Dr. Waldo explained. "The 'i,' of course, is for interuniversal, intelligent, interconnected, imagination, infinity, you have it. And the 'Pert' is in part for expert, because this device will make you an expert in all things! But also it is for Rupert, who as we all know is the heart and soul of the Hub. And without our hearts and souls, what would we have?" He handed them each an iPert, sleek and compact and made of a material that, with the push of a button, could camouflage the device, making it essentially invisible.

"Okay," said Emma, zipping up her backpack. "I think I'm ready. We all have pigeons and Dark MATTER spheres, water, ghost vaccines, iPerts, travel bracelets, change of clothes ...." She sighed. "Packing for vacation is hard enough! Packing for an infinity of possibilities, I don't know. If we just knew where to find more hubs, we could always go there and create what we need ... maybe? Ben, do you know how to make anything we need, if we find a hub?"

"I think so?" said Ben uncertainly. "Do you know where the hubs attached to Australia are, Dr. Waldo?"

Dr. Waldo shook his head. "Some but not all. There was the one I visited this summer, Point Quobba, out in the west. As for hubs near Lightning Ridge, well, let's see ...." He tapped and swiped through several screens on his computer monitor. "Well, there are indications the Fingal Head Lighthouse in New South Wales might house a hub, but it's not yet confirmed. Farther south, in Victoria, there may be one at Wilson's Promontory Lighthouse. But again, we have not yet confirmed it. Perhaps if you children have time while you are there you can visit these lighthouses and let us know? That would be just grand!"

"Let's not get ahead of ourselves," said Emma, though she was glad to see Dr. Waldo more or less back to his old self. "First, we need to find Eve's mom!"

Noticing that Eve had been unusually quiet as they gathered their travel necessities, Emma pulled her friend aside. "Is everything okay?" she asked.

"Yeah," said Eve. "It's just …." She faltered. "I don't know. Dad was called away on another dig, so he can't come with us, which scares me a little, not having him along, but it's probably for the best. My parents' relationship is awkward at best. I don't want to have to deal with that on top of everything else. But … I don't know. I'm nervous. I'm hopeful, like I want to hope we'll find her, but I don't want to hope too much and then just be let down. You know? If we don't find her, then what?"

Emma reached for Eve's hand. "If we don't find her, we keep looking," she said. "Now come on. The boys will be lost without us. We need to be strong and lead the way!"

Eve laughed. "You're right. What would we do without those guys?"

Emma looked over at the Charlies and Ben, who were improvising some strange dance, arms and legs flailing, while waiting for someone to tell them they were ready to go. *Crazy as they may be, I can always count on them to make me laugh,* she thought with a small smile. Each person in the group of five brought so many strengths and unique wisdom. She was grateful that on traveling into the great unknown, she had this group of friends alongside her.

Everyone rushed quickly to the living quarters to change into WaldoWear and make a final check before traveling. Their last preparations complete and a hearty meal hastily eaten, the teens and Dr. Waldo made their way through the elevator back to its Earth side. The elevator, as with all elevators on Earth, was in a lighthouse; in this particular lighthouse, the entrance was inside what seemed to the unsuspecting eye to be a storage closet.

On stepping into the lighthouse lobby, Emma marveled at its normalcy. "It's always so weird to think we're just inches away from ... well, everything. Like everything. How many people have come through here and never suspected a thing? If we hadn't been looking carefully at those pictures—"

"Wait," said Eve, holding up her hand as she looked around the lobby. "Where did the Charlies go? Did we lose them already?"

Before anyone could start to panic, Charlie and Chuck came bounding around a corner, dressed in Hawaiian-print WaldoWear T-shirts and shorts, sunglasses, and baseball caps, their travel packs on their backs.

"Hawaiian print?" said Emma. "Where did you get that?"

The Charlies just winked at Dr. Waldo, who winked in return.

"Aren't you cold?" laughed Eve. They were inside, of course, but the lighthouse was old, and the chill of a Pacific Northwest December afternoon seeped through the seams of the walls and permeated the air.

"The WaldoWear adjusts to the weather," said Chuck, "and where we're headed it's ninety-three degrees!"

"You all are quite overdressed, I'd say," said Charlie. "You wait and see, you'll regret it."

Emma looked down at her layers of clothing and had to agree. She wasn't quite sure about trusting the WaldoWear just yet, and had put on perhaps more clothes than necessary to keep warm. "Well, we'll deal with it when we get there. We've got to get going. Everyone ready?"

"Ready!" said Charlie with great enthusiasm. He was the only one of the group who had not yet traveled via the Dark MATTER sphere.

"Ready! Yeah!" said Chuck, pumping his fists in the air. "Dark MATTER! Dark MATTER!" he started chanting. Charlie quickly joined in, always up for a good chant. "Dark MATTER! Dark MATTER!"

"I guess ... ready!" said Eve, ignoring the boys. Emma reached out to hold her hand.

"Okay," said Ben, double checking coordinates on his iPert. "I think I'm setting us down just outside town. Everybody link arms!"

The others held hands and intertwined arms, ensuring they'd all be whisked away together on this journey. The Charlies changed their chant: "Australia! Australia!" they cheered. "Aussie Aussie Aussie!" cried Chuck, to which Charlie enthusiastically responded, "Oi Oi Oi!"

"Be safe, children, be safe! Come back soon!" said Dr. Waldo, a flash of concern crossing his face for just an instant.

"We will!" said Emma. "Don't worry!"

"I trust you!" he said to Emma, with a wink. "But I still worry!"

"All right, Lightning Ridge, Australia, here we come!" Ben swiped the face of the Dark MATTER.

They faded in from their edges, becoming nothing but breath and heartbeats. Silence and nothingness melded with awareness, and for the splittest of split seconds, the teens became one with the universes. A whoosh, and the process reversed, bodies reforming from molecules, miraculously reforming into five teenagers half a world away on Earth.

"I think I'm getting the hang of that," said Emma, waiting for her eyes to refocus before taking a step.

"Whoa!" said Charlie. "Dude, that was gnarly! Like, we were everything! For a second, we were totally ... we were infinite and eternal and *everywhere*. Did you feel that? That was amazing!"

Emma smiled, glad to share with her brother the indescribable feeling of not just being part of existence, but being all of existence itself. She released her grip from Eve on her other side, and punched Charlie affectionately on the shoulder. "Dork," she said, quietly.

He punched back. "Dork," he said affectionately. "That was unbelievable."

Eve was breathing heavy, bent over with her hands on her knees. "Sometimes I feel like my bracelet gets a little wonky when we travel. It doesn't give me the right amount of oxygen," she said.

"Wait, I thought Lero and Earth had about the same atmosphere? Isn't our air breathable to you even without the bracelet?" said Chuck.

"Mostly, I think," said Eve, "but it's sort of like being at the top of a mountain. The air is a little thinner. Normally I don't even notice it, but when we travel, it seems to take the bracelet a little time to catch up."

"That makes sense," said Chuck, still blinking. "I think it's taking my eyes a little longer to pop into place, too."

"Same," said Emma. "I feel like my eyes take the longest to readjust, too, every time. Plus, it's really bright here." She put up a hand to shade her eyes. The hot sun was already glaring down on them from above, amplified by the vastness of the horizon.

"That is so much better than flying," said Chuck. "I remember one time we flew from Minsota to London on a school trip. It was awful."

Charlie looked at Chuck. "Wait. You flew to London on a school trip? I never did that. Our paths, they are not the same." He frowned with exaggerated sadness.

Chuck's face fell. "I feel like I hardly know you, man."

"We'll get through this somehow, man," said Charlie, earnestly looking Chuck directly in the eyes. "We will."

"You are both such dorks," said Emma. The Charlies beamed.

"So where are we?" asked Charlie. "Are we where we're supposed to be?"

The group took in the unfamiliar landscape, trying to orient themselves. Based on the temperature, they'd certainly gotten what they'd expected. The air was hot and dry.

"I feel like the air is sucking the moisture out of me," said Chuck, wiping from his brow the beads of sweat that were starting to form on his forehead.

The narrow, two-lane road was paved but rustic, lined with a few feet of reddish dirt on either side. Scattered trees with fluffy clouds of dark green leaves mimicked the bright white clouds sprinkled across the deep blue sky. The silence was deep and broad. They were used to silence on the island, but the silence at Balky Point was muffled by forests of evergreens, hills and valleys and caves. The silence here felt like of an ocean of silence, miles and miles from anywhere.

Ben consulted his iPert. "Castlereagh Highway that way," he said, pointing behind them to the west. "Lightning Ridge this way," he said, pointing east.

They walked slowly east, the heat of the sun growing with the day. By their calculations they had arrived around 10:00 a.m., and the day was already quite warm.

"Couldn't you have gotten us a little closer to town?" said Charlie, wiping the sweat from his forehead. Emma reached into his backpack on his back and pulled out a bottle of water for him. He nodded his thanks.

"Sorry," said Ben.

"No worries, mate," said Charlie. "You did your best."

Finally, they came upon some buildings, sparsely scattered on the sides of the road. Shortly after that, they came to a sign that read:

Lightning
Ridge
Population
?

"This is it," said Ben, relieved to see he hadn't led them astray.

From the looks of it, though, they were still quite a ways from the downtown area—if there even was one. A few buildings were strewn here and there, but certainly there had to be more to the actual town. They trudged on.

A truck pulled up behind them. "Oi! Mates!" yelled a man from inside the cab. "Need a ride?"

The teens looked at each other, all of them hot and tired. They reached an agreement without speaking.

"Yes!" said Ben. "Thank you! We're heading to Lightning Ridge," he added.

The man laughed. "I should hope so! Not much else out here! Hop in!"

They scrambled unceremoniously into the bed of the truck and held tight to the sides. The man tumbled along the road until they reached a more populated area. He pulled into a parking area in front of a café, stopped, and hopped out of the cab.

"This good enough?" he said, helping the teens out of the back.

"Perfect!" said Emma, trying to keep her skin out of contact with the truck's hot metal sides as she climbed out. "Thanks so much!"

"Yes, thanks," said Eve, who had jumped out of the truck and was dusting herself off. "I'm Eve, by the way. This is Emma, Charlie, Chuck, Ben."

"Charlie and Chuck, you must be twins?" said the man. "Odd your parents gave you the same name!"

Emma was taken aback. Charlie was *her* twin, not Chuck's. She realized they might have to stretch the truth a bit so as not to arouse suspicion on their travels. *Maybe,* she thought, *we can be fraternal triplets.* She wasn't ready to give up her claim on her brother just yet.

For their part, Charlie and Chuck answered by just laughing it off. "Parents. Crazy! And your name?" said Charlie.

"I'm Mick. Did your car break down? We don't get too many people walking into town from that far out. Dangerous. And not too smart." His grin was wide and friendly.

Ben thought fast. "We, back there on the highway, we hitch-hiked, and someone, they dropped us off, they didn't want to turn down the road."

A squint in Mick's eyes indicated a hint of skepticism, but he just shook his head. "You've walked a long way. Good thing it's still morning. You know where you're going?"

"Opals," Emma blurted out. "We're, uh, looking for black opals?"

Mick laughed. "You're in the right place, then, missy. This is black opal country, that's for certain." With his arm, he made a gesture that swept across the landscape to include everything around them.

"Are you a miner?" asked Eve. "Black opal miner?"

"I do some fossicking on the odd occasion," said Mick, "but no, I'm a painter."

"Fossicking?" whispered Eve to Emma. Emma shrugged.

"You paint houses?" asked Chuck.

"Pictures," said Mick. "Scenery." He pointed down the road. "Gallery down there on the right has a show of my paintings right now, if you'd like to take a gander."

"We're definitely interested," said Emma, trying to hide her impatience. "First, though, can you tell us a good place to buy an opal?"

Mick guffawed heartily. "Take your pick!" he said. "Can't recommend one over another or's someone would have my hide. Just take a look around 'til you find one you like."

"That's great, thanks. And thanks again for the ride," said Emma, already turning to find a store.

"No worries, mate. Since you're new to town, if you have time later, you might enjoy a dip in the Artesian Bore Baths tonight, after it cools off a bit again. Closed for cleaning right now, but they open again at noon."

"Bore baths?" said Eve, confused again.

"Water from the bores," said Mick, as though it was the most obvious thing in the world. "Hot, though. But you kids might like it. Down the road that way," he said, pointing.

"Got it, thanks, down the road," said Emma, pretending she understood everything Mick had said. This man was quite friendly and kind, but she wanted him to leave so she could talk with her travel companions. "Thanks again for everything!"

"No worries. If you all need anything, just ask someone for Mick the landscape artist, they'll know me." Mick nodded, gave a slight salute, and headed into the café. The others waited until he was out of hearing distance before speaking.

"Fossicking? Bore baths?" said Charlie.

"Ah, I thought it was just me. I figured you Earthlings would know," said Eve.

"No, I don't know, either," said Emma. "But bore baths, that's water. Dark galaxy, water, magnet. Maybe that's the water?"

"What were you asking about an opal store for?" asked Eve.

"Don't you think we should buy a black opal? It seems like we might need one. I don't know what for, but it feels like we'll need one. And probably a magnet, too."

"Opals can't be cheap," said Chuck. "How are we going to afford one? I don't have that kind of cash."

Eve cleared her throat and patted her backpack. "I, uh, have a credit card."

"A credit card?" said Charlie, whose own backpack held only a minimal amount of money. "An Earth credit card?"

"It's … sort of universal," said Eve. "Dr. Waldo gave me and Dad each one, a year or so ago. It gets billed to the Hub … somehow."

"It gets billed to the *Hub?*" said Charlie in disbelief. "How does that work?"

"I guess … same way Ben gets paid, I think?" Eve said. She shrugged.

The Charlies and Emma looked at Ben. "Ben, how exactly do you get paid?" asked Chuck.

"Uh … it's direct deposit into my account. I guess I hadn't really thought about it?" said Ben. He was still living at home with his parents and didn't have too many bills. The chance to do science in the Hub was his motivating factor, far more than the money. He barely noticed when the paychecks were deposited.

"Man," said Charlie. "I gotta get me on that payroll." To illustrate his point, he reached into his pockets and turned them inside out: empty.

"Okay," said Emma. "We have the credit card, so Eve and I will go buy a black opal. You three, go find a magnet."

"Where are we going to find a magnet?" asked Chuck.

"I have no idea," said Emma, exasperated. *Do I have to figure out everything?* she thought. "Maybe ask the iPert. You can do this. I believe in you."

"It's 10:30 now," said Eve, looking at her watch. "Meet back here for lunch at … oh, 1:00 if not before?"

"Eve, do you have a picture of your mom with you?" asked Ben. Eve nodded. "Yes, why?"

"Maybe we should ask if people have seen her, while we're at it?" he suggested.

"Good idea," said Eve. "I … well, I already loaded some pictures of Mom and Dad onto my iPert, just … to have them with me. I'll message one to you all." She tapped and swiped the iPert screen, and in seconds the other four iPerts received notification alerts.

"Huh," said Chuck, looking at the picture and squinting. "She looks … sort of less human than you do."

Eve sighed heavily and slapped her forehead. "It's a picture, so she looks like herself. Leroian. Like she would look without a bracelet. Stupid me! That's not what she would have looked like to people around here. We can't show that picture around. I don't think I have any of her looking like a human!"

"That's not stupid," said Emma. "It's just complicated. So she'd look more or less like that, though, right? We can describe her to people without showing the picture. Shoulder-length blond hair, mid-thirties, funny accent, not from around here, talking about opals and water, maybe, start with that. They still might recognize her, you never know. It doesn't hurt to ask."

"Good point, Emma," said Ben. "Okay. We're off to find magnets and do some reconnaissance. You guys go get a nice black opal. Don't be cheap. Dr. Waldo owes us one."

Emma laughed. "He does indeed. Be safe, guys! See you at 1:00!"

Emma and Eve meandered slowly through the dry heat of the town. Mick was right: there were opal shops at every turn. They wandered into the first one they came across.

"There are so many," said Emma, looking at the huge variety of stones. "What if we get the wrong one?"

Eyebrows furrowed, Eve shook her head. "I don't know. Do you think only certain stones will work? Like the wishing rocks? The Universe Keys?"

"We don't even know what 'working' means," Emma said. "We don't know what it's supposed to do."

Eve scrolled through pictures on her iPert. "Well, maybe we should look for one as close to the original dark galaxy stone as we can find." She brought up an image of the stone her father had found all those years ago.

Emma peeked over Eve's shoulder to study the picture. "Okay. Very dark blue-black background, a cluster of bursts of all colors in the center. We should be able to find that," she said hopefully.

The variety of stones was endless. Some, like the dark galaxy stone, had multitudes of colors buried in their depths. Others were filled mostly with blue and green specks. In some, the colors formed stripes; in others, the hues glowed in flecks and shavings.

"So beautiful," said Eve in a hushed tone. "I can't believe these stones actually exist. They're amazing."

Emma, too, was awed. "Just ... I don't even have the word. Magnificent. Some of them really do look like you're looking into another galaxy."

They perused the offerings at the first store, but none of the stones struck them as the one they wanted.

"Let's try another store," said Emma. "We can always come back if there's nothing better."

Eve nodded agreement, and they wandered back out into the street.

"Earth is so big," said Emma. "I forget that sometimes. Like, I get used to my own little corner of the world, and I forget there's so much to explore even on my own planet."

"I know," said Eve. "I've only visited a few countries on Lero. I've probably visited more foreign planets than Lero countries."

Emma laughed. "That's so weird. Can you imagine? And I never would have imagined one of my best friends would be an alien!"

Eve blushed and looked at her. "Am I one of your best friends?" She caught herself. "Oh, you mean Charlie—Chuck, of course.

Well, that's natural, he's sort of your brother, too, in a sense."

Emma stopped in the street. "No, silly. I meant you. Dork." She punched Eve in the shoulder.

Tears welled up quickly in Eve's eyes, and she looked away. She'd seen Emma and Charlie use that show of affection too many times not to know its significance. "You're the dork," she replied, quietly, and she softly punched Emma's shoulder in return.

Emma beamed, and started walking again.

"Do you suppose there are alternate Leros, too?" Emma said. "And alternate Eves? We know there are more Emmas and Charlies. There must be more Eves. Have you ever met any?"

"Not yet," said Eve, her voice still a little tight with emotion.

"It's hard enough to imagine all seven billion people on Earth," said Emma. "I always thought that was a lot of people. But now I find out that's just a tiny percentage of all the intelligent life out there. All those billions and billions of minds, all thinking billions and billions of thoughts. I wonder if every single person is in their head as much as I am?"

"Every person is the center of her own universe," said Eve. "Every one of us. It's hard for any of us to imagine the universes aren't all here just for us. That's what Dad always says, anyway."

Emma smiled. "That's crazy. A mind is a universe in a way. And to have seven billion mind-universes, and then infinite times that." She shook her head. "I can't comprehend it. But it's cool to think about."

They headed into another opal store.

"G'day, girls!" called out the man at the counter as they walked in. "How can I help you today?" He was tall and tanned and blond, deep crinkles at the corners of his eyes.

"We're looking for an opal," said Eve.

"I just might have one or two here!" the man laughed, indicating his numerous showcases, each filled with opals in all forms: necklaces, rings, earrings, loose stones, and more. "Anything in particular?"

"Well," said Emma, "we're looking for one that might sort of look like a galaxy."

"A galaxy?" The man's face lit with surprise and delight. "You're in the right place, I'd say! They must have told you about my galaxy stone!" He nodded toward a corner of the store.

Eve and Emma looked at each other in shock. *His galaxy stone?* thought Emma. On seeing what the man had been directing them to, she gasped and felt a chill up her spine.

In one corner of the store, set apart with almost a shrine-like importance, was a large acrylic box. Inside the box was a pedestal, covered in black velvet. Propped up on the velvet stood an opal, about an inch high.

But what caught their eyes was not the opal. What caught their eyes was the sign over the box: "The Galaxy Stone."

"What!" said Eve.

The man was delighted at the girls' astonished reaction. He walked out from behind his counter to approach the object of their admiration.

"Right, the Galaxy Stone, found it myself about ten years ago, back when I was still mining. Brilliant, eh?"

Emma and Eve approached the stone with awe, hearts beating fast. They looked at each other. Was this a sign? Was this the stone?

In fact, the stone did not look much like Eve's dark galaxy stone. This Galaxy Stone had the same rich black background, but rather than having multitudes of colored flecks like stars and distant galaxies, this stone featured three fluffy swirling plumes of bronze-gold climbing up from the bottom of the stone in the foreground, with smaller curls of reds, blues, greens and golds embedded deep, hovering over and around the plumes.

"Looks like a nebula they once found, I reckon," the man said.

"Never saw another like it. She's a beaut, all right." He watched their reactions with pride.

"That's ... unbelievable," said Emma. "It does, it looks like those pictures I've seen. Like a nebula." She glanced around for a price. Surely this was the stone they were meant to buy? "How much is it?"

"The cost?" said the man with surprise. "Not for sale, little lady! Priceless. This one, she's priceless. Unless someone comes along with the right price, I reckon." He winked.

"How much ..." Eve cleared her throat. "How much would that be?" She, too, suspected it might be their stone.

"Oi, well," the man shook his head. "Upwards of three hundred thousand, I'd reckon." His amused eyes crinkled.

"Dollars?" said Emma, a nervous laugh escaping her throat.

Eve was less amused. She looked at Emma and shook her head. "I guess it's not for us."

The man laughed. "Can't blame you for trying! Maybe another stone, then?"

Eve nodded, a little deflated. She showed the man the picture of her own dark galaxy stone.

"This is some fancy technology you have here!" the man said, looking over the iPert. "New iPhone?" he asked.

"Uh ... no, well ..." stammered Eve.

"My uncle works at a tech company," Emma blurted out. "He's ... it's a test model."

"Ah," said the man. "These things, coming out faster than I can keep up. Let's see ...." He studied the picture Eve was showing him. "Yes, I think I have something similar anyway." He walked down a few counters and pulled out a tray from behind the shelf. "The opal is the only stone that has every color of every gemstone in it, did you know that?"

Emma and Eve gazed with reverence at the stones nestled in black velvet in the long, shallow tray.

"Ohhhhh," said Emma. "Gorgeous." These were, indeed, the kinds of stones they were looking for. Dark black backgrounds, richly spotted with specks of vibrant color, looking for all the universes like space, the galaxies and stars, frozen in time and made miniature in a stone.

"Can I …" said Eve, pointing at one stone in particular and looking at the tall blond man.

He picked up the stone Eve indicated and placed it in her waiting palm. "Did you know they found opals on Mars?" he said, casually.

Emma froze. Opals on Mars? What would make him say that? Did he know who they were? Did he know why they were there? She looked at Eve, whose jaw was dropped open.

Mistaking their reaction for amazement and tickled to have been the one who caused it, the man went on. "Right, unbelievable, you reckon? Sure, I heard they found opals on Mars. Nothing like these here," he said, "just trace amounts yet, opals like the ones we call 'fire opals.' Fragments. But maybe they'll find real stones one day, big ones. Now those will be priceless!" He guffawed at his own wit. "They say the opals could help them find evidence of life on Mars. Can you believe it!" He shook his head.

Emma and Eve shared a cautious glance.

"Amazing," said Emma, laughing nervously. "Do you think there's life on other planets? That seems a bit … I don't know, unbelievable, don't you think?"

"Completely believable," said the man, shaking his head. "All this space and you think we're the only ones? A bit arrogant, wouldn't you say? Besides, they've been to Earth, you know."

Emma found herself breathing shallowly and carefully; she could feel the hairs on her arms standing up straight. "They have?" She moved imperceptibly closer to Eve, protective of her friend.

"Right, sure have. You should go half a click down the road to the museum and talk to Agnes. She'll tell you all about it. A UFO came here once, Agnes saw it, sure enough."

"She saw a UFO?" asked Eve, subconsciously rubbing the stones on her bracelet that kept her alienness hidden in plain sight.

"That she did, so she says," he said, winking. "Some people think Agnes has a few kangaroos loose in the top paddock, but I say she's fair dinkum. Lightning Ridge has bonzer energy, mates, magnetic energy. There's something here; you can feel it. Wouldn't surprise me if one day we found out there's a portal from here to another universe!" His laugh shook his whole body.

Emma and Eve joined in his laughter. "A portal!" said Emma, laughing a little too loudly. "Can you imagine! Haha! Aliens! Haha! Can you tell us again, where's that museum?"

The man told them the name of the museum and pointed out the general direction. "Tell her Opal Ned sent you," he said. "Now, did any of these opals fit your fancy?"

Eve was still holding the stone that had originally caught her eye. "I think this one is perfect," she said, her mind racing, wanting to get out of the store and to the museum. "How much is it?"

As they walked away from the opal store toward Agnes and the museum, Eve tucked their new opal safely into a zippered pocket in her backpack. "Stay there," she said to the opal, patting the pocket as she closed it tight.

They walked with false nonchalance away from the store.

"Oh my gosh!" said Emma breathlessly, once they were sure Opal Ned could no longer see or hear them. "Did you hear that?"

"He said Lightning Ridge is *magnetic*," said Eve. "Did you hear?"

"I heard! And he talked about *alien life!*" gushed Emma. "Eve, we are in the right place. I know it for sure. I feel it!"

Their excitement quickened their pace along to the museum. "Down the street on the left," Eve mumbled, repeating Opal Ned's directions, her eyes scanning the buildings for the sign. "What was the name again?"

"Museum of Amazing Mysteries, I think?" said Emma. "It's got to be here … yes! There!" She pointed past another opal store to a building with a checkerboard of faded red and brown bricks on its face. Over the door, a colorful sign declared: "Museum of A-MAZE-ing Mysteries!"

"A-MAZE-ing," said Eve. "Interesting. I wonder what that's about?"

"We'll find out soon enough!" said Emma. "Come on!" Looking quickly to make sure no traffic was coming down the dusty road, they jogged across the street and into the museum.

The rush of cool air that met them was a welcome relief, and instantly calmed their haste. "Ahhhhh," said Eve. "Much better."

"Welcome, girls," said a cheery, short, gray-haired woman from behind a counter. "You've caught me, it's a dog's breakfast in here, I'm just cleaning up a bit. Have yourselves a look around, let me know if you have questions. Bikkie?" She held out a plate of cookies and smiled widely, squinting slightly behind her thick glasses.

"Bikkie?" said Emma half to herself, before remembering that in England, biscuits were cookies. Australia having once been a British colony, they must call cookies biscuits, or "bikkies," here, too, she reasoned.

"Yum, thanks!" said Eve, reaching for a cookie. "Are you Agnes? Ned at the opal store told us to come find you."

The woman's smile grew impossibly wider. "Yes! My stars, love that Ned, he's a cheeky one! I really should have him for a cuppa," she mused.

Emma gathered that the woman liked Ned, but all this Australian slang was starting to confuse her. "Ned said you have a great collection here," she said, not quite sure how to broach the subject of aliens.

"Oh, go on!" said Agnes, pleased with the compliment. "Well, a person's got to do something with her time, right? I like history. Australia's one of the oldest regions on Earth, you know. We have crystals that date back to only 165 million years after our Earth formed. Zircons. Almost four and a half billion years old! I'm telling you, lots can happen in four an a half billion years. A lot more than people want to believe." Her wink was filled with unspoken meaning.

Emma nodded slowly. Was Agnes suggesting what she thought she might be suggesting?

As Emma and Agnes had been talking, Eve had been wandering around the small, packed space. She stopped in front of a bulletin board on which articles and pictures were pinned.

"Agnes, what's this story?" she said, pointing at a weathered and faded article ripped from a newspaper, its torn edges brown and curling.

"You've found my treasure, there!" said Agnes, hustling over to stand by Eve. "That's from the night I saw a UFO fly overhead!"

"A UFO!" said Emma, feigning disbelief. "No! That can't be. Tell us about it!"

"Completely true," said Agnes, warming immediately to her audience. "Like I said, four and a half billion years, a lot can happen in that time. There's simply no way this was the first time they've visited us. But this was the first time I saw it. It was quite a while ago, twenty years even. I was out at the Artesian Bore Baths having a good soak, late at night, gazing up at the stars. You know the bore baths? Out to the east?"

The girls nodded slowly. *Yesssss. The bore baths,* thought Emma. *Water.*

Agnes continued. "It was winter. July. A bit chilly at night, just right for those hot baths, nothing better, right? It was quite late, or early, depending on how you look at it. I'd been up past midnight consoling a girlfriend whose old man had left her, all the better for her, if you ask me. I decided to go to the baths, and it was just me there, which is pretty rare, you know. I was sitting there, almost asleep, looking up, when suddenly out of nowhere I saw it." She looked at the girls and waited expectantly for their prompt.

"Saw what? What did you see?" said Emma.

"A bright white light, zipping across the sky, fast as can be. It stopped and hovered, and I swear it was staring right at me. Then it zipped off again, back where it came from, leaving me in the baths looking around for some other witness to corroborate my story. But it was just me," said Agnes.

Eve scanned the story from the ancient newspaper. "It says you heard a sound?" she said, pointing at the text.

"Sounded like a sonic boom, is what it sounded like," said Agnes, making a loud popping sound with her mouth to illustrate. "Pop! Thought I'd go deaf, I did!" She laughed at the memory. "Years ago. Haven't seen a UFO since, but I know they're here."

Emma waded cautiously in the discussion. "What makes you think they're still here?" she asked.

"Oi, you just know, don't you? You'd be silly to think it's just us! That was just the beginning. Out here, kilometers of nothing every which way, you'd be daft to think we know everything that's going on around us. Besides which," she said conspiratorially, "the labyrinth, you know. I'm sure it was made by aliens."

"The labyrinth?" asked Eve.

"The 'MAZE' in 'A-MAZE-ing,'" explained Agnes, pointing at her store sign. "Out on the outskirts of town, to the west, we have a labyrinth. Not much to look at, but you go on and visit it, and tell me you don't feel a vibration out there. I'm telling you, there's something out there. Why, I wouldn't be surprised if there are aliens living right here on Earth with us! Now people say I'm mad as a meat-axe; they say I fell asleep out at the baths and dreamed the whole thing. But I'm telling you," she leaned forward and spoke conspiratorially: "*We are not alone.*"

chapter eight

Deciding it was too soon to return to the café, Emma and Eve spent the remaining hour before the boys were to meet them again talking about what they'd learned and looking around for a place to stay that night. A quick search on their iPerts gave them a listing of nearly a dozen options for accommodations. Emma picked the one she liked best; Eve was less useful, absorbed in the possibility that maybe, finally, they would find her mother, down in the outback of Australia, of all places. They walked to the lodging, reserved two rooms, then wandered back toward their chosen meeting place. After buying cool drinks at the café, the girls sat outside in a shady spot, waiting for the boys to return to share their tales.

After not too long, a dirty pickup truck came bumping down the road, with three figures bouncing along in the back. The truck pulled up to the café, and the Charlies and Ben tumbled out of the truck's bed, all smiles.

"Cheers, mate!" Charlie called out to the truck's driver as the man pulled away, waving out the open window.

"Best day ever!" said Chuck, pulling up a chair to join Emma and Eve. "Where'd you get those?" he added, pointing to their drinks, which they'd nearly finished.

"Inside," said Eve, nodding at the café. "If you're getting one for yourself, get me another?"

Chuck gave Eve two thumbs up, and popped inside the café.

"What made it such a great day?" said Emma to Charlie, who had pulled up a chair beside her. He punched her in the shoulder. She punched back, then scooted her chair closer to his and leaned her head on his shoulder.

Charlie pushed Emma away. "Too hot!" he said. "You're all sweaty!"

Emma rolled her eyes and sat up. "Whatever, dork. You are too! And covered in dirt! What did you guys do today?"

"We fossicked!" said Ben, beaming. "Chuck found an opal!"

"A tiny, tiny, tiny opal," corrected Charlie. "But still an opal."

Eve laughed at the boys' bustle and buzz. "What is fossicking? We heard that word before. I thought I must have misheard it!"

"No, it's a thing!" said Ben. "Fossicking! It's where you search for gems through a pile of rocks that have been discarded. In this case, opals."

"Like a pile of gravel?" said Emma, looking in confusion at the rocks on the side of the road.

"No, rocks from the mine that they already looked over for opals," said Charlie. "You look to see if they missed any. And they do sometimes!"

"Indeed they do!" said Chuck, returning from the café interior carrying a tray of drinks for everyone. "I found one!" He put the tray down on the table, then rummaged in his pocket. Proudly, he displayed his incredible find.

"Um … huh," said Emma.

"Looks … like a chunk of rock?" said Eve.

Chuck shook his head. "You poor ignorant souls, not even able to recognize a pure treasure when you see one." Holding the tiny rock between his thumb and forefinger, with his other hand he pointed very carefully at a tiny speck of color on the gray stone. "There. Opal!"

Emma drew her head close to the rock and squinted. "Oh ... sure. I see it. Maybe."

Eve took her turn up close to the stone. "Where?" she asked, wrinkling her nose.

"Right there," Chuck pointed again. "It's probably worth a million dollars!"

"I'm sure it is," Emma said indulgently. "Why did we even bother to buy one today?" she asked Eve.

Eve shrugged her shoulders. "I guess we can take it back! Did you guys get a magnet, by the way?"

The Charlies and Ben looked at each other uncomfortably.

"Well, you know, there was the fossicking," said Charlie.

"And then while we were fossicking we met Banjo," said Ben.

"Banjo?" said Emma.

"And Banjo offered to take us on the car door tours!" said Chuck.

"Car door tours?" asked Eve.

"There's these car doors all over Lightning Ridge, and they're all part of little tours, the Red Car Door Tour, the Blue Car Door Tour, the Yellow Car Door Tour, and the Green Car Door Tour," said Charlie.

"Car door tours?" asked Emma.

"They use painted car doors to show you what spots are part of the tour. Who were we grand adventurers to turn down the opportunity to go on car door tours?" asked Chuck.

"So Banjo took us around on some of the tours. We didn't have time to do all of them. We saw the Beer Can House and a giant man made out of milk crates—" said Charlie.

"Green Car Door Tour," explained Ben.

"—and the Amigo's Castle and the Astronomer's Monument—"

said Charlie.

"Red Car Door Tour," said Chuck.

"—but then it was getting too late and we had to come back here," said Charlie.

"Wow," said Emma. "Sorry to have spoiled your fun."

"I can't believe you didn't take us along with you!" said Eve. "I would have wanted to go!"

"We still have two more tours to go on," said Ben. "We could all go together!"

"But we don't have a way to get around," said Emma. "Unless Banjo comes back and—"

A honk from the road startled everyone. There, as if they'd materialized him out of thin air by talking about him, was Banjo again, in his truck, waving at them and yelling out the window. "You forgot your bag, mate!"

Chuck, Charlie, and Ben looked around, and Charlie realized the one who had forgotten his bag was him. He ran to the truck. After a moment, he came back, his grin bigger than ever.

"Banjo said he can take us around to the other tours, if you young ladies would like an adventure?"

"Yes! Yes!" said Eve, hopping out of her chair.

Emma smiled. "Oh, all right. If Eve says yes, I'm in, too."

Later that evening, Banjo dropped the teens off at their cottages, telling them to give him a call if they needed another ride anywhere. They were exhausted and covered in sweat and dust, but happy.

"That was so fun," said Emma. "The tour of the opal mine was great. And I love Banjo. I love his name, too."

"The cactus nursery was beautiful," said Eve. "We have nothing like those cactuses on Lero."

"Cactuses?" said Chuck. "Cacti? Which is it?"

"You know what I meant either way," said Eve. "They were so pretty. And thanks for going back on the Red Car Door Tour again, guys. The way you talked about the castle and the monument, I really wanted to see them."

"Our pleasure," said Chuck. "We are nothing if not gentlemen, am I right?"

"Yes, that's how I think of you all, pure gentlemen!" laughed Emma. "Anyway, we need to regroup and get back on track. We don't have a magnet, but maybe that was just a clue about the area. Agnes—or was it Ned?" she looked at Eve. "One of them told us there's a magnetic energy here. I've been thinking," she said.

"You're always thinking," said Charlie.

"Nothing wrong with that, is there? One of us has to do it. Anyway, I've been thinking, Agnes told us she was out at the bore baths when she saw the UFO." While they'd been out on their tours, Emma and Eve had filled the boys in on everything they'd heard from their visits to the opal store and the museum. "We have an opal now, and we know 'water' is important. Maybe the bore baths are where we're supposed to go?"

"A dip in a pool sounds great either way," said Ben. "Even a hot pool. You think we should head over there?"

"I do think so," said Emma, "but I don't think we should go when it's crowded. It's open all night. Maybe we should go after midnight? Like, one or two in the morning?"

"Oi!" said Eve, catching on to the Australian slang. "That's so late! Or early!"

"We don't have to," said Emma, "I just think having fewer people around would be a good idea."

"No, I think you're right," said Eve. "And it's the only idea we have right now. May as well give it a try!"

◆

"I don't even know what time it is anymore," Eve said groggily as she changed into her swimsuit. The group had decided naps were in order before their trip to the bore baths, and the girls' alarm had just blared them awake. "Dr. Waldo needs to work on a cure for jetlag!"

"I agree," said Emma, yawning widely. "I think after our visit last summer, I slept for a week!" She pulled on shorts and a T-shirt over her swimsuit, then packed up her bag to take along. "Never know where we're going to end up," she said, closing the bag tightly and yawning again.

They wandered down the hall to the boys' room and knocked quietly. "You guys ready?" Emma whispered through the door.

Charlie opened the door, his hair a wild mane around his sleep-crunched face. "Whose brilliant idea was it to go at 2:00 a.m.?" he asked grumpily. He stepped aside and let the girls into the room.

Chuck and Charlie were still packing, but Ben was ready. He held up a Dark MATTER sphere. "I don't know what we'd need this for," he said, "but I'm going to keep it ready, just in case."

Emma nodded. If she'd learned anything in her travels through the multiverse, it was that one never could be too prepared.

"How far is it?" asked Chuck quietly. He slipped his arms through the straps of his backpack and saluted. "I'm ready!"

"About half an hour walk," said Eve.

"For people who can travel across universes, we sure do a lot of walking," said Charlie, securing his own backpack to his back.

"Stop whining," said Emma. "Let's go!"

The walk through the night air was refreshing after the extreme heat of the day. "Right now it's like the perfect temperature," said Chuck, his feet crunching along the road. To guide his way, he illuminated the path in front of him with a flashlight app on his iPert.

"Look at the sky," said Emma. "The constellations are all different. And the Milky Way. It's … well, it's milkier." She reached over for her brother's arm. "Can you believe we've been out there? Out in the stars?"

"Where's my Earth?" said Chuck, looking up. "Could you even see it from here? How does that work?"

Eve scrunched her face in the darkness. "I don't know. Dad describes the universes as layered, but I'm not sure they're *actually* layered. Some people think each universe is like a bubble."

"I've heard someone describe it like Swiss cheese," said Charlie. "Each universe is one of the holes in the cheese. The holes are getting bigger as the universes expand, but the space between them—the cheese—is expanding faster."

"So my Earth is in another hole in the cheese?" asked Chuck.

"Pretty much," said Charlie.

"Still confused," said Emma.

"Aren't we all," said Ben.

They padded along. Away from city lights, the darkness of the night was a thick, impenetrable cloak. The light from their flashlights kept their eyes from adjusting to the dark.

"Are there bears here, do you think?" asked Chuck, his ears alert for danger.

"No bears," said Emma. "Dingos, maybe. Wild dogs."

"And lots of killer spiders and snakes," said Ben.

Emma shuddered and wished she hadn't insisted on walking. "Spiders and snakes?" she said.

"*Killer* spiders and snakes," said Chuck.

"Stop it, you guys!" said Eve. "You're scaring me!" She changed the setting of her flashlight to spread a wider beam.

They walked on, yawning, alert now for snakes and spiders. Emma started to wonder if this was a good idea, after all. "Snake repellent," she said to Charlie. "Make note of that, please, to tell the committee, that the next time we travel anywhere we need to bring snake repellent. And spider repellent." Since they were little, Charlie and Emma had always told each other to "make note of that, please, to tell the committee." How it started, who the committee was, and what they had ever thought the committee would do about it, neither could remember. But the phrase was familiar, and automatic, and somehow brought Emma comfort.

"Noted," said Charlie, shuddering.

After a while, they saw some lights farther down the road on the right.

"Is that it?" asked Eve.

"I think it's just beyond that," said Emma, consulting her iPert. "Yes, almost there."

When they reached the baths, they were disappointed to find another couple in the smaller of the two circular pools.

"Great," whispered Charlie. "Now what?"

"Just get in," Emma whispered back. Seeing no chairs or benches, she set her bag down a few feet away from the larger pool and peeled off her shorts and T-shirt. She stuck a few toes into the pool to get a measure of its heat. "Oh, wow," she said. "That's hot." Clinging tightly to a railing, she stepped down into the pool and sat at the edge of a stair, her shoulders exposed to the night air.

Eve dug into her bag to find their precious opal. She carried it to the pool, holding it reverently over the water, and stepped in. "Ahhhhhh," she said. "Just what a girl needs after traveling a few thousand miles."

The boys followed, stripping down to their swim trunks and gingerly dipping their bodies into the steaming water.

Out of the corner of her eye, Emma checked on the couple in the smaller pool. "I think they might be leaving," she said. "I think we disturbed them."

"Good," said Eve. "I don't want company for this!"

"Exactly what is 'this,' anyway?" asked Chuck, twirling his toes in the hot bath. "Do we have any idea what we're doing?"

"We have no idea at all," said Eve. "We're just going on the clues we have. That's how science works, right? You make a guess, and you see if it goes anywhere."

"I suppose that's science more or less," said Ben with a smile. He watched as the couple from the other pool got out, holding hands, with a small glance toward the larger group. They dried off and walked languidly to their car, arms wrapped around each others' waists.

"They're gone," Chuck said as their car pulled away. "Now what?"

Eve looked at the opal glittering in her hand, its depths echoing the starry night sky above. Dark galaxy and water. That's what her mother had wanted her to know. What did it mean?

"I guess I put the opal in the water?" she said, but she didn't move.

Emma watched Eve closely. To the casual observer Eve might have looked calm, but Emma knew her well enough by now that she could see a touch of agitation. "Eve?" she said. "You okay?"

Eve looked at her. "Yeah, I guess. I'm just ... I mean, what if it doesn't work?"

"We won't know if we don't try," said Emma. "We don't even know what 'working' means. No expectations. Do you want me to do it?"

"No," said Eve. "I will." She tucked her long blond hair behind her ears, then cupped the opal in both hands. Slowly, she sank her hands below the surface of the pool. Water seeped over the surface of the opal, making the blue-black background look even darker, deeper, even more like the dark galaxy for which Eve's mother had named the stones.

Chuck, seated on Eve's side, held his breath.

"Is anything happening?" asked Charlie. He squinted his eyes. "I don't see anything. Does anyone see anything?"

Emma looked at Eve. "Eve, can you see anything?" she said softly. "Or feel anything?"

Eve sat still, quiet. Finally, she let out a sigh. "Nothing."

"Maybe you have to … think of something?" said Charlie. "Like Emma did. Think about wanting to go somewhere."

"But where?" asked Emma. "I always knew where I wanted to go."

"Maybe think about your mom?" suggested Chuck.

"I was," said Eve. She placed the opal on the cement edge of the pool, then turned to stare at it. "Mom, what did you mean?"

Emma looked at the boys. "Probably we needed the magnet," she said. She said nothing else, but her accusation was clear.

"Hey," said Charlie, "you guys were with us all afternoon. If you thought the magnet was so important, you could have said so then. You're the ones who thought Agnes's comment about Lightning Ridge being magnetic was enough."

"It was Opal Ned," said Emma. "Opal Ned was the one who said Lightning Ridge is magnetic, not Agnes." But she knew he was right. They'd been having too much fun on the car door tours. She'd thought, once, that they should ask Banjo to take them to buy a magnet, but then they'd seen another car door to follow and explore, and she'd forgotten all about it. As much as she wanted to blame the boys, she knew she was as much at fault as they were.

"It's okay," said Eve. "We'll get a magnet tomorrow and try again." Her shoulders drooped, and her normally cheerful smile was gone.

"One more day won't hurt," said Emma. But she knew all too well that in some cases, every second mattered.

After returning to the cottages around three in the morning, the exhausted teens slept late, finally gathering for a late breakfast shortly after eleven at a café near their hotel.

"I told the front desk we'd be staying another couple of days, and pre-paid, just in case," Emma told the others as they sat down to eat. "I figured we'd better just plan on it. If we leave early, we leave early."

"Good idea," said Ben, scooping some scrambled eggs onto his fork. "And I think I know where we can find a magnet. I found a hardware store. That iPert is really smart. It knows everything!"

"Nice job," said Eve with a smile. Emma looked at her friend and couldn't help but see how tired she seemed. Eve had tossed and turned in her bed the night before; every time Emma woke up through the night, she could sense that Eve was still awake on the other side of the room. Nonetheless, the girl appeared to be in relatively good spirits.

Emma's twin was watchful of their friend, too. "Feeling better?" Charlie asked Eve, shoveling some pancakes into his mouth.

"Yes, much," she said. "Not the first time I've been let down. I'm resilient," she said, her smile bright. "We'll find her, I know it. And I know we're closer than ever. The magnet, that's going to be the key. I can feel it."

"I feel something, too," said Ben, "but not that. Have you noticed the way the waitress is staring at us?" He tipped his head in the direction of the young brunette who had served them. "She keeps looking over here. And a couple of minutes ago she was on her phone, looking right at you, Eve. Like she was talking with someone about you."

A blush spread up Eve's neck. "She was?" she said. "How could she …" Eve checked the bracelet on her wrist. "Do I look normal to you guys? Is the bracelet not working?"

"You look fine," Emma said, with a glare in Ben's direction. "Don't worry about it. We're not from here, and she's probably just gossiping with someone about the visitors. It's probably because you're so pretty. That's all. Now let's finish up so we can get to that hardware store and get the magnet."

They gobbled down the rest of their breakfasts in silence. When they were done, Eve used her Hub credit card to pay the bill. The brunette waitress was nowhere to be seen.

When the clerk handed the credit card back to Eve, Chuck intercepted it. "How does this work?" he asked Eve, studying the card as they walked away. "Does it only work on Earth?"

"It … well, okay, it's not something everyone should know, so don't go telling all the world, but it works everywhere," she said quietly, once they were outside, well away from the clerk and any other listening ears.

"How can it work everywhere?" asked Charlie, taking the card from Chuck to study it himself.

Eve shook her head. "I don't know. Dr. Waldo worked it out. He said it somehow conforms to a society's method of payment."

"But that's impossible," said Emma. "That's not science. That's alchemy."

"What is alchemy but science we don't understand?" said Eve. "If it works, that's all that matters to me."

Emma was not convinced, but she let the matter drop. "Which way to the hardware store, Ben?" she asked, looking left and right down the street outside the café.

As Ben consulted his iPert once again, a young woman came running up to them.

"Eve?" she said, a little breathless from her run. She looked back and forth between Emma and Eve, her eyes finally resting on Eve. "Are you Eve? Evella?"

The color drained from Eve's face. No one called her Evella. No one on Earth, anyway.

"Who are you?" she asked.

"Are you Eve?" the woman asked again, wiping a drop of sweat from her forehead.

"I'm Eve," said Eve, hardly breathing, not taking her eyes off the woman. Emma reached out and put a hand on Eve's arm.

"A woman left a note for you. Kata? She told me to keep an eye out for you and if I ever saw you, to bring this to you?" She spoke with an uplift at the end of every sentence, making all her statements sound like questions. "My friend is a waitress in the café?" She nodded her head at the restaurant where they'd eaten. "She called me and was telling me about you guys … I mean, just gossip, you know, you're out-of-towners …" She looked a bit embarrassed to have been caught gossiping, but the words continued to spill out of her mouth. "But Nat was telling me about you guys and suddenly I thought, that sounds like Evella, that sounds like how Kata said Eve would look? A lot like her? Your blond hair, your eyes, and Nat said you were talking about magnets?"

Emma gasped. "What about magnets?"

"I work at the new-age shop down the street," she said, gesturing down the road toward the center of town. "I have magnetic bracelets and things like that. I gave Kata one once? She loved it, yeah? I just … well, I just thought I'd check, to see if you're Eve?"

"Where is she?" asked Eve, barely moving. "Where is Kata?"

"She's gone, yeah?" said the woman. "Left a couple of weeks ago."

Emma and Charlie exchanged a glance. A couple of weeks ago! But Eve and her father had been looking for Kata for a year! Where had she been before that?

"There's a note?" said Emma, reminding the woman why she'd come. "And I'm Emma, by the way," she said, holding out her hand."

"Right, sorry, I'm Sophie," said Sophie, shaking Emma's hand.

"Yeah, the note," she said, and reached inside her pocket. She pulled out a folded, worn envelope and tried to smooth out the wrinkles against her thigh. "Sorry, I don't have the first one," she said, handing the note to Eve.

"The first one?" said Eve. "What do you mean?"

Sophie pointed to the writing on the outside of the envelope. "Read this second," she read. "This is the only note she gave me. I don't have the one you're supposed to read first." The look of distress on her face was sincere.

Eve was stunned to silence, so Emma spoke on her behalf. "It's okay. We … we already … it's fine. We have the first note already. Thank you." *Read this second,* she thought. *This has to be for real.*

"How did you meet Kata?" asked Charlie. "How long was she here?"

"Yeah, right, she came to town months ago? I mean, there are lots of tourists, right? So we don't hear about every one, but there was something about Kata, well, people talked. And she was here a while, then she left, then she came back, and then she left again, but she gave me this note."

"Why you?" asked Emma. "Did you get to know her well?"

"Yeah, right? She liked to come into my shop. She thought it had good energy." Sophie smiled. "She's right, it does, yeah? It's nice. You should come by?"

Ben suddenly remembered how the conversation had started. "You said you gave her magnets?"

"Right. Yeah. A magnetic bracelet? She just seemed a little lost, right? She was out at the baths all the time, I saw her there, too. Looking for peace. I could tell she was a seeker, yeah? I knew she was seeking something. Magnets can help with balance, tension, oxygen in the blood, all sorts of things." Sophie paused. "I don't know if I actually believe all that? But a woman in town makes the bracelets and they're quite nice. I gave Kata one, once, when she came into my store, just because she seemed a little lost, yeah? That was the first time she was in town. Then she left, and came back, oh, several months later. I almost didn't remember her, but she still had that lost look, and she still had the magnetic bracelet. The second time she was here, she'd been here a couple days when she gave me this note to give you, and then she left again. We talked a long time when she came into the store, about life and the universe and everything. She told me she likes to travel, misses her family, tried to find them but they were gone. Sad, really, yeah? Do you know her family?" Sophie looked at Eve, expectantly.

Eve hesitantly shook her head: No.

"Right?" said Sophie. "I thought you might? You look a little like her? Anyway, she was a good woman. If you see her, tell her Sophie said hello? If she comes around this way again she should stop by."

Eve was still clutching the note tight in her hands. "Did she say anything else? Do you know where she went?"

Sophie shook her head. "Sorry, mate, that's all I know, just the note." She smiled broadly. "I'm so glad Natalie called me! I thought the chances of ever finding you were none in a million! Right, that's a load off my mind, yeah?" Sophie looked at her watch. "I'd better get back to my shop, right? Left my boyfriend in charge when Nat called, and he doesn't know a cash register from his bum!" She laughed and turned. "Good luck," she said. She waved and ran off again.

They watched as Sophie raced back down the road. "Oh. My. Gosh," said Emma. "Eve! The note! Read the note!"

Hands shaking, Eve carefully opened the envelope. Before reaching inside, she reverently turned it over again to read the back for herself: "Read this second," she whispered. "It's from her," she said. "I know it is."

"Well, why are we waiting to find out?" said Chuck, bouncing with excitement. "Read the note! Read the note!"

Charlie joined Chuck in the chant. "Read the note! Read the note!" they cried.

"Hush!" Emma said. "Shhh! We don't want to draw attention to ourselves!"

"Apparently we already have," said Chuck. "That's how Sophie found us!"

"Hush!" said Eve, then to herself: "Focus!" She pulled the note out from the envelope and unfolded it. "Read this second. That means the first letter of the second word. Okay. Here it is." She read the note aloud:

> *My Love,*
> *So. Australia. You've found me. Good girl.*
> *I've been trying to find you,*
> *but you were gone when I went home.*
> *I really hope you are well.*
> *Me, I've been traveling.*
> *It's never easy.*
> *But the universes call and I answer.*
> *I hope to see you soon.*
> *Love,*
> *Mom.*

As Eve read, Emma took out a notebook and wrote down the first letter from the second word of each line:

L–A–B–Y–R–I–N–T–H

"Labyrinth!" said Emma, a chill running down her spine. "Eve, that woman at the museum, Agnes, didn't she mention a labyrinth? The 'maze' in 'A-MAZE-ING'?"

"Yes!" said Charlie. "We saw one! We were there! There's a laby-rinth out on one of the car door tours! We saw it!" He was bounc-ing with excitement, now, too.

"The Green tour!" said Ben. "Yes! Banjo took us there!"

"You've been there?" said Emma. "We have to go there!"

"Wait. We still need to get a magnet," said Ben, determined this time not to let the task be forgotten.

"Right," said Emma. "That woman, Sophie, she gave Kata a magnetic bracelet. I think we should get one just like it. If that's what your mom had," she said to Eve, "then I think that's what we should try, too."

Eve nodded. "Where's her store?" She peered in the direction So-phie had run.

"If you give me the credit card," said Chuck, "I'll go get it, yeah?"

Eve smiled. "Only if you promise not to buy anything else!" She handed Chuck the card, and he ran off.

"How far is the labyrinth?" Emma asked Ben and Charlie. "Can we walk?"

"And were there lots of people there?" asked Eve. "We don't know what's going to happen. I don't think we want an audience."

"There wasn't anyone else there when we were there," said Ben. "I don't think we have to worry too much about that. But how far was it?" He looked to Charlie for help. "It's walkable," he said without enthusiasm. The day was already quite hot.

Charlie shrugged. "To be honest, we were all goofing around and talking. I wasn't paying attention. I'd say at least a mile." He glanced at the sun, beaming down its unforgiving summer heat. "I suppose you're going to tell me we have to walk there again."

Shading her eyes, Emma gazed up at the sun. It was after noon, and the heat hadn't yet peaked. She'd overheard someone at the café discussing the day's weather: 41 degrees celsius, which she'd calculated to be about 106 degrees fahrenheit. Definitely hot. Walking a mile or more in the heat would be anywhere from uncomfortable to dangerous.

Emma caught Eve's eye. Eve nodded.

"Ben," said Emma, "do you think you can target the labyrinth with the Dark MATTER? Do you know the coordinates?"

Charlie pumped his fist in a gesture of triumph. "Yes!" he said.

"I can probably find the coordinates," Ben said. He went to work on his iPert. "Got it," he said after a few moments. "Yeah, I can probably get us pretty close."

"So humble," said Eve. "I have faith in you, Ben!" Eve beamed at the young man.

Ben waved off the compliment, but blushed. He was saved further embarrassment by the commotion of Chuck's return.

"I got it!" said Chuck as he approached at a slow trot. "Dang, it's hot! Any chance we could, you know, transport to the labyrinth instead of walking? That few blocks there about did me in."

Charlie patted Chuck on the back. "I got you, Chuck. We have arranged special transport on the Ben Express. Our man has the site in his targets, ready to beam us over."

"What did you get?" asked Emma. "Can we see?"

Chuck reached into his pocket and drew out a bracelet of beads and magnets. "Sophie said this is like the one she gave your mom," he said to Eve. "I figured we should get something as close to it as possible."

"Smart thinking," said Emma.

"Yeah, naturally, right? Mate? G'day? Bonzer?" said Chuck, tossing out all the Australian slang he could think of.

Eve rolled her eyes but laughed. "Right!" she said. "Okay. Do we have everything? We might not be coming back for a while, so we should make sure we're ready to go."

Emma looked around. Even though she'd told the hotel manager they would be staying a few days, they'd brought all their belongings with them. It was still a strange notion to her, the idea that they weren't heading out on a simple road trip, but literally into the unknown. She knew from experience that using their various modes of interuniversal travel could land them anywhere. Setting the coordinates where they wanted to go did not guarantee that they'd actually get there.

"This still makes me a little nervous," said Charlie, echoing Emma's thoughts.

"You're the one who didn't want to walk," said Emma. She reached out and punched him softly. "Dork."

"Dork." He punched back, but looked her straight in the eye: stay with me, his eyes said. Charlie had almost lost his sister once from this traveling through the universes. She'd been unconscious. He'd been the one who'd had to deal with the possibility she was gone for good.

Eve was watching this exchange with a bit of reverence. She'd never had siblings, much less a twin. The deep connection Emma and Charlie shared was something she envied. "You guys ready?" she asked.

"Ready," said Emma.

"Ready," said Charlie.

Chuck affirmed his readiness with a salute. Ben gave a thumbs up.

"Okay, then. Ben, take us to the labyrinth!" said Eve.

As usual, it took the travelers a few seconds to recombobulate after they transported. "Is the heat making the air wavy like that, or is it just me?" asked Chuck.

"A little of both, I think," said Emma, rubbing her temples.

She looked around to try to orient herself. Ben had intentionally dropped them a few hundred yards away from the labyrinth;
landing smack in the center could have caused alarm if someone
else were present. Shielding her eyes against the sun with her hand,
Emma turned to see if she could find the maze. Though the surrounding area was dotted with the low trees familiar to the area, the
labyrinth itself lay in a dry, flat clearing. They were, it seemed, right
in the middle of a whole lot of nothing. The arid air and the deso-
late landscape suddenly brought to her mind a memory of the time
she'd landed herself and Charlie on a deserted planet with a man
who sought to destroy the universes. She shuddered involuntarily.

"Looks a little like that planet where we found Vik, eh?" said
Charlie.

Emma nodded.

"There," said Eve, pointing toward the north. "Is that it?"

Ben squinted in the direction Eve was pointing, then checked his
iPert. "I think it is. Good eyes, Eve."

Still a little wobbly on their legs, the group trekked the short
distance to the labyrinth.

"This is it?" said Eve, puzzled. The labyrinth was not what she
was expecting. This was no shrub-lined maze; it was nothing at all
like the maze in Dr. Waldo's Thought room back in the Experimental Building in the Hub. No, it would have been easy to miss this
labyrinth from a distance: it was low to the ground, nothing more
than earthen paths delineated by stones. The thousands of jagged
rocks that lined the outer circle and the diminishing circles within virtually blended in with the surrounding dirt. It was only the
shadows of the stones that revealed their presence.

"Yeah, this is it," said Charlie. "Surprised us, too, yesterday. Banjo
told us a labyrinth is not really supposed to be a maze. It's just a
path; you walk it to sort of meditate and think. You could just walk

straight to the center, but walking the path is supposed to sort of, I don't know, put you in a trance or something."

"A trance?" said Eve. "Really?"

"Well, maybe not a trance," said Charlie. "But it's supposed to sort of calm your mind. I think."

"It's not supposed to be a maze," said Ben. "Just, like Charlie said, a meditation thing."

"So do you think your mom intended us to walk the path?" Chuck asked Eve. "I mean, what else would we do here?"

"Your guess is as good as mine," said Eve. She walked to the entrance, a path about two feet wide, lined with stones. From there she could see that the labyrinth was made up of four equal quadrants, the paths within each winding around within each quadrant, before leading on to the next, and, ultimately, to the center.

"One, two, three …" Chuck counted the number of rings within the outer circle. "I think thirteen?" he said.

"However many there are, let's go," said Emma, taking Eve's hand.

By unspoken agreement, Eve led the way. This was her mother they were seeking; this was her quest. With her left hand she tightly grasped Emma's hand, and in her right, she carried the opal. The magnetic bracelet was wrapped around her right wrist.

The group walked the meandering path in silent expectancy, not knowing what might happen, or when, or even how. Part of Emma thought nothing would happen; after all, they were nowhere near water, and she was convinced water was important. Another part of her half expected to be transported to another world at any moment.

They walked slowly, as if already in a meditative state. The sun beamed down on them, its heat so thick it became part of the air. As they neared the center of the labyrinth, Eve paused, letting out a big whoosh of air. "Just realized I'd been holding my breath," she said, looking nervously at the others.

Emma grasped Eve's hand tighter. "Are you ready?"

Eve nodded. "Link up, people!" she said. With her free hand, Emma reached for Charlie's hand. Charlie reached for Chuck. Chuck caught Ben's hand, and the line was complete.

"Let's go!" said Ben.

Eve led the group again, winding around the last few tight turns, the chain of people serpentining behind her.

At the very edge of the center circle, she gasped and jumped back, bumping into Emma.

"Did you see that?" she cried, her shock causing her to unintentionally drop Emma's hand.

Not wanting to be left behind again—that had happened to her before—Emma quickly linked her arm with Eve's elbow. "See what?" she said, staring tightly into the center.

"Shimmering. The air shimmered." Eve looked around. "Or was it just the heat? Heat makes the air shimmer sometimes, right?"

"It does," said Emma, hesitantly, "but I'm guessing whatever you saw was more than heat."

"Crowd around," Eve instructed the others, gathering them closer to her. "And watch."

The group clustered tightly around Eve.

"When I say move, everyone walk forward," she said. "Like, two steps. Then stop."

Emma wrapped the arm that held Charlie's hand close around his arm. Charlie laughed. "Calm down, sis," he said. "I'm with you."

"Move!" said Eve.

As if in a comedy film, the group shuffled clumsily in a cluster toward the center.

And they all saw what Eve had seen. The air in the center seemed to shift in shimmering waves, like ripples on a lake dispersing from a stone's throw. The air, invisible, seemed to take on weight and shape, no longer invisible but instead thick, like a see-through gelatin.

"What's happening?" said Chuck.

"Shhh," said Eve. "Wait. Watch." Her arm linked with Emma's, Eve grasped the opal and the magnetic bracelet in both hands.

Suddenly, the air in front of them changed completely, and a new landscape appeared momentarily, parting from a center point then dissipating out to the edges.

"What was that!" said Charlie. He gripped tighter to Emma's arm.

Before anyone could answer, it happened again. Another landscape emerged from a point in the center, growing out several feet to the edges before disappearing. Then another, and another, slow at first, then faster and faster. Each image opened like a window before them, a screen door, so real it seemed they could walk through. Flickers of landscape after landscape passed before their eyes.

"Step back!" said Eve. The others obeyed. The images disappeared.

"What!" said Chuck. "What the heck!"

Emma looked at Eve. "Do you think those were other planets?" she asked.

"I think they might be," she replied. "Other planets, in other universes."

Emma's heart was beating fast. "Do you think ... we're supposed to jump in? Walk through that window?" She glanced around the area, checking for onlookers, people watching from afar. No one was anywhere to be seen.

Eve let out another whoosh of air. "I don't know, but that's what I was thinking."

"How do we know which one to jump into, though?" asked

Charlie. "And then what happens?"

"I think," said Eve, "that's where 'water' comes in. As for what happens next, I don't know."

Emma had been thinking the same thing. "Okay. So, we wait until we see a water landscape. But what if there's more than one planet with a water landscape? What then?"

"I think I'll know," said Eve. "I just … I think my gut will tell me which is the right one. You guys ready again?"

"Ready as we'll ever be," said Chuck. "Lead the way!"

"Okay," said Eve, bracing herself. "We'll walk forward again until we see a water landscape, and then when I say go, everyone walk through. I don't want to leave anyone behind."

They huddled together, everyone clinging to everyone else. "Walk forward," said Eve calmly, and as one they moved toward the center of the circle.

The air shimmered again, changed, transformed until once again it had weight and substance. And then, as before, the landscapes started to emerge. A dry desert, not terribly different from the one they were in. A craggy mountaintop, snow-covered, the chill of the air bursting through to cool them for the briefest second. A market-place, filled with sentient beings.

"Can they see us?" whispered Chuck, but before anyone could answer, the landscape changed again.

A nighttime forest filled with dark, twisted trees, illuminated by two enormous moons.

An underground cave sheltering a crystalline lake, stalactites dripping in an eternal journey from the ceiling.

"Is that it? There's water …" said Emma.

Eve shook her head no. "I don't think so."

When the next landscape flashed open, they all knew. This was it.

"Now!" cried Eve. "Jump!"

chapter nine

They jumped. Or rather, they dived—because what they saw before them was not a lake, or an ocean, or a pond, but rather a complete wall of water. In the universe they were jumping into, wherever that might be, this window opened up deep under water. Some law of physics or the universe or interuniversal travel somehow kept the water on the side of the water universe, though in the split second the teens saw the wall of water, Emma half expected it all to start spilling into their own world.

So when Eve said "Jump!" they dived, headfirst, into a wall of water, clumsily holding on to each other as, incredibly, impossibly, they stepped over a threshold from one universe to another.

Once in the water, Emma glanced back to where they'd been, to the hot Australian desert side of the portal. The window to their own world closed the instant after Ben's foot made it through.

"Phew," she said. "That was close." Even as she started to speak she realized—or assumed—she was about to get a mouth full of water.

She did not.

It hadn't occurred to her until that moment to wonder whether the rock on her bracelet, the one which allowed her to breathe normally in other atmospheres, would also work under water. Luckily for them all, it seemed that it did. A field of air hovered around each of the teens' heads. The air bubble thickened at noses and mouths and faded out to blend imperceptibly with the water about five inches from their faces. Looking at each other, the teens could just barely make out the pockets of air. About the only clue to the existence of the air pockets was the fact that they could breathe.

Emma kicked lightly to maneuver herself in the water. She tested her ability to breathe, taking deep, tentative, shallow breaths to try to calm the panic she felt rising inside her. The teens had not landed anywhere near the surface of the water, it seemed, but neither were they at the ocean floor. They were simply floating in the depths of some vast ocean on some unknown world. "Seems like we have air around our eyes, too," Emma observed. "Hadn't thought of that, but that's good."

What the others heard was "Eeemmiiee rrmmm err ooo. Aaddnaao aaa ooo."

"What?" said Charlie.

The others heard "Ahhh?"

"Talking. Under water. Of course! We can't understand each other!" said Eve. She shook her head and waved her arms slowly through the water.

The others couldn't understand, but from her frustration, and their own, they knew what she was saying.

What were we thinking? thought Emma. *We weren't. We just jumped. We should have known better!* She glanced over at Charlie, who was watching her. She knew he knew what she was thinking, but that didn't help their situation at all. She shook her head at him. "What do we do now?" her look said.

Figure out more about where we are, she told herself. *Look around. See if there's a way to the surface. If there's even a surface, that is,* she thought.

Emma took another cautious, deep breath within her tiny bubble of air. *Assess the situation,* she told herself. *Figure out what you know for sure.*

First, she thought, *we're alive. So that's a positive.*

Second, we're floating in mid-water, not sinking. So that's a positive. I guess.

Third. Look around. Okay. There's water. That's pretty obvious. Wait, it's not too dark for me to see, she thought, *so either the stones are giving us the ability to see under water, too, or we're near enough to the surface for light to shine down. So that's a positive.*

Emma noticed that Eve and Ben were trying to pantomime a conversation, but she couldn't make heads or tails of what they were saying. She continued with her assessment.

Fourth. I don't see Eve's mom anywhere. So that's a negative. On the other hand, I don't see any beings, so that's probably a positive, because we are, pretty much, defenseless.

She squinted, trying to see farther into the murky depths. *Is that … are those buildings over there?* She looked closely but couldn't interpret what she was seeing. In the distance, on what she thought might be the ocean floor, were large structures that seemed to have some intentional form. Not just rocks and caves, but structures that could have been built, could have been put together with some thought. *Which would indicate intelligent life. Which would indicate …*

"They live here! People live here under water!" she blurted out.

The others heard: "Ayyierr! Eehhhhrrrdrrrarr!"

Emma pointed and gesticulated toward the structures, trying desperately to communicate. The others followed her line of sight, but could not figure out what she was trying to tell them.

"Buildings! Homes!" Emma cried out futilely. "They're …"

And then she saw movement.

Dark forms rushed toward them, with the grace and agility of creatures that lived under water. And with a speed and precision that implied intent.

The others couldn't understand the words Emma was crying out, but the look of alarm on her face was enough to alert them. They turned just in time to see six creatures of the sea surging at them, carrying between them a giant, roughly formed net.

They were trapped.

The aquatic creatures scooped them up faster than they could react. The net that imprisoned the teens seemed to be made from some strong form of seaweed. They struggled against it but their confusion and fear, combined with their lack of underwater agility, left them helpless.

"My bag!" Emma screamed into the air bubble surrounding her head. In the chaos, her backpack, with not only her spare clothes and food and iPert but also an extra Dark MATTER and pigeon, had been ripped from her back. Emma watched with dismay as it floated slowly toward the ocean floor. Squinting, she saw two other dark masses swirling alongside it. In horror, Emma realized those were two other backpacks, each full of items they needed to survive and return home.

She didn't have a chance to watch the bags land, as the beings pulled their captives along through the water at breakneck speed. Emma felt the pressure of the water tearing at her face and tangled limbs. Trying to remain calm, she studied their captors as best she could from her awkward position, sandwiched between Eve and Chuck, all of them pressed up against the sides of the net, arms and legs trailing. The creatures looked a lot like octopuses, she thought; at least, that's the best reference point she could think of. She thought she counted nine legs, though, or arms, she wasn't sure which. Maybe both. At the end of each arm or leg were several long tentacles, sort of like fingers. Emma couldn't quite figure out how the beings moved so swiftly through the water. They seemed to pulse; the movement was not steady. But with all of them acting together, they were fast.

The force of water somehow pushed the air pockets that allowed them to breathe closer to their faces. Emma was just about to panic for real when the beings thrust them all into a giant, solid room—more box-like than cave-like—that very definitely looked man-made. *Or made by something, anyway,* thought Emma.

Unceremoniously, the creatures pushed the teens into the box. They gathered up the net with no apparent concern as to whether they might be taking any fingers and arms and legs or anything else with them, and rushed out. A wall closed behind them, sealing the teens inside ... and sealing out all light.

"Aaahhh!" "Rrrgagaahh!" In the darkness, Emma could hear the muted mumbles of others yelling, but she still couldn't make out their words. Her heart raced so fast she thought it might pound out of her chest. She flailed, trying to find someone's arm, a leg, something to cling to, someone to hold on to. A hand caught hers, and whoever it was pulled her close.

Suddenly, lights went on in the box, blinding them.

The water that filled the room started to gush out through a drain as the teens looked on in both hope and horror. Quickly, the level of the water lowered enough for them to stand. Emma looked and realized it was Chuck she was clinging to.

"Can you all hear me now?" asked Emma tentatively, still holding tight to Chuck's arm.

"Yes!" cried Eve, collapsing onto the floor. "Oh my gosh, where are we? What is happening? I lost my bag!"

"Me too," said Emma. "It fell when they caught us. I lost every-thing."

"Me three," said Chuck. "Gone."

"I had mine," said Ben, "but it's gone now. It must have been tangled in the net when they took it away."

Everyone looked at Charlie.

His backpack was still attached to his back but it was hanging completely open, mostly empty, its few remaining contents spilling out the sides.

"Your iPert?" said Emma. "Or a Dark MATTER globe? A pigeon?"

As the others watched on, holding their breaths, Charlie reached deep into the pockets of his bag. "The iPert, I think!" he said, his fingers pushing into a far corner. He pulled the object out triumphantly. The look on his face quickly fell. "Cracked," he said, holding it up to show the others.

"'Cracked' is an understatement," said Chuck, reaching out for Charlie's iPert. "Demolished is more like it. How did that happen?" As he held the iPert, water dripped from its core.

"Make note of that, please, to tell the committee to make the iPerts shatterproof and waterproof," said Emma bleakly.

"Noted," said Charlie.

"Anything else?" said Eve, the hope in her voice noticeably diminished.

Charlie rummaged through his pack some more, then dumped all the contents onto the floor. Everyone went over to help search for any device that might help them get home, but they found nothing.

Emma inhaled deeply. "Well, at least we can still breathe, anyway, right? And we can hear each other again, so that's good?" She watched as the last of the water seeped down the drain. They were, if nothing else, on dry land again.

"But where are we? Are they going to let us out? And how did they know we weren't like them? I thought the bracelets were supposed to disguise us?" said Charlie in a rush.

"And I thought the bracelets were supposed to enable us to communicate with each other?" said Chuck. "But not under water, apparently."

Eve shook her head. "I have no idea. This was so stupid of me, telling you all to jump into the water! What was I thinking?" She started to cry.

"It's not your fault, Eve—" Ben began, but stopped mid-sentence when another side wall started to slide open.

The door inched open slowly. The teens stood watching, barely moving, afraid of what was to come next. Charlie moved protectively in front of Emma. She reached for his hand and held tight.

Whatever was on the other side, the teens were relieved to see it was not filled with water. As the door's opening widened, it revealed what seemed to be a rather plain hallway, its floor tiled in a deep ocean blue, its walls a simple off-white.

But the teens hardly noticed the walls or the tiles, because standing there in front of them was a woman, tall and blond, looking a great deal like someone they already knew.

"Hello?" the woman said tentatively.

Eve saw the woman and leaped from her place on the floor. "Mom?" she cried, hardly believing her eyes. "Mom! Is that really you?" She rushed into the woman's arms.

"Oh my gosh, Evella, you found me! Is that really you? I can't believe you're here!" Kata hugged her daughter tight. "You're all wet! Come inside, change your clothes, you'll catch a cold like this." But she didn't budge from her spot, holding her daughter like she'd never let her go.

"You're Eve's mom?" asked Chuck, though the answer was obvious. Kata looked exactly like an older version of Eve.

Kata nodded, tears squeezing out of her closed eyelids.

"You mentioned inside?" said Emma, who was, in fact, starting to shiver a bit, and wanted very much to get somewhere warm, where they could discuss this turn of events. "Inside where? Where are we?"

"Inside, inside," said Kata, releasing her daughter from her hug but keeping an arm around her. "We'll make introductions when you are all dry and warm. Do you have dry clothes or is everything wet?" she said, looking at the contents of Charlie's backpack, strewn all over the floor.

"We lost everything," said Emma, holding back tears. "Including our way home. All that's left is …" She gestured at the mess. Charlie squeezed his sister's hand.

"All right, now, don't start worrying. Inside!" admonished Kata, herding the teens from the damp, dark box into what looked like the hallway of a home. "We'll deal with all that later," she said, gesturing at their spare belongings. "There are dry clothes inside; I'm sure you can find something." She pushed the boys through the house and off into one room to change, and then led the girls into another.

Emma had only caught a glance of the rest of the home as Kata rushed through it, so she took her time looking around the room where they were changing. For all intents and purposes, it looked like a bedroom of some sort. There was a wide, raised platform with a long, soft mattress, which Emma assumed served as a bed. Small tables on either side held up what Emma assumed were lamps. Across from the bed, a large section of the wall was bound by a rectangular frame of what seemed to be wood, but as far as Emma could tell, there was nothing within the frame. Just outside the frame to the right, a small glass-fronted panel was embedded into the wall. Sliding doors hid what Emma thought could be a closet, and a door led into another room. The doorknob, while similar to Earth doorknobs, was about half a foot higher than what Emma was used to.

Kata pulled open a dresser drawer and tossed some dry clothes at the girls. "It won't fit exactly, but it's good enough," she said. "Extra arms, it seems," she said, unfurling from around her neck two extra sleeves on the shirt she was wearing, which Emma had at first thought were a scarf.

Emma held up the clothes Eve's mother had given her. The soft, stretchy pants seemed normal, but, sure enough, her shirt also had four sleeves. It was dry, though, and that was all she cared about right now. She peeled off her wet clothes and put on the strange but warm garments with gratitude.

"Where are we?" Eve asked her mother as she pulled on a pair of dark green pants. "And how did you get here? And what were those creatures that brought us here? And what was that room they pushed us into, and how did they get the water out? And where are we now? How long have you been here? Why didn't you come home?"

"Shhh," said Kata, laughing and stroking her daughter's hair. "One question at a time!"

"And I know you're eager, Eve," said Emma, wrapping the extra sleeves around her neck in the same way Kata had done with hers, "but the others will want to hear it all too. Let's wait until we're back with the boys so your mom doesn't have to answer everything twice." She extended her hand to Kata. "I'm Emma, by the way. I'm from Earth. It's nice to meet you."

Kata beamed a bright smile. "Nice to meet you, Emma from Earth. I'm Kata from Lero, but I'm guessing you know that." She glanced at Eve. "Yes, you two finish up here. Put your wet clothes on the tiles in the hall and we can deal with them later. I'll go make something hot to drink. Come on out when you're ready." She left the room. Emma opened what she thought was the closet. She wanted to explore more, but knew now was not the time. Looking on the floor, she found what she'd been seeking: footwear, including thick, soft slip-on shoes that would keep their feet warm. She slid her feet into a pair and brought an extra pair to Eve, then the two followed the sounds of the others back out into the main part of the house.

The boys had found clothes and changed quickly, made their introductions to Kata, and were already waiting for the girls, mugs of some sort of tea warming their hands. They were sitting in what appeared to be a living room, with couches and chairs, end tables and knick-knacks. What especially drew Emma's attention was a bookshelf, chock full of books.

"Oh!" she gasped, pulling one book off the shelf. The cover was soft, smooth, almost silky in her hands. She opened the book reverently. Books contained worlds, she knew. She couldn't even imagine what might be inside these. The pages of the book she held were made up of something quite paper-like, delicate and beautiful and covered in ink. "What!" she said, gasping again. "I can read this! Is this in English?"

Kata laughed and held up her arm. There, around her wrist, was a bracelet just like the ones Emma and the others all wore, complete with the stones that allowed them to breathe, to disguise themselves, to be understood when speaking to aliens, and to read. "It's not English," said Kata. "But I am glad to see Dr. Waldo equipped you with bracelets!"

"Emma, come over here," Charlie said impatiently, patting the seat beside him. "We've been waiting for you guys so Kata can tell us what the heck is going on." He noticed how Emma had wrapped her shirt's extra sleeves around her neck, and followed suit.

"You haven't been waiting *that* long," Emma huffed. She sat next to her brother on the couch, bringing the book with her, cradling it like it was priceless. "Does this couch seem a little high?" she asked, noting that her feet were almost, but not quite, dangling above the floor.

"I think you're right," said Kata. "I haven't seen anyone else since I've been here, but everything seems to be made for beings slightly taller than we are."

"So where are we?" asked Emma, settling into the cozy couch. She had no idea what time it was or how long it was since they'd slept the night before, but she suspected nothing but adrenaline was keeping her awake at this point. "What is this place? And how did you get here?"

"You were gone so long!" Eve said, unable to contain herself any more. "Why were you go gone so long?" She was seated on a wide chair with her mother, head resting on her mother's shoulder, her arm wrapped around Kata's arm, holding her hand tight as if she'd never let go.

Kata gently kissed Eve's forehead. "I wasn't, though. That's what happens when you start thinking you can control time. Time lets you know who's boss." She sighed. "Where to begin. So much has happened. Well, you know, I had a lot of thinking to do." Eve nodded slightly, knowing her mother was talking about her relationship with her father. "I was out for a bike ride on Lero one day, just thinking, and I had my Universe Key on my necklace." She pulled out her necklace, with its wishing rock secured tightly to its end: a small gray rock with a band of white around the center. Some of these wishing rocks, which could be found all over Earth and Lero and probably many other planets, were more than just rocks; they were keys that could unlock the entrance to the elevators they used to travel; keys, in essence, to the universes.

"Out of nowhere, I was riding along, and the key started to vibrate," Kata continued. "You know how it does that?"

They all nodded.

Kata went on. "It started vibrating, so I knew I was near an elevator. One that I hadn't discovered before; that no one had, as far as I knew. Of course, I had to find it." She looked at Eve. "Can't help it; I'm curious. You get that from both your dad and me. So I searched around until I found the elevator, and took it for a ride. It took me to a lighthouse out in the east of Australia. And you know," she said to Eve, "I've always wanted to spend more time in that country. It's one of the oldest places on Earth. Australia's rocks contain an infinity of stories."

"Dr. Waldo told me you liked Australia, but I didn't know," said Eve, her mouth in a pout.

Kata looked chagrined. She held Eve's hands in both of hers. "Well, Dr. Waldo was right. So I started wandering around. After a while I realized I was seeing dark galaxy stones in stores everywhere. Just everywhere! I had the one your dad found long ago … I always carry it with me. He never knew, but back when we … when things started to go bad, I went into the storage unit and, uh, borrowed it. It reminded me of better times. The times I wanted to get back."

Eve wriggled in her seat next to her mother, the turmoil in her mind clear on her face. Finally finding her mother after more than a year of searching was more than enough to deal with, let alone trying to sort out her parents' relationship problems.

Sensing Eve's discomfort, Kata moved on. "Anyway, I learned that the dark galaxy stones are mostly mined out at Lightning Ridge, so I hopped on a bus and headed out there."

"How do you pay for the bus?" asked Chuck, ever curious. "Did you just happen to have Earth money?"

"Chuck!" said Emma. "Seriously?"

"Well, the company I work with, which does interuniversal research, gave me a credit card that works pretty much everywhere," Kata explained.

"You have one, too?" Chuck said with envy. "I gotta get me one of those cards!"

Kata continued. "I wanted to have some time to think, and like I said, I'd always wanted to go back to Australia. I thought the universes were telling me something by randomly sending me there. Not so randomly, maybe. So, I got to Lightning Ridge, and I was just wandering around town, going in and out of shops. One shop I wandered into was what Earth people call 'new age'—healing stones, incenses, soft music on pan flutes, that sort of thing. The woman at the counter took one look at me and knew I was lost. Not physically—I knew where I was—but emotionally. She just knew. She showed me some magnetic bracelets and told me about their healing power. She gave me one, saying she could tell I needed it. And then she directed me to the labyrinth, telling me to walk its path and meditate; that it would be good for my soul."

"We met her," said Eve. "Sophie. She's the one who gave us the note you left."

"Of course," said Kata. "Of course, that's right. We talked a lot, Sophie and I. She's sweet. Well, she told me about the labyrinth and said I should go out there. I'm assuming you found that, too?"

They all nodded.

"I went out to the labyrinth, wearing the magnetic bracelet. As always, I had the dark galaxy stone in my pocket. As I walked the labyrinth, I took the stone out of my pocket to help me meditate on what I wanted, on the good times, on our family. At first, I carried it in my right hand, and the magnets were around my left wrist. But before I reached into my right pocket again to get out a handkerchief—it was quite warm—I passed the dark galaxy stone to my left hand, just as I reached the center of the circle. And that's when it happened. Through whatever combinations of forces and time and energies and serendipity and fate, the universes all opened up before me. You saw it, too."

"It was amazing," said Ben. "Just incredible."

"I had no idea what I was doing," said Kata. "I jumped in, stupid-ly. I know better than that. But I wasn't thinking clearly. I thought it was all meant to be. I jumped into one of the first universes I saw, and I ended up getting caught in a vortex of time and space. I think …" she looked around at the teens, hanging on her every word. "Well, to be honest, I think it might have been a dead universe."

"A dead universe!" said Emma. She remembered all too well her experience on a dry, desolated planet, where she'd confronted Vik about The Void. That planet had not, she thought, been dead, but it wasn't far off. "What is a dead universe? How did you know?"

"I can't say anything more than that," said Kata. "Not because I don't want to; I just don't know. Something in me, when I was there, something told me, 'This is a dead universe.' I don't know if I was right. I jumped back out immediately—I'm still not even sure how I did that—but in the moments it took to jump into and out of the dead universe, months had passed on Earth." She looked at Eve. "I wouldn't have known that except that the weather was dif-ferent when I returned, and the time of day. I didn't find out until later how long I'd been gone. Before leaving the labyrinth, though, I opened up the universes again—put the dark galaxy stone and the magnets together—and watched the planets unfold in front of my face. I saw this world here, a world under water, and I wanted to explore. But I didn't want to leave again without telling you. I raced home, but you guys were gone."

"We were out looking for Vik," Eve murmured, calculating the timeline in her head.

"That's when I left the notes," said Kata. "You must have found them? The ones that told you about the dark galaxy and the magnet and the water?"

"We did find them, but why did you have to be so cryptic?" asked Eve. "We almost didn't figure it out. We might never have found you if it weren't for Ben."

Kata scratched at her knee. "You can never be too careful in my line of work," she said. "You know that, Eve. You don't always know who's on your side." She lay her head down on top of her daughter's. "I'm sorry."

Eve let out a deep sigh. "I know, I know."

"Anyway," said Kata, resuming her story, "after leaving the notes, I went back to Lightning Ridge and left a note with Sophie, and then I went out to the labyrinth. I jumped into the water world and ended up here, just two days ago, if I'm measuring time right. The underwater creatures brought me here the same way I assume they brought you."

"Two days?" said Charlie. "That's not possible! You left Lightning Ridge *weeks* ago, according to that Sophie woman."

Kata shrugged. She was familiar with the ways of the universes, and no longer tried to fight them. "This universe, or at least this planet, must not be on the same timeline as Earth. You get used to it."

Emma's forehead furrowed as she contemplated this new information. If Kata had been there for only two days, but in that time weeks had passed back on Earth, then had they themselves already been gone for a week? She shook her head. The more she thought about it, the more confusing it became.

"Okay, so we have no idea how long any of us has been gone, that's established. Do we at least know where we are?" asked Ben. "We were under water, but now we're not anymore, right? How did that happen?"

Kata laughed. "Oh, you're still under water," she said. She unwound herself from Eve, got up, and crossed to a large wall of curtains opposite the couches. Kata pushed a button on the wall, and with a mechanical whirr, the curtains parted. Behind them were two giant window panels framing another section of wall. The enormous center section was about the height and width of both windows put together, and resembled the section of wall opposite the bed that Emma had noticed in the bedroom earlier. Another glass-covered panel was embedded into the wall next to the button Kata had pushed.

"I don't get it," said Ben, looking out the windows into utter darkness. "Are you showing us that it's night?"

"No, not night, said Kata. She tapped the panel, and lights on the other side of the wall illuminated the space outside the windows.

"Oh my gosh!" said Emma, jumping up. "We are still under water!" The field of outside lights filtered through the water to reveal fish of all kinds and sizes swimming by. Looking down, Emma could see that the building they were in did not rest on the ocean floor. Water distorted perception, she knew, but from her best guess they were still several stories above the sandy coral-covered bed below. The fish themselves ranged from those that looked quite Earth-like to creatures Emma never imagined possible. As she gazed out in wonder, a school of luminescent fish swam by, their bodies aglow in a bright green-blue.

"What are they?" said Eve, who, along with the others, had joined Emma at the window.

"No idea," said Kata. "Your guess is as good as mine. Since those octopus creatures—they remind me of octopuses on your Earth—since they left me in the box, I haven't seen another being up close. And I definitely haven't talked to anyone." She pushed another button on the glass panel by the window. "But I have been fiddling with all the gadgets. Watch this."

In the blink of an eye, the middle panel seemed to change from wall to window.

Ben studied the windows on either side of the panel, and the panel in the middle. "Is that … that's not a window is it?" he said. "The scenery is different. It's not a continuation of the windows on either side."

Emma looked more closely, comparing the scene in the panel to the scenes outside the windows. "You're right. It's not. It's something else?" Her words were a question to Kata.

Smiling, Kata nodded. "As far as I can tell, it's a projection from elsewhere in the sea, or ocean, or lake, or wherever we are." She pointed at a section of the image somewhat to the right of the center. "See this here? If you look closely, I think that's a collection of buildings. Not as sophisticated as what we might be used to when we think of buildings, but they definitely have structure. It's not just random rocks. It was planned. I've been watching, and I think those might be homes."

Emma nodded slowly, remembering that she, too, had thought she'd seen structures that were more than just caves on the ocean floor.

"Homes," said Chuck, pressing his nose up close to the screen for a closer look. "Homes for whom?"

"Or what?" asked Charlie.

"Homes," said Kata, "for those octopus creatures. There's not enough light to tell for sure, but I think that's where they live."

"Are you sure they're not just caves?" asked Emma. "Do octopuses live in caves?"

"First of all," said Kata, "they're not actually octopuses, as I know you know. We're just calling them that because that's the closest thing we can think of. That's our frame of reference. But they worked together and communicated together differently, and they have nine arms, not eight."

"That's what I thought," said Emma, recalling how she'd counted their tentacles earlier as they'd tumbled along in the net. "But did they make this building we're in? How could they? I mean, not to be rude, but it seems rather … sophisticated."

"I don't think so," said Kata, "but I don't know. I'm really hoping someone will come along at some point and tell us something, because I can't find a way out." She put her hands on her hips and stared out the windows, thinking.

Charlie looked around the room for inspiration, seeing nothing. He cupped an elbow in one hand, holding his chin with the other hand. His gaze rested on the blue tiles that led down the hallways. "The box?" he suggested. "The way we came in?"

"Code-protected," said Kata, pulling herself back from her faraway thoughts. "We can get into it but not out the other side. I tried everything. And there's another door, the one door I can't go through, that's also code-protected. I'm guessing it goes out, too."

"Out where?" asked Eve. "Into more water?" The idea of getting out was appealing; the idea of being stuck under water again was not.

"Good question," said Kata. "What's interesting is that both mornings—or rather, both times I woke up from sleeping, which I guess I may as well call morning—there's been fresh food in the kitchen. It wasn't there when I got here. I snooped around the whole place, and I'm sure it wasn't here before. And I'm definitely sure it was fresh the second day."

"So someone's coming in to feed you, but they're not talking to you?" said Charlie.

"It would seem so," said Kata.

"That's sort of creepy," said Emma, shuddering. If someone was bringing food when Kata was sleeping, that meant someone was watching, from somewhere, to see when Kata slept.

"Not the creepiest thing I've ever encountered," laughed Kata. "I tried to stay awake last night to catch the person," she continued, "but I couldn't help myself. Fell asleep. Woke up, and there was food again."

"So someone is watching you," said Eve, echoing Emma's thoughts.

"Watching all of us, now, probably," said Kata.

"What I don't understand," said Ben, "is how those octopuses knew we weren't from here?" He pointed to the bracelet on his wrist. "Isn't this supposed to make other beings think we're like them? Isn't it supposed to disguise us somehow?" He plopped himself back on the couch.

Kata followed, finding a cushiony chair for herself. "I don't understand that either. My best guess is that it has to do with the water. Their eyesight might be better, or maybe they see differently. I don't know."

"So the stones don't work here then?" said Chuck, looking at his own bracelet with suspicion. "We were able to breathe under water, though. For sure some of the stones work, because in ordinary life, I can't breathe under water. That much I know." He sat down. "I'm confused."

"Maybe we don't have the right stones. I have no idea," said Kata. "All I know is that it's obvious they knew we didn't belong. They brought us here, and clearly the beings who live in this house don't live in water. If the octopuses had meant to hurt us, they could have. I think maybe they brought us here for someone else to find."

"But the person or people who are bringing you food," said Emma. "Why won't they show themselves? What are they waiting for? Who are they?"

Kata shook her head. "I have no idea. All I know is, based on these clothes, I'm pretty sure they have four arms."

"I'm not really concerned with who's who at this point," said

Charlie. "What I want to know is, how do we get out of here? We lost everything. Our Dark MATTERS, our pigeons, even the iPerts. Have you tried the opal and magnet again?" he asked Kata.

A flush of red burst over Kata's cheeks. "I ... I dropped the opal when the octopus creatures grabbed me," she said. "I have the magnetic bracelet still, but not the stone."

Charlie looked at Eve. "What about our opal and stone? Do you have them?"

A blush creeping up Eve's neck mirrored her mother's. "I dropped both of them. The octopuses, the net ..."

"It's okay," said Emma. "It was chaos. I would have dropped them too, I'm sure." She shot a look of warning at Charlie, and he backed off. "We'll find a way home. We always do."

Not knowing what else to do, the group waited in the hopes the beings who lived there would return.

On the first day, Kata showed them around the home.

"Did you notice?" said Eve. "There are no pictures."

"Weird," said Chuck. "Maybe it's a vacation home?"

"Underwater vacation home?" said Ben. "Could be, I suppose?"

"Maybe they hide the pictures when they're away?" said Emma.

They had many questions but few answers.

They'd figured out that the panel in the bedroom that matched the panel by the windows to the ocean world had the same function: different buttons brought up different views from around the sea.

"Do you think there are, like, TV channels in there too?" asked Charlie. "Underwater soap operas? Cop shows? Cartoons?"

"You'd think, right?" said Ben. "I can't imagine a world without something like TV."

"At the very least to get news," said Eve. She poked and prodded the panel buttons, but couldn't bring up anything other than the silent views of what they assumed was the underwater world around them.

Eve, having opened every drawer and cupboard that could be opened, was particularly fascinated by the clothes. "All the shirts have four sleeves," she noted. "So they must have four arms. Pants have two legs but they're really long. And the shoes, they're pretty much just shoes. But no high heels. Maybe only men live here?"

"Or maybe there's just one gender?" suggested Ben.

"Or maybe the women here don't subject themselves to the ridiculousness that is high heels," said Kata. "That would make them very smart women, in my opinion!"

The colors of the clothes also intrigued Eve. Many items had subtle ocean designs on them, but many others were simply one solid color.

"I wonder if that's a trend?" said Eve.

"Or maybe they don't see color the same way we do," Kata pointed out. "We don't know."

"Don't see color the same?" said Chuck. "What do you mean?"

"Eyes are different," said Emma. "Like a fly's eyes are different from our eyes. Or a dog's eyes."

"We did wonder about those octopuses' eyes," said Eve. "I mean, after all, there had to be some way they knew we weren't like them."

"Aside from the fact that they swim like Olympic athletes and we were practically dead in the water, you mean?" said Charlie.

"Well, there's that," Eve admitted.

Later that day when they were gathering up the items they'd left behind in the box the creatures had locked them into, Ben discovered his iPert in his jacket pocket. When he picked it up, water dripped from its core. As the others watched anxiously, he tried making a call, but heard only silence.

◆

On the second day, Chuck asked Emma whether she couldn't just think them home.

"Well, there's this thing called telomeres …" she said, and Charlie explained that the previous travel had possibly shortened Emma's life.

"We'll wait," said Chuck decisively. Emma hugged him.

On the third day, Emma tried.

"You can't, Emma!" said Charlie. "That's just for emergencies!"

"Is this not an emergency?" said Emma. "I don't know what you call an emergency, but I think this might be it." She tried to calm her mind, to imagine them all back at the Hub, safe in the lounge, playing with Rupert and laughing at Dr. Waldo's antics. She visualized them on the couches and chairs they'd created, recounting their tales from the peaceful security of the place she was starting to think of as a second home. She squeezed her eyes tight and imagined with all her might.

The others looked on, holding their breaths.

Nothing happened.

"I don't know," said Emma. "Maybe I was too stressed. Or I did it wrong. I'll try again." *Or maybe I've forgotten how to do it,* she thought silently.

She tried again. Nothing.

"It's okay, dork," said Charlie, punching his sister lightly on the shoulder. "We will find a way home. We always do."

On the fourth day, they discussed universes.

"We've always thought the universes were layered," said Kata, stacking one hand over the other to show what she meant. The others nodded. They remembered Eve's father's explanation, that the universes were like layers of batting in a quilt, all piled on top of each other. "I have a new hypothesis, now," Kata continued. "I think maybe some universes are layered, like yours and ours. And other universes, I think, might be interwoven."

"Interwoven?" said Emma. "What do you mean?"

Kata pushed a loose strand of hair back behind her ear. "I've been trying to figure out what happened when we used the opal and the magnet. It's possible that the labyrinth was at a thin spot and we opened up some kind of elevator. After all, we've never seen an elevator from the outside, right? Maybe that's what it looks like. But I think it might have been something else. I think instead … have you ever wondered about atoms? There's so much space within an atom. Have you ever wondered what's in that space?"

"I knew there was space, but I've never wondered what's in that space," said Charlie.

"Yes!" said Emma. "Yes! An atom is about 99.999999999 percent empty space!" She recalled having that very thought back when she and Charlie were discussing Dr. Waldo, how everyone on Earth could fit into a sugar cube if you took out all the empty space in their atoms.

Kata nodded and smiled at Emma. "Exactly, Emma, that's exactly right. My hypothesis is that maybe what's in that space is other universes. The atoms and molecules from other universes are interspersed with the atoms and molecules of our own. All the universes together take up all the space, but we only ever see one universe at a time. The opal and magnet together somehow revealed the different atoms from the other universes. They're all there, all the time, but normally we can't access them. That's my hypothesis, anyway. If we get back to the Hub, I'm going to start exploring the idea."

"*When*," said Chuck. "When we get back to the Hub."

"When," agreed Kata with a smile.

"Multiple universes existing right here in the exact same space?"

said Ben. "That's an amazing idea. Somewhat unbelievable, but amazing. So you think some universes are layered, and some are interwoven?"

Kata shrugged. "I don't know, could be. That's why I want to study it. There are infinite universes. They all have to fit somewhere."

Every morning when they awoke, more food awaited them.

"It's enough for all six of us, so obviously someone is paying attention," said Ben.

They tried to catch the provider by taking turns staying awake, but whoever was bringing the food was too clever. The person on watch would fall asleep for just a few minutes, or go to what they had decided, and hoped, was the bathroom, and the food would appear while they were away.

"It's like trying to catch Santa Claus," said Charlie. "Only harder."

"At least someone's feeding us," said Chuck. The others agreed.

On the fifth day, the house's residents came home.

chapter ten

When Emma first heard the sound, she wasn't sure whether she was awake. She'd been dreaming about the underwater world they were trapped in, her mind re-living the terror of the capture, the net, the box they'd been pushed into, the water rushing in and filling the room with darkness and fear. In her dream, she was gasping for air, but her lungs were taking on water. In her dream, she was panicking, frightened, drowning. In her dream, the octopus beings were closing in on her with fury and venom and giant saber-tooth-tiger-sized fangs, their tentacles tipped with vicious-looking claws. In her dream, there was no escape.

Therefore, when she heard the sound, at first she thought she'd awakened herself with her own screams. Which might have been true, too, but there was another sound, this one definitely not human. This was mechanical. Something in the house was moving; something that had not moved before.

Quietly, so as not to awaken Eve in the other bed, Emma pulled back her covers and padded softly to the door. Her heart filled her throat as she silently turned the doorknob. Peering out into the hallway, she wished they'd left more lights on. She'd wanted to suggest it, but hadn't wanted to seem scared. But she *was* scared, and now her fears were heightened.

"Emma!"

Emma jumped on hearing a whisper from her left, down by the room the boys were staying in. Emma blinked in the darkness. "Ben?" she whispered back, willing her heart to calm down. "Is that you?"

"Did you hear something, too?" whispered Ben, creeping down the hall toward Emma.

"I thought I did. I wasn't sure if it was a dream."

"It sounded … almost like an elevator," said Ben. He switched on the flashlight on his iPert, which had finally dried out. He'd tried several times to make calls on it with no results so far. But the flashlight, at least, was working again.

The hairs on Emma's neck stood up as the sound began again. "It's … is it coming from that room we can't get into?" she asked. Her heart raced. "Should we wake the others?"

But Ben was already on his way to the code-protected door that led to parts unknown. "It's definitely coming from there," he said, moving along like a leopard in the night.

Emma followed, more so that she wouldn't be left alone than because she wanted to find the source of the noise. "Maybe it's just the person who brings the food?" she said.

"Could be," said Ben. He stopped outside the locked door and flipped on a nearby light switch. "We'll find out."

As they stood waiting, the seconds felt like hours. Emma realized she was holding her breath and forced a deep inhale. As she exhaled, she heard noises from behind the door. She grabbed Ben's arm. "That … that sounds like voices," she said. "Like people—beings—talking."

Ben nodded, straining to hear. "And they're getting closer," he said.

Footsteps echoed on the other side of the door, then stopped.

Ben and Emma stepped back from the door, alert.

They heard a "click," and the door slid open.

Emma's bloodcurdling scream awoke the others.

It wasn't that she was afraid, really. She'd faced aliens and alien worlds before; she'd battled them and won. It was more that she, like the others, was bone-tired from sleeping sporadically and not sleeping well, and her nerves were shot with worry and fear. And there was that dream she'd just had, which she couldn't quite remember anymore, but she knew that in it, she had not fared well. Seeing two alien beings come through the door put her over the edge. She screamed. And then she fainted.

The aliens, for their part, had been informed that odd, unfamiliar creatures were inhabiting their home, and were better prepared. They reacted to Emma's scream not with threat but with kindness, helping Ben lift her up and carry her to the living room, while all the others came running from their various bedrooms.

Now they were all gathered together, seated on the couches and chairs, in the borrowed clothes they were using as pajamas, bundled in blankets. Eve sat with Emma, holding her in her arms, in part to comfort Emma and in part to comfort herself. One of the aliens had brought Emma a glass of water, which she accepted with embarrassment and a great deal of apology.

"I'm so sorry," she said. "We've just been ... we don't know where we are and we can't figure out how to get home."

"Shhh," said the being who had brought the water. "Our fault, we should have sent warning that we were coming."

"We've been away at our daughter's wedding," said the other being. This being's voice was deeper, richer, than the first, so Emma assumed the first was female, and the second, male. "My wife is the Science Ambassador to the Klyvnini. This is our home while she is

Ambassador," he said. "Our caretaker let us know you were here, but we could not get home sooner. Our apologies."

Emma wasn't sure what she'd expected these alien beings to look like. On the ghost planets she'd visited, she'd seen ghosts from dozens if not hundreds of planets and universes. While the life forms certainly ran the gamut in terms of body shape, a good majority more or less conformed to the same basic shape as the Earthlings and the Leroians: a head (or two), some arms, some legs, most walking upright; these features were all surprisingly common. These new beings were in the same general category. As they'd guessed, the people (it was easier, Emma thought, to call them people) had four arms and two legs. They were slightly taller than your average human, she decided, but with only two people to judge by, it was hard to know if that was true of just them or of the whole species. Their torsos, however, were shorter. It was their legs that added height. As Eve had suspected, their legs were very long, as were their arms. At the end of each hand they had six digits—but rather than a thumb and five fingers, it seemed they had two thumbs and four fingers, with a thumb on either side of each hand. *Four hands, eight thumbs,* thought Emma, *imagine how many things you could do at once!*

Their skin was smooth, like human skin; the color was a deep shade, dark brown-black with a tinge of green, like twilight mixed with the forest. *Or,* thought Emma, *like silky smooth, dark seaweed.* She couldn't get a good look at their eyes without staring, but she thought they were a little larger than her own, and the pupils seemed to be wide rectangles rather than circles. Their noses were similar to human noses, but their mouths had only the vaguest hint of lips, and while Emma assumed they must have some way to hear, she could not see evidence of any ears.

"I am Alykas," said the woman. "Ambassador Alykas Aantu. People call me Aly. My husband is Bek, Doctor Bek Aantu. We welcome you to our home." Her tone was pleasant and kind, but it was clear she expected some explanations to be forthcoming soon.

"I'm Kata," said Kata, extending her hand to Aly. "Thank you for your welcome, Ambassador, Doctor. Your husband said you're the Ambassador to the Klyvnini? Is that a country?"

Aly stared at Kata's extended hand.

"Oh, sorry," said Kata. "A handshake. It's a way of greeting people."

Aly nodded. This, too, would need an explanation later.

"We cross hands here," said Bek jovially. It was clear that as an ambassador's husband, he was used to diplomacy and to easing uncomfortable situations. He held out his lower set of arms, hands palm down. Aly placed the hands of her lower arms on top of Bek's. Bek then put his other two hands on top of Aly's, and she finished the hand-piles with her last pair of hands.

"That is a lot of hands," Charlie said under his breath, elbowing Chuck in the ribs. Chuck laughed softly.

Aly noticed. "You'll excuse me, please," she said with calm and grace—and directness. "There seems to be a trick of the eyes here. You seem to look like us, but at the same time I think you are not. And furthermore, everyone knows the Klyvnini. Forgive me for being so forthright, but you'll understand, you are in our home. You are welcome, but we need some answers."

"Of course," said Emma. She held out her two hands the same way Bek had held out his. Aly placed her lower hands on Emma's. "I'm Emma. The first thing I guess we should tell you is that we're not from this planet. We only have two arms. I can't do your greeting right."

Aly blinked with surprise, but quickly recovered her serene demeanor. She wrapped her upper set of hands around Emma's and smiled. "Thank you for your honesty, Emma. Honesty builds trust.

And if you are not from our planet, then yes, indeed, we have many long conversations ahead of us."

"Aliens from another planet! Just like our caretaker thought!" said Bek, his smile beaming as wide as ever. "We thought she was joking. You're lucky. Aly is, as I said, the Science Ambassador. You couldn't have landed anywhere better. Anyone else might have hurt you, but we, well, let's just say we are prepared. Aly may pick apart your brains, but only metaphorically." He winked. "This is going to be good."

Aly smiled at Bek and shook her head. "It's my duty and responsibility," she said.

"You love this sort of thing. The crazy stuff," Bek said. To his guests, he explained, "Aly not only is the Science Ambassador, she also serves on the board of the Ka'Jovo Investigatory Committee. She loves the paranormal! She loves interrogating people! For once, I won't be the one being interrogated!" He laughed.

Emma squirmed. Paranormal? Interrogation? Was this woman going to arrest them? She seemed nice, but anything was possible.

"Now," said Aly, "Let's begin. Who are you all, and why are you here? And, if I may ask, how did you get here? You are clearly not Klyvnini, but they found you in the water, and I'm told you were able to breathe under water as well. And you say you only have two arms, but my eyes want me to believe you have four." She looked at the five strangers, one by one. "Who would like to begin?"

Eve looked at the others nervously, then spoke. "Well, actually, we're from three different planets."

"Three different planets!" exclaimed Bek with a burst of joy. "This just keeps getting better! Can you all tell my wife I arranged this? This would be good for ten years of anniversary presents!"

Aly shook her head with indulgent amusement. "Calm down, Bek. We have not yet established the motives of these people. They could be here to harm us, for all we know."

Bek laughed. He crossed the room to a cabinet, from which he extricated a glass and a bottle filled with fluid. "I think I need a drink for this. Anyone else?"

Charlie looked at Emma, who shook her head at him. "I guess not," he said.

Bek filled his glass with an amber liquid, and returned to his seat. "Please, do continue," he said.

Eve looked at Aly, who nodded. "Well, like I said, we're from three planets. My mom, Kata," she gestured toward her mother, "she and I are from a planet called Lero. Emma, Charlie, and Ben are from a planet called Earth." Emma, Charlie, and Ben raised their hands to identify themselves. "And Chuck, well, Chuck is from a planet called Earth, too, but not the same one." Chuck confirmed this by bobbing his head.

"Wait," said Aly. "These two, they are not brothers?" Aly looked from Chuck to Charlie and back. Emma wondered what they must look like to Aly, disguised as they were by the bracelet. Whatever their appearance, they must have still looked like twins.

"Parallel universes," said Chuck, as though that explained everything.

"There's ... well, I mean, if you're Science Ambassador, you know there are infinite universes, right?" said Emma. She looked at Aly to see whether the woman already knew that much, but Aly's face remained stoic, giving away nothing. Emma continued. "So, there are infinite universes, and for every planet, we guess there are parallel planets, the same but not quite the same, and last time we were out traveling we met Chuck ..."

"Emma and I are twins," said Charlie. "Chuck and I are just exact duplicates." Charlie and Chuck high-fived.

"You're from different planets ... parallel universes," Aly repeated, absorbing the information. "The same planet, but different."

"Yes," said Emma, laughing nervously. "It's sort of confusing."

"And you all met ... traveling through universes." Aly said.

"Right," said Emma. "See, Eve and her dad were on our Earth trying to find this guy, Vik, who wanted to destroy the universes, only it wasn't really him, it was The Void, which, by the way, maybe we should warn you about. Anyway, we found Eve and her dad, Milo, in the lighthouse, with Dr. Waldo, in the Hub." Even as she spoke she realized she was making no sense.

"The Hub?" said Aly, taking in every word. "What is the Hub?"

"The Hub is ... well, so, universes are all layered ... sort of like how you stack your hands in your greeting. That is, we *thought* the universes were all layered, until we found this universe, and Kata thinks maybe your universe is interwoven with ours, but other universes are layered, and there are thin spots where they meet, and at those thin spots, there are hubs. A hub is a place where everything is possible."

"Universes are layered and interwoven. Everything is possible," Aly repeated, almost to herself, carefully sorting and filing away in her mind the deluge of information.

"This is *good*," said Bek, taking a drink of the amber liquid. Whether he meant the drink or the conversation wasn't clear.

"Right, everything is ... and at hubs, you can travel to other universes by elevators ... well, they're not really elevators, but ..." Eve said.

"But Dr. Waldo, he's a scientist from Eve's home planet, Lero, he's made ways to travel with other devices, like the pigeon or the Dark MATTER," said Emma.

"A pigeon?" said Aly. She looked like she might have been a little sorry she asked.

"Not an actual pigeon—that's a bird," said Emma. "It's just called that because it takes you home, and there are these birds, homing pigeons …"

"And while we were out looking for Vik," Eve said, "we lost Mom. So then once we caught Vik, we started tracking Mom's clues, to try to find her and bring her home. So we used the opal—the dark galaxy stone, and the magnets, and out at the labyrinth it opened up all the universes—"

"—and we saw the water universe," said Charlie, "because Kata left us a clue, 'water,' so we jumped in—"

"—and that's how we got here," said Ben.

"—and when we lost our backpacks we lost all the Dark MAT-TERs and pigeons," added Chuck, sighing heavily.

Aly sat, blinking, not saying a word.

Bek shook his head with an ever-growing smile, revealing a double row of bright white teeth. He poured himself another drink. "This is *so good*."

Aly shook her head. "So, Kata is the one who was at our home first? Our caretaker said one of you was here before the rest."

"I was," said Kata, nodding.

"All right, they came here looking for you. Why did *you* come here?" asked Aly.

"Sheer curiosity," said Kata. "It's gotten me in trouble before, but never anything I couldn't get out of." She smiled sheepishly.

Suddenly, Aly burst out laughing. "Bek is right. This is *good*. Never in my life … do you know, at the Ka'Jovo Investigatory Committee, we've heard stories of aliens—we keep it quiet from the general public so as not to cause a panic—but I've heard reports of aliens coming here before. I never quite knew whether to believe it. Certainly never in my life did I imagine I would find some real live aliens right here in my home. You are indeed lucky you came here. Not everyone would be so welcoming. But as for me, I welcome you. This is incredible. If what you say is true … But wait. Emma, you said you only have two arms, but I'm seeing four. How are you doing that? How are you tricking my eyes?"

Emma squirmed. Were there rules in the multiverse, rules about who could know its secrets, or how they were to be revealed? Or was it all random? Did everyone stumble on the secrets of the universes in the same way she and Charlie had? Were there initiations, repercussions of sharing her knowledge? And who was she to make that decision, anyway?

While she was pondering, however, Charlie was being his usual headlong self. "It's these bracelets," he said, without a care for whether any interuniversal judges would rain judgment down on him. "One of these stones has … I don't know, properties, I guess, that make us look like whoever is looking at us. Another stone is a translator; it lets us understand you and vice versa."

"It's never failed us before," added Eve, rubbing her own bracelet. "It's sort of weird that you guys can tell we're not like you. Sort of scary, really."

Aly reached out to Emma's wrist and ran a finger over the stones on her bracelet. "Would you be willing to take it off?"

Emma looked at Kata. "The atmosphere stone. Will I be able to breathe without it?"

Kata frowned. "I'm not sure. Aly, do you know what your air is made up of?"

"Mostly nitrogen, a good amount of oxygen, some pilogen, that's the main part of it," said Aly. "One of your stones allows you to breathe?"

"It's how we were able to breathe under water," said Kata. "Pilogen, I'm not familiar with that. But with mostly nitrogen and oxygen, it shouldn't kill us right away … I don't think. Take a deep breath before you take it off," she told Emma.

"Okay," said Emma. She exhaled deeply, then took in a deep breath and pulled the bracelet off her wrist, giving it to Kata.

Aly and Bek gasped. Without the stone in her bracelet, however poorly it might have camouflaged her, Emma looked intensely different from their own species. Her two arms seemed useless in comparison with their own four. Her legs seemed stunted and clumsy. But it was her hair and face that fascinated them most. Next to their own bald, earless heads, Emma's long auburn locks and protruding ears seemed almost wild.

"Oh my goodness," said Aly, one of her hands fluttering to her chest, as another reached out for Bek's knee.

"I cannot believe this," said Bek. "An alien. A real live alien." He laughed again, his chuckle contagious and deep.

Aly reached out to Emma's hair. "May I?"

But Emma, without the bracelet on, suddenly couldn't understand anything Aly or Bek was saying. She could tell from the inquisitive expression on everyone's faces that one of them had asked her a question. She looked helplessly at Charlie and pointed at her ears, then his bracelet.

"Oh!" said Charlie. "The translator stone! She can't understand without the translator stone! Aly wants to know if she can touch your hair."

Emma nodded, still holding her breath, her lungs starting to burn.

With her two right hands, Aly caressed the waves of Emma's shoulder-length hair. "It's so smooth," said Aly. "It's like the hair of an animal."

Unable to hold her breath anymore, Emma exhaled. Instinctively, before she could catch herself, she inhaled again.

"Oh!" she said. "I breathed!" Cautiously, she inhaled and exhaled shallowly. "I think it's okay," she said.

"Better safe than sorry," said Kata, handing Emma's bracelet back to her. "Put this on."

Emma stared at Kata. "I can't understand you, either. This is weird. I mean, it's normal, because why would I be able to understand aliens? But it's weird."

"Put your bracelet on," translated Charlie.

Emma did as she was told.

"We couldn't understand you, either, with your bracelet off," said Aly. "That is a powerful tool. I would like to study it more later, if I might?"

Emma nodded.

"Now it's my turn," said Kata.

On hearing this, Emma realized that other than the photo Eve had shown them of Kata, she had never actually seen either Kata or Eve without their bracelets. Emma usually almost forgot Eve wasn't from Earth.

Kata threw a glance at Eve, and together they removed their bracelets, Kata handing hers to Emma and Eve handing hers to Chuck.

"Why do you give them to someone else?" asked Aly. It was clear why she was a scientist: she was curious about everything, full of questions, eager to learn.

"I think if we were still holding them we might still be protected," explained Emma, realizing that Kata and Eve would not be able to understand any of them now. Aly nodded.

On seeing Kata and Eve, the shock was less for Aly and Bek; to them, these two were not much different from Emma. This time it was Emma, the Charlies, and Ben who stared.

"Your hair," said Emma. She remembered the first time she'd met Eve, how she'd been jealous of the girl's long white-blond hair. She remembered thinking it shone like a full moon. Seeing it now, unmasked, she felt the assessment was more accurate than she'd realized. Eve's hair, and Kata's too, was so shiny and smooth it almost glowed. No curls or waves interrupted the cascades of hair that fell from their heads to well past their shoulders.

"And your skin," said Charlie. The skin of the Leroians was so delicate as to seem almost translucent. Emma thought if she looked closely enough she might be able to see not just veins but organs; that she might even be able to see straight through to their bones.

As for their bodies, they were, more or less, like those of the Earthlings. Their fingers were slightly longer and more delicate, as were their necks. Their eyes were spaced slightly wider apart; their pupils were similar but slightly larger than those of the people they'd been traveling with, round and dark in contrast to Aly and Bek's wide rectangular ones. Eve was about Emma's height; Kata was a little taller.

Aly nodded: she was done with her assessment. Kata and Eve put their bracelets on again.

"And these three?" said Bek.

Ben, Charlie, and Chuck removed their bracelets.

"Are you sure these two are not twins?" asked Bek, looking at Charlie and Chuck. "They look exactly alike."

"Parallel universes," said Emma. "Parallel Earths. There's another Emma, too, Chuck's sister, but he says she didn't want to come along. I wish she would have."

"So there is a parallel to every being?" asked Bek, his curiosity intense, his delight overflowing. "There is a parallel me somewhere?"

"Infinite universes," said Eve, "so infinite everything. Probably several parallel yous. Technically, I suppose there are infinite parallel yous."

"One is enough," said Aly with a twinkle in her eye. Bek roared with laughter.

Charlie, Chuck, and Ben put their bracelets back on so they could join in the conversation.

"I would like to have a Bek convention!" Bek continued. "For all the infinite Beks to come together and meet! Can you imagine! Charlie and Chuck, I envy you. What a treasure, meeting your alternate self! What an extraordinary opportunity."

Charlie nodded heartily. "We have to agree, twice the Charlie is a pretty fabulous thing."

Emma rolled her eyes so hard she thought she might break her eyeballs.

"So that's us," said Eve.

"Inadvertent travelers, exploring while we can," said Kata.

"I am jealous," said Bek. "Maybe I will come with you sometime."

Kata smiled. "So what about you? Where are we? What is this planet called? And who were those creatures who so generously brought us here?"

Bek got up to refill his glass. "Is anyone hungry?" he asked. "I can make us up a plate of something."

Charlie and Chuck shot their hands in the air.

"Starving," said Chuck.

"Ravenous," said Charlie.

While Bek went to the kitchen to prepare some food, Aly started in on the story of their planet. "This planet is called Jovo," she said. "Or rather, that's what we, the Ka'Jovo, call it. Ka'Jovo means the people of Jovo. We share this planet with those creatures you saw. We call them the Klyvnini. They call themselves oo'broo, and they call us ah'broo."

"They speak?" said Chuck. "Those octopuses?"

"Octopuses?" said Aly, pronouncing the word carefully. "I am not familiar with octopuses. Can you explain?" Her peaceful demeanor and air of profound interest made it clear why she'd been selected for the office of Ambassador.

"Octopuses," said Chuck, "they're animals in the sea where we live. They look a lot like your … uh … oo'broo."

"That's right, oo'broo or Klyvnini," said Aly.

"I'm not an octopus expert, frankly," said Chuck. "They're sea creatures. They have eight tentacles with suckers on them, and I think they're smart, and that's about all I know."

"Your octopuses," said Aly, "you don't communicate with them?"

Charlie laughed. "Well, no. They're animals." He squirmed.

"But you say they're smart," said Aly. "How do you know they're smart? And if they have intelligence, why don't you communicate with them?"

"Well," said Emma, "they're … they're not *that* smart. I mean, they don't have language." Even as she said it, Emma realized the error in her argument. "That is, they don't … I guess they don't understand our language."

"But do you understand theirs?" asked Aly. Her questions were non-judgmental, pure curiosity.

"No," said Ben. "We don't. At least I don't. I'm sure some scientists do, or at least they know part of it. Our language is a lot more sophisticated than theirs, I guess. They have intelligence, but not like human intelligence."

"'Human,' that's you?" asked Aly.

"Yes," said Emma. "Charlie, Chuck, Ben, and I, we're humans. Our planet has lots of creatures, but we're the only ones … well, we're the smartest." She blushed, realizing how arrogant that sounded, even if it was true.

Aly nodded. "We Ka'Jovo thought the same here, not so long ago. We thought we were the only intelligent life. Just a hundred years ago, even. Because the Klyvnini are under water, and we are above water, we didn't really see or study them. We dismissed them. And I will tell you," she shifted her eyes left and right, as though she was checking to see who might be listening, "to be honest, the intelligence of the Klyvnini is … not the same as the intelligence of the Ka'Jovo. But they are sentient beings. They have consciousness. They have awareness of themselves and their society. They have some degree of community and civilization. And they are aware of us. More than we have been of them."

"Why is that?" asked Eve. "How can they know more about you, if you're above ground and they're under water?"

"We were somewhat careless about the oceans," said Aly. "They're vast. Our planet is almost all ocean, about eighty-seven percent is covered by water."

"What percentage of Earth is covered by water?" Eve asked, looking at Emma.

"I think … like seventy percent?" Emma replied uncertainly. "Somewhere around there, I think."

Ben raised his hand. "I actually studied that recently in a project back at the Hub. You're right, Emma. It's about seventy-one percent. So Jovo has even more ocean than Earth does."

"Interesting," said Aly. Emma thought she could almost see Aly creating a file in her mind, a folder labeled "Earth," in which she was carefully storing the information they gave her. Emma had the feeling that if they came back to visit Jovo in three years, Aly would still be able to pull these facts out of her memory stores. "How much of Earth is covered by water?" someone might ask. Aly would pause, a faraway look on her face, and then, "Seventy-one percent. About seventy-one percent of the planet called Earth is covered by oceans. In these oceans are creatures called 'octopuses,' which are rather smart and which have eight tentacles."

"You were saying about eighty-seven percent of your planet is covered by water?" said Kata, prompting Aly to continue.

"Yes, yes. Our planet is mostly a water world, with only two large land masses, one of which is at the northern pole and mostly covered in ice. With the exception of a few scientific expeditions and explorers, all our people live on the other land mass. Ka'Jovo, the above-ground people, for a very long time in our history thought that meant the oceans were somewhat disposable. That we didn't really have to be concerned with them. What we can't see can't be important, right? But there have always been people who are fascinated with the waters, scientists among them. And one day, as I said, about a hundred years ago, we discovered that the Klyvnini have greater intelligence than we previously imagined. They had, as I said, awareness. Some scientists started an intensive study on them and learned their language, and found that they were quite intelligent enough to learn ours, as well. At that time, a very tentative relationship began. This home," she said, spreading out all four arms to indicate the full space around them, "was built about thirty years ago when they first introduced the position of Science Ambassador to the Klyvnini. I am the fourth Ambassador to hold this position. There's also a Diplomatic Ambassador, who has a similar home elsewhere in the ocean. You won't have seen our conference rooms, they're locked away in a secure area, but we have rooms where we can 'meet' with the Klyvnini, talk with them through specially designed communication tools."

"Are relations between your two species good?" asked Kata.

Bek returned with a tray of food, which he placed on a short table in reach of everyone. Overhearing the question, he exchanged a look with Aly. "They aren't ideal," he said, serving himself a morsel from the tray. "The Klyvnini would prefer to pretend we don't exist. They don't think too highly of us. But our activities affect their world, and vice versa, so we have to maintain relations."

"Why don't they like you?" asked Chuck.

"They think they came first. Which is both true and not true. Our ancestors climbed out of the ocean while theirs stayed. But technically, we come from the same roots, just a different branch of the same tree, a long, long time ago," said Bek.

"They have exceptional eyesight," said Aly. "Ours is pretty good but not as good as theirs. You say those bracelets disguise you, but I'm sure they didn't fool the Klyvnini for one moment. Our eyes are good enough that we can tell there's something different about you. You look like us, but at the same time you don't."

"Okay, so, back up," said Chuck. "Conference rooms? Do they … the Klyvnini, do they, you know, walk? Out of water? How do you have conference rooms?"

"Dual-sided rooms," said Bek. "They stay on the water side; we stay on the dry side."

"I would love to see that," said Emma. "Can we see those rooms?"

"One thing at a time," said Aly. "We'll get to that." She was not a woman who would be rushed from her agenda, and control of the conversation would be hers. "As I was saying. The Klyvnini and the Ka'Jovo have had difficult, tentative relations at best, since we learned we can communicate with them."

Emma sat, taking this all in. Two species trying to get along on one planet? It was hard enough on Earth for one species to get along. "Are there other animals on your planet," she asked. "Other animals with, I guess, with less intelligence? Animals you can't talk with?"

"'Animals' is not a word we use anymore," said Aly. "It implies too much distinction between 'us' and 'them.' We try to refer to all life as 'beings' or 'life forms.' After all, it was not that long ago that we didn't realize the Klyvnini were of higher intelligence. We can't assume there's more we don't know. And yes, there are other beings, quite a gamut, from the tiniest microbes to other life forms in the sea, to birds and other forms flying in the sky, to giant beings on the land; a wide variety of beings."

"Do you eat them?" asked Chuck. Emma shot him a look. "Hey, I'm just being curious. Do your higher life forms eat the lower life forms?"

Aly sighed. "That's a difficult question, isn't it? Yes. Some do. Ka'Jovo evolved by eating the meat of other life forms, as did the Klyvnini. There are many who do not eat meat any more, but many others who still do."

"I, for one, enjoy a good baftoi steak," said Bek. "Mmmmmm!"

Aly laughed. "I suppose I do too, now and then. I try not to eat meat very often, but … it can be delicious."

"What about the Klyvnini?" asked Chuck. "Are they vegetarians?"

Bek laughed heartily. "No. No, indeed, the Klyvnini are not vegetarians."

"Would they eat … us?" asked Chuck.

"Well, they didn't this time, so that's a start," said Bek with a wink.

Emma shuddered. "I think we're all very glad about that. Thank you, Aly and Bek, for telling us about your people and the Klyvnini," said Emma. "And I don't mean to rush. I could ask a zillion questions. But what I want to know right now is, how do we get home?"

Another chuckle burst out of Bek. "You're asking *us?*" He shook his head and laughed.

"We need to either find an elevator, or find the stones and magnets we dropped," said Eve. She looked at Aly and Bek with hope. "I don't suppose the Klyvnini have, like, an underwater lost and found?"

Aly shook her head. "If they do, I've never heard of it. But, we can ask them. I'll arrange a meeting."

Emma's heart skipped. A meeting with the Klyvnini! She was so curious how that might happen, but realized she would just have to wait and see.

chapter eleven

Aly went off immediately to set up a meeting with the Klyvnini. Emma wanted to follow and watch—she could see Aly was using something like a computer, and Emma was curious to find out how advanced (or primitive) the technology was. Was Aly calling the Klyvnini on some sort of phone? Texting them? Could the Klyvnini even have phones or computers under water? But even though Aly was alien to Emma, Emma could read her body language: she wanted privacy.

Emma turned back to Bek, who was encouraging the others to try the delicacies he'd brought out on the tray.

"Looks sort of like cheese and crackers," said Chuck, digging in to a few of the treats. Following Bek's lead, he piled some of a soft, light brown substance onto one of the cracker-like pieces, topped it with a small, firm object that may have been a nut, and popped the whole concoction into his mouth. "Orrmmm!" he said with his mouth full. "Mmm!" He chewed and swallowed. "That is good, Bek! What is that?"

The others tried the food as well while Bek explained. "This," he said, pointing to the cracker, "is something we got at the market, made from … well, I suppose it's ground-up grains, salt, some oil, and some seeds, all mixed and baked."

"It *is* a cracker!" said Emma. "That's pretty much what crackers are made of, I think." She nibbled the corner of one of the crackers and her eyes lit up with delight.

Bek's smile increased on seeing his new friends enjoy the treats. "This," he said, pointing to the light brown substance, "is mashed beans, mixed with some nut butter and flavorings. And this," he said, pointing to the firm nugget on top, "is a nut from the sweet-nut tree. It's sweet," he said, with a laugh.

"Clever name for it," said Chuck.

"Delicious," said Eve.

"Mrrrmmmm," said Charlie, his mouth full.

Aly rejoined the group, a look of purposefulness on her face. "They will meet with us at eleven. That doesn't give us much time. Do you know what you want to ask them?"

Emma realized she'd lost all track of time. Was it morning? Evening? Had Aly and Bek returned in the middle of the night, or had the rest of them all been sleeping during the day? What with the underwater home, the artificial light, and all their travel through the universes, she was completely disoriented.

"Eleven?" she said. "What time is it now? We were asleep. Is it day?"

Bek laughed. "You really are off your center, aren't you! Yes, it's midday. Our day has twenty cuts. That is, the day is cut into twenty pieces, each one is called a cut."

"Like our hours," said Ben. "We have twenty-four hours in a day."

"Yes, much like that, I'd guess," said Bek. "It's now just past tenth cut. Up above ground, it's the middle of the day."

"Can we go above ground?" asked Chuck. "I'd like to see it."

"Me too," said Emma, "but we need to figure this out first." She looked at Aly with hope.

"We shall see," said Aly. "One thing at a time. First, let's talk to the Klyvnini, and then we'll go from there."

In the end, Aly decided it would be best to limit the number of people in the conference room.

"I'd like to minimize exposure," she had said. "The Klyvnini don't communicate with Ka'Jovo very often. Their ideas, their views of the world, they're very different from ours. Some Klyvnini, I'm told, those who live in farther reaches of the ocean, don't even believe we Ka'Jovo exist. They don't believe there's a world above the water. They believe we're just made-up stories told to bad oo'broo young ones, to make them behave."

"Understood," Kata had said. "I'd like to be there, since my dark galaxy stone was one of the ones lost."

"Me too," Eve had quickly added, claiming her spot at the table.

"And me?" Emma knew she wasn't really needed, but she'd wanted to be included.

Aly had agreed. "But the three of you, that's more than enough."

Realizing they were all still dressed for bed, Kata, Eve, and Emma had run off to change into regular clothes. Now, they were all reassembled in the room with the giant windows.

"Almost time," said Aly. "Everyone ready?"

"Ready as we can be, I think," said Emma. "Nervous, but ready."

With a nod to Bek, Aly rose and indicated the designated three should follow her. "This way," she said.

Aly led them along the hallway to the door from which she and Bek had emerged what now felt like days ago, when they'd frightened Emma and awakened all the rest. Stopping outside the locked door, she entered a code into the panel. The door slid open.

For a moment, Emma feared that passing through this door would lead them to something like the box that had been their first introduction to the house. She shuddered, remembering the fear of being inside that dark room, of being submersed in water and not knowing if they'd ever find a way out. She quickly realized, though, that this door led to a hallway and multiple rooms behind more closed doors.

"Lots of security here," said Aly. "Just to keep us safe. One never knows." She waved at the ceiling. Emma looked up and saw what she guessed must be a security camera of some sort. Emma gave a tiny wave, too.

"Through here," said Aly, turning left down the hall. She reached a hand up to the keypad next to the door, but then paused. She turned to the others.

"I told you that we've learned to understand the language of the Klyvnini, and they more or less understand ours. But their vocal cords are very different from ours, and neither we nor they can speak the other's language very easily. We use translators in the conference room, but I'm not sure how the translators will work with your bracelets. Things that can fool live beings sometimes cannot fool technology. If that's the case, leave the talking to me as much as possible." She paused. "Now, the Klyvnini are a very story-loving species. Chances are, they will have made up stories about who you all are already, and these stories may not be kind to you. If that's the case, to the extent possible, I won't correct them. I want to raise as little suspicion as possible. Whatever they say about you, even if it seems ... uncharitable ... I would prefer you not try to correct them." Aly gave them a look that clearly indicated this was more command than request.

"Of course," said Emma. "We'll follow your lead."

Aly nodded, then reached again for the keypad. She pressed five buttons, and the door slid open.

The Ambassador led her alien visitors into a bright and sparsely furnished room. One wall was completely made up of a giant empty frame, much like the one in the living room. A long, wide table, shaped somewhat like a kidney bean, sprawled in front of the window. Sturdy chairs stood guard behind it, and in front of each seat were a microphone and a small console.

"We're early," said Aly. "I wanted to show you the setup. I'll sit here," she pointed to the seat in the middle, "and you may sit wherever you like. They can't hear you unless you're pressing the button at the base of the microphone." She demonstrated briefly. "They are seated on the other side of this wall, but this is not a window. They did not like the idea of having lights shining on them, and we can't see them well in the dark under the water. We compromised with a dual-sided panel and underwater cameras that compensate for the darkness. Essentially, what you see is what is on the other side of the wall, but via video rather than through a window."

Aly pressed a button on the panel next to the frame, and an underwater scene appeared in the frame before them. "They designed it," said Aly. "We helped with the technology. The Klyvnini ... do not really have technology of their own." Her words were carefully chosen.

"Are those rocks their chairs?" asked Eve, pointing to what seemed more like stacks of volcanic rock than seats.

"Yes, that's what they prefer. If you look closely, you can see the microphones hanging from the other side of this wall, and the speaker consoles." She pointed through the frame as best she could. "Those panels there, on the side of the seats, that's what they push so we can hear them speak."

"They can push the buttons?" asked Kata.

"They have nine arms, each with nine 'fingers,'" said Aly. "They are quite dexterous."

Emma nodded absently, taking everything in. She couldn't help but wonder about the animals in the oceans back home on Earth. Were any of them capable of communicating like this? She didn't think so, but maybe, one day ...

"Here they come," said Aly. She sat in her chair and the others followed suit. "Oh, one last thing," said Aly, "they prefer that we call them oo'broo when talking to them, rather than Klyvnini." She pasted on a diplomatic smile, watched the frame in front of her, and waited.

Two Klyvnini glided through the water, then curled and slithered onto their rocky seats. Emma couldn't help but stare. The last time she'd seen these creatures had been under less than pleasant circumstances. Now, from the safety of the conference room, she studied them. The more she looked at them, the more she realized she didn't really know what an octopus looked like, not really, and so she couldn't tell how alike or different they were. The Klyvnini's heads were enormous, elongated bulbs, with a slight bulge at the top. Their eyes were widespread, mounted on the ends of short protuberances. Their wide, rectangular pupils mimicked those of the Ka'Jovo, and the eyes seemed to be able to move independently of one another. Emma couldn't see evidence of mouths or ears, but she assumed they were there, somewhere. The skin of the creatures was mottled, and almost seemed to move.

"Are they changing colors?" whispered Emma.

"They are able to do that, yes," Aly replied. "They can change their skin to hide, or to express emotion."

"What emotion are they expressing now?" asked Eve.

"I'm not an expert on Klyvnini skin changes yet," said Aly, studying the new arrivals carefully, "but my guess is they're annoyed."

Once the Klyvnini seemed settled in their seats, Aly pressed the button at the base of her microphone. "Greetings, Ambassador Mroo, thank you for meeting with us. These are my friends Kata,

Emma, and Eve." She spoke clearly and slowly.

One of the two Klyvnini moved an arm, unwinding a finger to press the button to activate its own microphone. "They must be your mutants." The words came through the intercom translator, a nondescript voice filling the air.

With the slightest look out the side of her eye, Aly indicated, "What did I tell you?" but she said nothing.

The Klyvnini continued. "We assumed you had discarded them into our space because of their deficiencies. Throwing into our ocean the things you do not want, as always. Did the others die?"

"No, the others did not die. Thank you for delivering them to us. They had gotten lost," said Aly, revealing as little as possible.

"What do you want?" said Ambassador Mroo. "We are very busy."

Aly pursed her thin lips. "We appreciate your time, Ambassador. We have two questions. First, when you found these young ones, they had some special stones with them, which they lost in the confusion. Did any of the oo'broo happen to find them?"

"Special?" said the other Klyvnini. "They are valuable?"

Emma, sitting beside Aly, could almost feel her tense up. Emma started to speak, but Aly stopped her with a gentle hand on Emma's knee.

"Special only to the young ones. But not valuable," Aly said.

"Why do you want them so badly, if they have no value?" said the second Klyvnini. "A meeting between Ambassadors? They must be worth something."

"I'm sorry, I don't believe we've met," said Aly pointedly. "Ambassador, might you introduce your colleague, please?"

"This is Bloo. He was one of the oo'broo who rescued your mutants."

"Rescued!" said Eve under her breath. Aly hushed her with a stern look.

"I am pleased to meet you, Bloo. Thank you for showing the young ones back to our home, we are grateful."

"It seems you already owe us," said Bloo. "And now you want us to tell you where to find your valuable rocks. You ask very much. As always." Bloo's skin whirled through a variety of colors and patterns.

"I'm no expert on Klyvnini skin changes," whispered Kata, "but I'd say he's angry."

Aly cleared her throat. "I am sure, Ambassador Mroo and Bloo, that you can agree our species each help the other whenever we can."

Ambassador Mroo's skin erupted in swirls of blossoming color. "It is not so! The oo'broo are always accommodating the ah'broo. You have nothing we need. We give everything."

Aly took a deep breath. "Ambassador, we do not have anything specific to give at this time. We would ask that you consider this a diplomatic request and treat it as such."

The oo'broo did not reply, though their skin spoke volumes.

Finally, Ambassador Mroo broke the silence. "What is your second question?"

"We are wondering whether you, Bloo, believe you might be able to find the exact spot at which you first found our friends?" Aly asked.

The kaleidoscope on Bloo's skin calmed. "Of course. We have superior memories, as you know. We have two brains. We forget nothing."

Ambassador Mroo broke in. "For what purposes? Why do you need to return to this place? Is it 'special,' too?"

But Aly had had enough. "Would you be able to take us there?"

Ambassador Mroo's skin cycled through blues, grays, browns, deep red, even a plummy purple, but he did not speak. Aly, too, stood her ground, saying nothing more. Waiting.

"We do not have the stones," Mroo finally said.

"No one does?" asked Aly. "Are you certain of this?"

"We are done here," said Mroo. As quickly as they had arrived, the Ambassador and Bloo floated away into the dark depths of the ocean.

"Floating seaweed!" said Aly, fury in her voice. She looked at her guests. "I'm sorry. That was rude of me. I sometimes just cannot understand the Klyvnini. And I suppose they probably feel the same about us. I don't think we'll be getting back your stones, and I definitely don't think they'll be taking us to the spot where they found you—if they could even find it themselves."

"Do they really have two brains?" asked Eve.

"They do, but it doesn't always seem like it," huffed Aly.

"So they won't be helping us at all?" asked Ben.

On the delegation's return from the conference room, everyone had gathered again in the living room while Aly, Emma, and Eve brought the others up to date. Bek was again relishing his role of host, having brought out a sort of dark, sweet tea for everyone to try.

"It doesn't sound like it," said Aly, dipping something round and cookie-like into her tea.

"This is really good," said Chuck, following Aly's lead.

"You and Charlie, you'll eat anything!" Eve said, laughing, but then her face turned serious. "Without the help of the Klyvnini, we will never find the place where we got here. It's literally in the middle of an ocean. We're going to have to find another way."

"Those Klyvnini don't sound too helpful," said Ben.

"Or smart," said Chuck.

Aly nodded. "I suppose that's true. If I'm honest, they don't seem as intelligent as we are. But that's how it is with all species, isn't it?

We are the smartest on our planet, and I imagine your species is the smartest on yours, but are you smarter than we are? Are we smarter than you? Surely there's a species out there far more advanced and far more intelligent than any of us; does that make our intelligence worthless? Does that make our knowledge and our existence any less important?"

Chuck shrugged. "I guess I see what you're saying. Still, they seem pretty uncooperative."

"It can be difficult working with the oo'broo, because their view of the world is so different from ours," said Aly. "As I said, some of them don't even believe the above-ground people exist. Or the sky. The universes, the galaxies. The moon. To them, those things are all just imaginary fantasies, and why would they believe them to be anything more? Still, we can't ignore their existence, and it's our duty to treat them as we would want to be treated."

While Aly was talking, Emma was distracted, her mind churning on the matter of getting home. "Are there elevators on every planet?" she asked Eve and Kata, hardy realizing she was interrupting another discussion.

Kata shrugged. "We haven't seen every planet yet. There's no way to know."

"Every planet you've been to so far?" Emma asked.

"Well, that's sort of a circular question," said Kata. "We've gotten to almost every planet by using the elevators, so by definition, there are elevators on those planets. But we all got here using the dark galaxy stone and magnets. I have no idea whether there are elevators here. And even if there are, there's no saying whether they have stops at our planets."

"But if there are elevators, then they should be attached to hubs, right?" Emma pressed. "And if we can get to a hub … well, it wouldn't be our Hub, but at hubs, everything is possible, so …"

"Good thinking, Emma!" said Ben. "If we can get to a hub, that's definitely one step closer."

"Does every hub have a Dr. Waldo and a lab, though?" said Chuck, skeptically.

"No," said Ben. "But if all hubs are like our Hub, then once we find one, we should be able to build our own lab. After Vik destroyed everything in the old Hub, I helped Dr. Waldo recreate everything from scratch. Remember? I think, maybe, I could create a lab, or, I don't know, maybe even a Dark MATTER."

"Using the power of intention," said Charlie, nodding and grinning like a fool. "Yes! We can find a new hub and it's all ours! Bwa ha haaaa!" He twiddled his thumbs like an evil scientist.

Aly was listening to this conversation with deep interest. "You create things in this Hub with the power of intention?" she asked, doubt tinging her tone. "Your brains, you mean? No tools?"

"The power of our minds!" said Chuck with delight. "Yes! We just have to find a hub! Bwa ha haaaa!"

"That should be easy," said Emma sarcastically. She liked the idea, but she knew finding a hub was not as easy as simply wishing for one.

Aly broke in. "Tell me more about these elevators and the Hub. How do you find elevators on your own planets?"

"On Earth, it's a little easier because every elevator is in a lighthouse. A lighthouse is … well, it's a building on the edge of the land near the ocean, that has lights and, I'm not even sure, I think fog horns, too, to help guide ships. Make sure they don't crash into the land," said Emma. "The elevator we first found was inside a lighthouse. But not every lighthouse on Earth is an elevator. And on most other planets we've been to, the elevators haven't been in lighthouses. I mean, on Chuck's planet they are, but that's because he's on a parallel Earth. So it's the same as our Earth."

Eve pulled her Universe Key rock out from under the neck of her shirt. "This unlocks hubs," she said. "It looks like a rock, but ..."

"... rocks are the foundations of the planets," Aly said, half to herself. She reached out a hand and gently lifted the stone around Eve's neck, rubbing her fingers over its surface. "Yes, I see. We have rocks like this on our beaches, too. Are you saying all those rocks will open the elevators?"

"No," said Emma, "only some of them. They're rare, but they're out there."

"When you're near an elevator and you're wearing a Universe Key, there's this ... there's a vibration. In the air. You can sort of feel the pull of it," said Eve. "The key lets you know when there's an elevator, a portal, nearby."

"And remind me of the features of an elevator, a hub? I mean, how else you might suspect you were near one," said Aly, the set of her eyes showing that the wheels in her mind were turning.

Charlie looked at Emma. "When we were on the island last summer, we went out one night to watch the stars. We thought we saw some weird lights," he said. "Eve's dad explained to us that it's what they call a 'thin spot.' Looking back, we think maybe we were seeing through universes. Seeing lights from other worlds."

Aly looked at Bek. Their eyes exchanged unspoken information; an agreement was made without a word being said. Bek nodded.

"Well," said Aly. "I will tell you, because of my position I am familiar with something that may just be what you are referring to. There's a place nearby that used to be the source of mysterious occurrences, or energies. People would go out and watch the skies for unexplained activity, flashes of light, that sort of thing. Some people used to report that they thought they could see whole cities in the sky. The government officially denied everything, of course, but we kept files. The place where people saw these phenomena used to be on public land. Then an eccentric writer bought it and built up walls around the land, and she's been getting more eccentric ever since, though her books are selling better than ever. She seems to disappear for great stretches of time; no one sees or hears from her, and then she'll suddenly return and put out a new book very shortly after. It's incredible how prolific she is. Now that you have explained these elevators, I have to wonder if there is what you call an elevator there, and she's using this portal to travel through space and time."

"She's traveling!" said Eve. "It sure sounds like it!"

"We have to go talk to her!" said Emma. "Maybe she can help us!"

Bek shook his head and held up his right arms. "She is a private, unusual woman. She might not talk to us. She hardly talks to anyone."

"She keeps to herself almost all the time," added Aly.

"The Void!" said Eve. "Maybe The Void has got to her!"

"The what?" said Aly.

"The Void?" said Bek. "You mentioned that once before. Why does that sound familiar?" His brow furrowed.

"The Void!" Emma repeated. "The Void, it's this … it's emptiness, emptiness so complete you can't even imagine it. And the guy we were fighting against last time, when he started using elevators on his planet, he awakened The Void in the elevator." Emma turned to Eve. "You don't think he's introduced this planet to The Void? I don't want to face that again!"

"Let's not jump to conclusions," said Eve. "It might be completely unrelated to The Void. Tell us more about this woman?"

Bek looked at Aly. "We used to be close acquaintances with her, actually," he said. "Back before she was famous. She was a writer with mediocre success. She writes possibility fiction."

"Possibility fiction?" said Ben. "What's that?

"It's ... well, stories about things in space, aliens, things that we don't know could happen, we haven't seen it, but maybe it could happen. Some people call it space fiction, but it doesn't always take place in space."

"Sort of like our science fiction or fantasy," mused Emma. "Interesting. Go on."

"Yes," continued Bek, "that sounds right. She was always interested in science and would often come to our meetings and conferences. Even though her books didn't sell too well at the time, she was well known, a friendly woman. But after she bought the land, her stories just took off. At the same time, she became more reclusive." He shrugged. "We always figured it was the fame. It can be hard on a person, having everyone wanting to know all your business."

Emma turned to Eve. "We have to get up there and talk to her. And we have to find a way to tell Dr. Waldo! What if this is The Void? If it's still spreading, we need to let him know!"

With a nod to herself, Aly stood. "I think it's time for us to get you all back on dry land."

chapter twelve

"Outside! Above ground! Yes! Yes!" Chuck and Charlie were ecstatic at the idea of getting out of the fishbowl they'd been trapped in for the past several days. They danced and chanted their joy.

"Outside! Outside! Outside!" cheered Charlie, pumping his hands in the air.

"Fresh air! Dry ground! Fresh air! Dry ground!" exclaimed Chuck, swinging Eve around in an improvised square dance, reminiscent of Dr. Waldo.

Emma laughed and rolled her eyes. Dealing with twice the Charlie was sometimes annoying; still, she couldn't help but love her twin and his otherworldly doppelgänger. Life would be much more boring without them.

"We must be careful," Aly said, smiling indulgently at the boys' antics. "Even with your bracelets on, Bek and I were able to discern there was something unusual about your appearances. Others on the surface will be able to see this as well. We need to keep you away from people as much as possible."

"Is it crowded up there?" asked Ben. "Are we in a city, or out in the country?"

"We're outside of the city," said Aly. "And our population is not large, not like it once was. A powerful, rampant virus killed off more than half our people when Bek and I were young. It devastated our world. We have not yet fully recovered."

"I'm so sorry," said Eve. "That must have been horrible."

"Aly was an only child, and lost both her parents," said Bek. "I lost all my siblings, two sisters and a brother. New families were created as people came together to support each other. That's how Aly and I met. She came to live with us." He smiled, but his eyes betrayed an underlying sadness. He reached out to hold Aly's hand.

"But that was a very long time ago," said Aly, smiling but shaking off the conversation. "The point is, it is not crowded, but many people have lost so much within their lifetimes. The Ka'Jovo are wary people. We must be cautious."

"Can you tell us more about this eccentric writer you were talking about?" asked Kata.

Aly stretched her arms out over her head and to her sides. A giant yawn escaped her thin lips. "Please excuse me! I have not had much sleep lately!" she said. "Yes. This woman, Gesil Eendu, was one of those who lost almost everything when she was quite young, younger than I was. She was placed with another family and seemed to be doing fine, but as with so many of us, I am sure it was difficult for her. Water churns deep in the oceans of the heart. We knew each other, of course; as I said, our population is small. When I became Ambassador, I often saw her at science events. She was always quite friendly. This is before she became so famous." Aly shifted in her seat. "But then, that land I mentioned went up for sale. It was never technically public land; just unclaimed land. There was a lot of it after the virus. This particular land encompasses a wide, clear, open-sky area, so scientists and stargazers were known to go there often. When it went up for sale, Gesil bought it. There was a small outcry, as the sale had been conducted very quietly; many didn't know the land was even for sale. Some small groups said they would have bought it for their own use if they'd known it was available, but whether that's true is unimportant. Now Gesil has built a giant fence around it, and from what I hear she has built a small but functional house on the grounds, too. It seems the peace and quiet of having a secluded space are good for her. After she bought the area, she started writing prolifically and became one of our planet's most widely read authors. She writes several books a year, more than you could imagine possible, and all with the most fantastic, unbelievable stories about space and other worlds." Aly's lips curled up on one side in a wry smile. "Perhaps we now know why?"

In the middle of Aly's explanation, Chuck yawned too, a big wide yawn that the others could not help but catch. Soon, everyone was yawning and laughing at their own inability not to yawn.

"Our sleep schedules are completely off," said Kata, covering her own yawn with her hand. "We had no idea what was morning and what was night. You guys came back in the middle of our sleep— don't get me wrong, we're glad you did—but I think we all could use a little more sleep before we do anything else. I don't want us making bad decisions because we're too tired."

"Good point," said Aly. She looked at their borrowed clothes. "I see you've found everything you needed? Did you not bring anything with you?"

"We did," said Emma, "but most of it ended up on the ocean floor. Charlie managed to save some of his things, but the rest of us lost everything." She was glad she hadn't brought anything too personal, but the loss of their technology and devices was an incredible blow.

"Hmmm," said Aly, with a look at Bek. "I'll tell you what. You all go back to sleep, and Bek and I will see what we can figure out. And we'll work on a plan for approaching Gesil, too."

"But I want to get up to the outside world!" said Chuck, just before he interrupted himself with another wide yawn.

Aly laughed. "Back to bed with you all. Sleep as long as you need, and Bek and I will work while you dream. We will get you home."

Several hours later, the well-rested visitors straggled back into the living room, one by one. As they did, Bek fed them each a hearty meal, the first real meal they'd had since they'd arrived. Not knowing what everything in the kitchen was—including, at times, whether what they'd found was even food—they'd eaten warily. The hot stew and chewy bread Bek served them were more than welcome.

"This is the best food I've ever had," said Chuck, eating as though he'd never eaten before. He ripped off a chunk of bread and dipped it into the stew. "Mmmmmm." The juices dripped down his chin.

"So delicious," said Emma. "I'd ask for the recipe but I'm guessing I won't find the ingredients at home." She poked at the various components of the dish. The meat looked like meat; the vegetables were similar to root vegetables on Earth. Still, the taste was, she thought with a chuckle to herself, *literally out of this world. Or out of mine, anyway.*

"Mmmmmphmm," said Charlie, serving himself up a second meaty, chunky bowlful. "Delicious." He reached out his hand, indicating that Chuck should pass him the plate of bread. Chuck complied, grabbing another piece for himself as he passed it.

"You eat up," said Bek, clearly delighted to have people to cook for. "There's plenty for everyone, and I can always make more!" He took some empty platters back to the kitchen, and returned them, full again, to the table.

Aly laughed. "I am so spoiled. My husband is quite a catch." She planted a quick kiss on his cheek. "Now then. While you all were sleeping, we got some work done. First, we managed to find some of your things."

"You did? How? Did you go diving?" asked Eve, incredulous. "You didn't have to! Thank you!"

"No, no," smiled Aly. "It's not for naught that I'm Ambassador. I have connections, people both above and below the surface who are willing to help when they can. It cost me a few favors, but I got some young Klyvnini to do some salvage diving for me."

"Did they find the stones?" asked Charlie. "The magnets?"

"If they did, they didn't bring them up," said Aly. "Mostly they found clothes, and two of those devices like Ben's."

"The iPerts," said Ben. He protectively patted his own iPert, resting on the table beside him. Even though it still wouldn't make phone calls, he didn't want to let it out of his sight.

"Yes, the iPerts," confirmed Aly. "Rather waterlogged, but I've sent one of them off to my lab to see if they can dry it out for you. I hope you don't mind."

Emma shook her head. "Not at all," she said. She suspected Aly's kindness was not completely without self-interest; she could tell the Ambassador was bursting with curiosity at all their tales. Likely, Emma thought, Aly wanted to see what she could learn from the technology. But Aly and Bek had been more than generous. Whatever knowledge they could glean from the iPerts, they had earned.

"We've put what clothes we found, plus the dirty clothes you'd been wearing, into the wash," Aly continued. "They should be ready for you soon. I also looked at that bag Charlie was carrying. We don't have anything exactly like it, but I managed to find something that should work. New bags will be delivered here for you in the next cut."

Aly looked at what apparently was a clock on the wall. "We have come up with a plan, but will have to wait until tomorrow to do anything about it. It's almost bedtime now, for those of us who didn't sleep the day away."

"And I definitely could use some sleep!" laughed Bek. He started to clear the table. Kata got up and helped him carry dishes back to the kitchen. Under his instruction, she put them into the Ka'Jovo version of a dishwasher.

"What's the plan?" asked Eve, shifting forward in her seat. Now that she was rested, she wanted to get going right away.

"As I said, we have to be careful about taking you out into society. People will be suspicious quickly. We think, perhaps, that we should instead invite Gesil here. It makes perfect sense. As Ambassador, it is not unusual for me to entertain people of all sorts. And she does know me, though it's been a while since we've talked. I can tell her I'm interested in hearing more about her books; that is not only believable but true. Many of the books on our bookshelves are books she wrote." She nodded in the direction of the shelves full of novels that had so fascinated Emma days before.

"Just think of all the books in all the universes," said Emma with awe. "I thought all the books on Earth were a lot of books, but if every intelligent species writes books? So many books!" She wanted so badly to read them all. *Maybe,* she thought, *Aly will let me take one of them home with me.*

"Can you call her tonight?" said Eve, not wanting to get off track. "Set up dinner for tomorrow, maybe?"

Aly looked at Bek. "Do you think you could get everything ready for dinner by tomorrow night?"

"I'd need to get to the store for groceries," said Bek, already making a mental list of what he would need to purchase for the meal, "but I'm sure I can make it happen." He looked at the others. "Not the first time I've had to put together an Ambassador's dinner on short notice!" he laughed. "I am a professional!"

"I agree," said Chuck. "You can cook for me anytime!" He wiped his mouth with a napkin and handed his clean plate to Kata.

Aly checked the clock on the wall again. "I suppose it's not too late to call. I'll see if I can reach her. To be honest, I couldn't even tell you if she's reachable without my actually going up to her home. She's become quite secluded. But, I have connections." She smiled and winked, then went off to her office, leaving the others behind.

"Bek, can you tell us more about Jovo?" asked Ben. "If we leave soon, we won't have much chance to explore it. That's the downside of this traveling we've been doing. Seeing the universes without actually seeing anything. What's it like up there?"

"I can, indeed, young man! In fact, give me a minute …" Bek raced off without another word, leaving everyone else wondering what he was up to.

"I wish we could stay, too," said Emma. "One of these days I'd like to plan a vacation somewhere, off Earth. To go and visit, not just go and rescue Dr. Waldo, or fight Vik, or find Eve's mom." She looked at Kata. "No offense. I'm glad we found you."

"I'm glad you did, too," said Kata with a smile. The table was cleared so she sat back down with the others. "I'm sure I would have found my way home eventually, but it's good to have company."

"The problem is not knowing where to go," said Charlie. "With all the possible universes and planets, the chances are good that if you just randomly pick a place you'd end up in Nowheresville."

"Nowheresplanet," corrected Chuck.

Charlie nodded. "You and me, Chuck, we could start a travel company, where we research different places and tell people what they're like. Write books and put stuff on the internet and stuff."

Chuck's eyes lit up. "We could lead tours! 'Visit Parallel Earth!' 'Discover the Plassensnares!' 'See an Underwater World!'"

"I like the way you're thinking, there, Chuck," said Charlie. "It would not surprise me to find you are the smartest person on your

Earth. Am I right?"

Chuck nodded with faked humility. "You are probably right, there, Charlie. And I suspect the same is true of you?"

Emma rolled her eyes once again, but Eve giggled. "I would so love to see you two start a travel company! I would definitely be interested in knowing some planets with nice, undiscovered sandy beaches!"

"Or waterfalls," said Emma. "I love waterfalls!"

"We have waterfalls here," said Bek, returning with a small object in his hand. He took the object to the panel between the two large windows that faced the water and plugged it into a slot on the wall. "Time for you to see more of Jovo!" As he spoke, a giant image of a lush green world appeared on the wall.

"Ohhh!" said Emma. "Beautiful! This is your planet?"

"Part of it," said Bek. "We have many climate zones on our land mass, as I imagine you do on yours?"

The others all nodded.

"This is one of the tropical areas, near the equator, where it rains all the time. There are waterfalls aplenty here for you, Emma. I'm sure there's a picture of one in here somewhere ..." He pushed a button and flipped slowly through image after image. First on the screen was an image of giant-leafed trees with rainbow-hued bark, surrounding a dark sapphire-blue lake, rimmed with large, jagged, gray boulders. "A favorite swimming hole," said Bek. "Aly and I like to go there a lot." Next he brought up a picture of a flat, sandy desert, with rugged pillars of stones rising high out of the ground. "It does not rain much in this area," he winked.

"It doesn't?" said Chuck, jokingly.

The next picture was of a cliff overlooking the ocean, taken from a distance. The side of the cliff revealed layers of rock in shades of the sunrise, from a fiery orange to a deep amber and everything in between. Tufts of verdant grass covered the top of the cliff, while fluffy clouds dotted the cerulean sky.

"Can we have a picnic there sometime?" asked Eve, her eyes savoring the scene.

Next, Bek brought up a picture of a bustling market on a city street. Beings like Bek and Aly, with their long legs and multiple arms and hairless heads, walked up and down the aisles, perusing stalls where people were peddling strange produce.

"Is that where you get your groceries?" asked Ben.

"It is," said Bek, "but sometimes I go to a store that has a greater variety of products. Depends on what I need, and how fancy dinner is going to be." He winked. "Tomorrow might be pretty fancy."

A rush of happiness spread through Emma. It may not have been her preference to be stuck for days in what basically amounted to a reverse aquarium, but she was glad to have met this strange couple who were not, she thought, so strange after all.

"I hope we can come visit you again, after we figure out how to get home," she said.

Bek looked at her with a wide toothy grin and nodded. "Yes, I would very much like that, young Emma," he said. "You are welcome here any time." He reached out to stack hands in the gesture of the Ka'Jovo before remembering she only had two arms and couldn't complete the stack. Charlie rushed over and gave Emma a smile. Emma stacked her two hands on Bek's proffered hands. Bek stacked his other two hands on top of hers. Charlie completed the stack with his own two hands.

"We'll be back," said Charlie. "You can bet on that."

"We're all set," said Aly, walking back into the room and filling it once again with her confident presence. "Gesil will be delighted to join us. I suggested lunch, so you all don't get anxious waiting all day," she continued. "Bek, you'll need to get to the market first thing tomorrow morning."

"Not a problem at all, my love," said Bek, releasing Charlie and Emma from his grasp. "I know just what to make."

"And with that," said Aly, "I need to go to bed. This has been a long but interesting day. You all may stay up or go to sleep again, whatever you'd like. I will see you in the morning."

Bek shut down the impromptu slide show, and with a small bow, made his leave behind his wife. "Goodnight, new and fascinating friends," he said. "You have brought me much to dream about. Sweet sleep to us all."

chapter thirteen

After having slept all afternoon, and with the excitement of po-
tentially meeting Gesil the next day churning in her head, Emma
spent the night with her eyes closed but her mind wide awake. In
the room she shared with Eve (who apparently was able to sleep
anywhere and anytime, and fell asleep again rather quickly), Emma
tossed and turned most of the night. Before they went to bed, Bek
had explained to them how to read their clocks. Emma watched
hers all night as the time passed, eagerly awaiting the moment they
could reasonably get up again.

At some point in the night, though, her adrenaline crashed, and
Emma fell into a deep slumber. She awoke abruptly to Charlie
bouncing on the side of her bed.

"Emma! Get up! Wake up! Bek showed us how to work the showers, and sister, you need a shower. Time to get ready!" He stopped
bouncing and put his face right next to hers. "Emma Emma Emma
Emma Emma Emma," he chanted mercilessly until she groaned.

Emma pushed her brother's face away from hers as she rubbed
her eyes. "What time is it?" she asked.

"If I told you, would it make any difference?" asked Charlie. "You
have somewhere you gotta be?" He put his face right up next to
hers again.

"Stop it, Charlie," said Emma. Somehow, even with all the sleep she'd had, she was more tired than ever. She dropped her head back on her pillow and closed her eyes.

"No, no, no!" said Charlie, shaking her arm. "No more sleep, Emmz! Time to wake up! Wakey wakey!"

"Oh for gosh sake," said Emma, punching Charlie's chest. "I'm getting up." She looked over at Eve's empty bed. "Am I the last one?"

"Last one," said Charlie. "We've all been up for hours."

"Hours?" said Emma. "I think you mean cuts. And you can't have been up for many cuts. Bek told me how to read the clock and I know it's not midday yet."

"You know what I mean. Time to get up!" He gave the bed one more rattle.

"Stop, Charlie!" said Emma. "Don't break it!" She rolled out of the bed, and as her brain woke up she grew excited again for the day. "Did Aly hear back from Gesil?" she asked.

"Yup," said Charlie. "She'll be here in two cuts. Bek is cooking now."

Sure enough, as if to prove Charlie's point, mysterious but delicious aromas wafted into the room from the kitchen. Emma shook her head. "I think I'll miss Bek," she said. "And Aly. Crazy to meet aliens who already feel like friends."

"What do you mean?" said Charlie. "Eve feels like a friend, and she's an alien. And Chuck, too!"

Emma laughed. "Can you believe it? Eve feels so much like a friend I keep forgetting she's not from Earth. And Chuck, well, he's just another you."

Charlie nodded solemnly. "I am sure it is hard to believe how lucky you are, having two of us now. That is, truly, almost unimaginably amazing."

Emma rolled her eyes. "Unimaginably. Show me how to use the shower, dork," she said.

The shower turned out to be a room they'd seen before, but the purpose of which they hadn't been able to discern. To the unsuspecting eye it was nothing more than a fully enclosed space with smooth, apparently waterproof walls. When Bek showed them how to activate the shower, though, the room transformed. The press of one button started a process in which various shower heads at various body heights sprayed powerful but yet comfortable jets of water at the person in the middle. Then, a misty, soapy substance spritzed out from all sides and above; and then, the water jets returned, whirling and spraying from all angles to clean off the suds. A blast of warm air followed, and the shower purred back into silence.

"It's like being in a car wash for people!" Charlie told Emma with great joy.

"Just keep your eyes closed, and let the shower do the rest," Bek told Emma, before she stepped in to try out the room for herself.

He was right.

"Oh my stars," said Emma, emerging into the living room feeling refreshed and energized after her shower, and back in her own WaldoWear, which Aly had returned to her fresh and clean. "I feel like a new person! That shower was fantastic!"

"You smell a lot better now, too," said Charlie.

"You're one to talk," Emma quipped back. "You were getting pretty ripe yourself."

"That's enough," said Aly, smiling. "Now we know to keep instructions on the walls in case more aliens show up at our home unannounced. Sorry we didn't think to get you cleaned up sooner. At any rate, we have just a short time before Gesil gets here. I have been trying to decide whether it's better for us to meet with her alone, or if it would be safe for you all to be present, too."

"We have to be there!" said Emma. The idea that she might not get to be a part of the meeting distressed her. "Besides, how will you know what to ask her if we're not there? Even though we've told you a lot, she might ask something you don't know. And it could be something critical to our getting home. We have to be there!"

"I made food for everyone," said Bek with his immutable smile. "It's up to you, Ambassador."

Aly tilted her head. "I suppose you have a point, Emma. You're right. I'm just worried about the risks, but I think that's a risk we'll have to take." She clapped all four hands, top left hand to top right hand, bottom left hand to bottom right hand. "All right, no time to waste. She'll be here soon. We'll set the table for …" she counted the people in the room. "I guess we are nine. Quite a party!" She laughed. "You are putting Bek in his element. He may be a doctor, but I can tell you, entertaining is his passion."

"I am here to help," said Bek. "Lunch for nine, coming up!"

While Chuck and Charlie helped Bek set the table, Ben, Eve, and Kata worked to tidy the rooms they'd been staying in. Emma grabbed the opportunity to talk with Aly, who was putting the living area back in order. She felt a little shy about it; still, she knew the opportunity might be gone soon, and she wanted to take advantage of her time while she was there.

"You said you've heard of some things before, alien things," Emma began, feeling her way into her questions. "Like, what kinds of things?" She picked up some pillows that were strewn all over the couch and arranged them neatly.

Aly dusted the low end tables with a fluffy cloth. "Well," she laughed, "it's all moot now. I think we're beyond the point of questioning whether there's life on other planets, or even whether ours is the only universe." She looked at Emma. "Seems we have those answers." She looked around the living room and gave it an approving nod. "I think we're good. Shall we sit?"

Emma nestled into what had become her favorite chair. After tossing the dust cloth into a basket by one of the end tables, Aly sat on the couch.

"When I was young," Aly continued, "and I lost all my family, I felt completely alone. I'd say that's what got me interested in the idea of life on other planets. I wanted to know that there was someone else out there ... anyone else. I suppose what I really wanted was to see my family again, somehow. Now I know that's impossible, of course, but at the time, I thought maybe they still existed somewhere."

"They might!" said Emma excitedly.

"What?" asked Aly, suddenly tense. "What do you mean, 'they might'?"

"There's a ghost universe," said Emma. "At least one, maybe more than one. We've been there. Where ghosts from all sorts of planets and universes live."

"People's loved ones?" asked Aly softly. "People who have passed on?"

Emma realized what she'd done. "Oh, but you can't go there. I'm sorry."

"You said you've been there, though? Why couldn't I go there?" asked Aly.

"It's dangerous, is why," said Emma. "People who are alive and go to the ghost universe, to the ghost planets, they don't always come back." She looked at Aly with great seriousness. "We almost lost Dr. Waldo on a ghost planet recently. It's dangerous."

Aly didn't reply. Her eyes glazed over briefly, lost in thought, lost in time.

"I mean, maybe, maybe Dr. Waldo knows more now, since he's been there and back, and he's always inventing things. And we have a vaccination now, too, for people who are allergic to ghosts."

"Allergic to ghosts?" said Aly, snapping out of her reverie. "My goodness, Emma. I have so many questions. I really hate to think of you all leaving so soon." She looked at her watch. "But, there's no time for that now. Gesil will be here any moment."

True to Aly's words, in the next instant the room was filled with a gonging noise.

"That must be her," Aly said, rising from the couch. She looked at Emma. "Are you ready?"

Emma stayed behind while Aly went to the door. Bek joined Aly, and the others came to sit with Emma, all of them bursting with nerves and adrenaline.

"I don't know why I'm so nervous," said Eve, fidgeting with a loose button on her shirt. "It's not like we haven't met people from other planets before."

"And if she won't help us, we'll still find a way home," said Ben. "Emma will think of a way." He smiled.

Emma blushed. "We'll all find a way together," she said modestly, but inside she was delighted with Ben's vote of confidence.

Muffled voices from down the hall grew nearer, and then Aly and Bek arrived in the living room with their guest. Everyone stood.

"Gesil Eendu, I'd like to introduce you to our guests, Eve, Chuck, Charlie…" began Aly, pointing at each in turn.

Gesil nodded at Eve, Chuck, and Charlie as they were introduced, her demeanor reserved but kind.

Emma was standing next to Gesil, and as Aly was about to introduce her, Gesil reached her hands out to perform the traditional hand stacking. Just as she did, Aly suddenly cried out, interrupting the introductions. "Oh my!" she said, pointing out the windows into the ocean. "Did you all see that?"

"What?" said Emma, rushing to the window and gazing out into the water.

"I couldn't even say!" said Aly, peering intently into the darkness. "It was enormous! Well! We will have to keep an eye out to see if it comes by again! Everyone, please, have a seat."

With admiration, Emma realized Aly's cry had actually been a distraction to prevent Gesil from discovering Aly and Bek's other visitors were cursed with only two arms each. Taking advantage of the distraction, Emma sat down quickly. The others all followed.

"It's so nice to meet you, Gesil," said Chuck, who was sitting beside Emma. "I love your books!"

Emma elbowed him in the side.

"Thank you ... Chuck, is it?" said Gesil. "Which was your favorite?"

Chuck stammered. "Uh, oh, well ... I mean, they're all so good. What was your most recent one?"

"*The Layers of Time*," said Gesil. "I particularly enjoyed writing that one." A small smile spread on her thin lips.

"Yes, *The Layers of Time*," said Chuck. "That was the best. Loved it!"

Discreetly, so Gesil couldn't see, Emma stomped on Chuck's foot.

"Ahhh!" Chuck cried out.

"What? Are you okay?" asked Gesil.

"Ahhh!" said Emma. "I think I saw it too! Did you see the thing in the ocean? That must be what Aly saw earlier! It was huge!"

Everyone turned back to the windows to look. Emma elbowed Chuck in the ribs again and shook her head. "What are you trying to do?" she whispered.

"Just trying to act natural," Chuck whispered back. "If she's a famous author, wouldn't we have read at least some of her books?"

"You're going to get us in trouble!" whispered Emma, plastering on a smile as the others returned to the conversation.

"I didn't see anything," said Eve, puzzled.

"Maybe it'll float by again," said Aly. She had caught Emma and Chuck's exchange and was trying to pretend she wasn't a little amused. "Strange things happen in the sea sometimes."

"They certainly do," said Gesil.

Bek, the consummate entertainer, broke in. "Gesil, I have to say, Chuck is right. *The Layers of Time* was an excellent book. Where did you get the idea for it? All your books, they're absolutely fantastic. Creative. I envy you your imagination," he said warmly.

Bek's bright smile seemed to melt Gesil's cool manner. "Thank you, Doctor," she said. "That's very kind. All I can say is my home inspires me. Looking out at the moon at night, walking my land, it just has a way of sparking ideas. The land takes me places I'd never imagined."

"None of this 'doctor' business. Call me Bek," said Bek. "That's wonderful. You are lucky indeed, as are all of us who benefit from your imagination."

As Bek spoke, Emma realized Gesil's gaze kept shifting back to her, out of the corner of her eye. *Can she tell?* thought Emma. *Does she know we don't belong? Or am I just being paranoid?* But Emma kept watch out of the corner of her own eye, and she was certain Gesil's attention wandered to her more than to anyone else. To her, that is, and occasionally Ben, but mostly her.

"What are you working on now?" asked Aly. "Are you writing currently?"

"Oh yes," said Gesil, "always writing." Her previously furtive glances at Emma were nearing an all-out stare.

Emma flushed with fear. What was happening? Could Gesil see

right through her disguise? She checked her wrist, pulling her sleeve back to make sure the bracelet was still there, supposedly doing its job of hiding her from detection. "Come on," she whispered at the bracelet. "Work!"

Gesil was watching. On seeing the bracelet, she nodded, as though she'd seen something she'd been waiting for. "I knew it. Emma? Emma Nelson, from Earth, is that you?" she said.

chapter fourteen

Emma's jaw dropped. She was speechless.

Charlie, of course, was not. "You know Emma?" he said, befuddled. He looked from Gesil to Emma and back again, as though doing so would give him some clue. "How do you know Emma?"

"And you," said Gesil, ignoring Charlie and looking at Ben, "... are you ... Ben?" This time, her tone was much less certain.

Ben's astonishment matched Emma's. He shook his head. "What? How do you know me? How do you know us?"

Emma looked at Aly and Bek. "What is this? What kind of trick is this? Did you tell her?" She felt betrayed, that these new friends had somehow turned out to be untrustworthy. What else had they told this woman? The hair on her neck stood up as her body prepared for danger. If she had to fight, she would.

But Aly was just as shocked as the rest of them. She raised up her left hands to halt Emma's protests. "I promise you, I have no idea whatsoever," she said. "Gesil, it seems you have us all at an advantage. How on Jovo can you possibly know these two young people? Have you been to their planet?"

"I have not," said Gesil, studying Emma and Ben intensely, her eyes sparkling with recognition.

"But we haven't been here before, either!" said Emma defiantly.

"You can't know us. That's impossible!"

"Emma," said Gesil, her smile warming, "you should know as well as anyone it is not impossible. You are the one who always told me: *Everything is possible.*"

The blood rushed out of Emma's face and a chill spread over her body. Of course, it was true. Everything was possible. In the Hub, everything was possible. With all the possibilities in all the universes, everything was possible somewhere. "Everything is possible" was certainly something she might have said. But when? How?

Bek burst out laughing. "People, this just keeps getting better and better." He walked to the cabinet that held his favorite amber drink and poured himself a glass. "Anyone else?"

"What is that, Bek?" asked Charlie. "You keep drinking it. Is it alcohol?"

Bek tossed his head back and guffawed. "No, no!" he laughed. "It's a juice made from fruits and roots, good for the body, sweet and strong, just like my Aly. That's why I love it!"

Emma laughed, her tight nerves and the turmoil of the conversation making her suddenly giggle uncontrollably.

The sight of Emma laughing made Gesil look at her and smile. "It's good to see you laugh. We didn't have much to laugh about last time we met," she said.

Aly put up all her hands. "Wait. I think we need some explaining here. Gesil, please. How can you possibly know Emma and Ben?"

"And do you know the rest of us, too?" asked Charlie. The look on his face revealed his confusion. How could Gesil know Emma and Ben but not know him?

"Sorry, I only know these two young ones," said Gesil, shaking her head. "I guess I'll need to figure out where to begin." She paused, gathering her thoughts, folding her hands over themselves in her lap. The room was filled with quiet tension. No one spoke, nor hardly breathed. The anticipation was unbearable.

"Since I know who you are, I know there's no reason to hide anything, really. Still, I can't tell you everything," Gesil continued mysteriously. "Dr. Waldo warned me about time travel and its potential consequences. There is still much to learn."

"Dr. Waldo!" cried Emma. "You've met Dr. Waldo?"

"Be quiet and let her tell her story!" said Charlie, more impatient than unkind.

"Yes, I've met Dr. Waldo, and you, Emma," said Gesil with a nod to Emma. She moved her gaze to Ben. "And you, too, Ben. We all met in my past ... but in your future."

Seeing that Emma was about to burst out again, Charlie clamped a hand on her mouth and kept it there. He nodded at Gesil. "Continue?" he said.

"I met you in your future," Gesil said, addressing her words to Emma. "You were much older. I think you told me you were twenty-eight of your Earth years when we met."

Emma pried Charlie's hand from her face. "Twenty-eight!" she said. "That's eleven years from now!" A chill passed through her. She had no idea what would transpire over the next eleven years, but now she knew that in eleven years, she'd still be traveling the universes. Still? Or again? Would she travel that whole time? Or would she be called back for a special mission? And why was she there with Ben? Her mind overflowed with questions.

"I think that's right. Enough older that you don't look quite the same. But you told me the Ambassador introduced us, so when she invited me here and I saw you all, I suspected this might be our meeting. The bracelet confirmed it," she said, gesturing toward Emma's wrist. She paused. "Our meeting actually was a while ago, in my timeline. I'd almost forgotten."

"How long ago?" asked Eve.

"Two of our years, maybe?" said Gesil. She laughed. "There is so much to tell. We are getting way ahead of the story. Let me go back." She settled all her hands into a neat pile in her lap again, getting her body organized as well as her mind. "I am a wanderer, and a curious soul. Before I bought the land I now own, I, like so many others, used to go there to walk, or to sit and write, or to think. It's an area that is charged with energy. Everyone feels it. No one really knows why, I don't think, but when you're there, you can tell there's a powerful force in the air. Rather, you might not know exactly what you're feeling, but you know you feel something. Some don't like it; it can be unsettling. It's like walking into a question. Not everyone likes that. But me, like I said, I'm curious. The feeling energized me and excited me.

"One day, I was feeling particularly fidgety. I'd already been wandering a lot that day. Earlier in the morning, I'd been down to the beach, picking up stones." She pulled a necklace out from under the collar of her shirt. At the end of it was secured a small gray stone, encircled by a narrow but unbroken band of pure white.

"A wishing rock!" said Charlie.

"A Universe Key," said Kata, softly.

Without thinking, Emma pulled her own wishing rock necklace out from under the collar of her shirt. "We all have them," she said, half to herself.

"I had no idea at the time, of course, that there was anything special about this rock. Something compelled me to pick it up, take it with me. Or maybe nothing compelled me to. Maybe it was pure coincidence."

"There are no coincidences," said Emma, repeating the words of a woman she'd met on a ghost planet that summer. "You were supposed to find it. The universes wanted you to find it."

"Maybe so," said Gesil. "You told me that before. I'm not sure I believe there are no coincidences. It doesn't matter, though. I found the Universe Key, or wishing rock, or whatever you call it, and I had it in my pocket. Still restless after going to the beach, I then went to the park that is now my land, and walked around. Aimlessly. Driven, I suppose some might say, by a greater force."

Emma desperately wanted to see the land Gesil was talking about, so she could envision it in her own mind. She tried to piece together some of the images Bek had shown them in the photographs, to imagine what this park would be like.

"Sometimes there would be dozens of people at the park, sometimes just a few. On this day, I was one of the only ones there. It was a work day, and late morning, so I suppose most people were off doing their jobs. As a writer, I have the luxury of a more flexible schedule," she said, "and on days when I get restless, I like to walk. It helps me write."

Emma shifted in her seat, trying to keep herself from telling Gesil to hurry up and get to the point. How had they met? How, in all the universes, had they come to encounter this same person twice? Regardless of what Gesil thought, in Emma's mind, there certainly were no coincidences.

"So you were at the park?" said Emma, guiding Gesil to continue.

Gesil smiled a small amused smile. "Yes, I was at the park, walking. You have Universe Keys, so you can guess what happened. I had the stone in my pocket, and I was absentmindedly rubbing it between my fingers."

"Do your coats have pockets for all your hands?" asked Chuck. "Four pockets?"

"Chuck!" said Emma sharply. "Is that really relevant right now?"

Chuck scowled at Emma's scolding. "What? I'm curious, too! If I don't ask now, I might never find out!"

"Infuriating," huffed Emma under her breath.

Gesil laughed. "I'll show you my coat later. But yes, Chuck, our clothes have pockets for all our hands. That's an excellent question. I hadn't really thought much about alien clothing before. That's wonderful. Thank you." Her mind trailed off momentarily on another thread, but she brought it back to the matter at hand.

"Anyway," she continued, "I was walking along, hands and stone in pockets, and suddenly, I felt a vibration in the air. You know exactly what I mean."

"Yes," said Eve. They'd all felt it many times.

"Something was happening, somewhere. I had no idea what. But we have a saying on Jovo, 'Curious minds find hidden doors.' How apt that was in this situation! So on point, it makes one wonder if the first person who said it hundreds of years ago had the same experience with a Key and an elevator."

"You found an elevator!" said Charlie.

"Of course she found an elevator," said Emma, exasperated at all the interruptions. "Have you not been paying attention?"

Bek burst out laughing. "Aly," he said, "No offense to you about our wedding day or the birth of our children, but I do believe this is one of the best days of my life. I am enjoying this very much!" He got up and poured himself another glass of his favorite fruit juice, then brought a tray with the decanter and some glasses back to the group, setting it down for others to serve themselves.

"Thank you," said Gesil. "I'm not used to talking so much anymore. My mouth is a bit dry." She poured herself a glass and took a long sip, her face infused with pleasure. "This is the best, Dr. Aantu. You have excellent taste."

"Call me Bek!" insisted Bek. "And I will take that as a high compliment. At the market, I've heard stories that you are quite a connoisseur of flavors."

"The park?" said Emma, who was not in any way interested in the flavor of the fruit juice. "The Key? The vibration?"

Gesil laughed. "Emma, if you could only see yourself in eleven years. You are much more patient in the future!"

Emma blushed. She didn't like being thought of as impatient, but the interruptions were getting ridiculous.

"I'll continue," said Gesil, seeing Emma's discomfort. "I know, you're eager to hear. I would be, too. All right, yes, Charlie, you're correct. I found what you call an elevator. Of course I didn't call it that, and I still don't. I call it a portal. I do remember Emma and Ben calling it an elevator, though, because I know at the time it confused me. You told me you'd explain later why you call it that, but we were rather busy not getting killed."

"Not getting killed?" said Emma. "Why? Where were we? What was happening?"

"Patience, Emma," said Gesil. "Stories must be told in order or they won't make sense."

You're the one who started telling it out of order, thought Emma, frowning inside her mind, *telling me we were trying not to get killed.* But she said nothing and waited. She poured herself a glass of the juice to give herself something to do.

"I found an elevator, or a portal," continued Gesil. "I was walking along, and suddenly the air shifted and shimmered, and the scene in front of me changed in a way I would not have believed had I not seen it. An open door. A room. As it was, I stood and blinked for a good while … well, you've been there. You know what it's like."

Except for Aly and Bek, the others nodded.

"I stepped into the portal, and the door shut behind me. I stood there a good long time, not knowing what to do next. My heart was beating in double time. I was both frightened near to death and thrilled beyond comprehension. At one point, the door into my Hub opened up, but of course there was nothing there yet, so it was just a vast, dark expanse of emptiness. That got my heart going into triple speed. Sheer fear. I backed away and that door closed again, much to my relief."

"Your Hub?" Charlie started to say, but Emma slapped a hand across his mouth to keep him from interrupting again.

Gesil ignored him this time. "Eventually, I noticed a panel on the wall. I'm sure you've seen the same. I pushed some buttons, not knowing what to do at all, not knowing the consequences, but at that point, I was curiosity personified. I pressed buttons, and after I'd put in a good number of numbers, the room started to shift. That feeling of the world falling out from underneath you, that queasiness."

"We know that feeling," Ben confirmed.

"When the door opened, I didn't know where I was, but I knew I wasn't on Jovo anymore," said Gesil. "My park was lush and green, with a little lake near where I'd been walking. The door opened, and I was on top of a mountain, the cold air and snow blasting into my tiny sanctuary. I was terrified. What had I done? What had happened? How would I get back? I cowered into the corner, not knowing what to do. The door closed, and I was in the room again, alone, but I hadn't any idea how to get home. I sat in there a very long time. I couldn't say how long but it felt like half a day. Eventually, the portal took pity on me and returned me to Jovo. The door opened, and before me was my beautiful park, the crystal clear pond. I walked out of the portal back into my home. As far as I could tell, it was only a short time after I'd left. I don't know if I time traveled that day or if I merely lost track of time, but I was home, and that was all that mattered."

Gesil swallowed what was left of her drink, and poured herself another glass. "Walking away from the portal, I told myself I wouldn't go back there," she laughed. "But even as I thought that, I knew I was fooling myself. Dangerous as it might be, I couldn't stay away. I managed to keep my promise to myself for a short time, very short, but two or three days later, I returned. I didn't know how I'd gotten to the mountain top the first time, so I didn't know how to replicate it. I suppose I thought I'd always end up at the mountain top, but on my second excursion, I realized that wasn't the case. On the second trip, I ended up in a dry, uninhabitable desert. Once again, not knowing how to get back, I simply sat in the portal, looking out, and then waited for the room to bring me home."

"I didn't know the elevators would do that?" said Ben, looking at Eve. "I thought you had to enter the home coordinates?"

Eve shrugged. "There's lots we don't know about the elevators yet," she said. "Maybe this one wanted to make sure Gesil always got home safe."

"Whatever the reason, the portal did always seem to protect me, somehow," Gesil said. "I started experimenting. I had a little notebook I kept with me, and I wrote down the numbers I entered into the panel, just so I'd know how I got to any place, in case I wanted to go back. Eventually I found a combination that seemed to bring me home. Either that, or the portal was playing with me and wanted me to think I was in control. I would talk to it, you see, telling it what I wanted. Occasionally I would get what I wanted—a forest, an ocean, whatever—but I suspect that was just pure chance. Still, I grew to think of the portal as almost a being. Like it was communicating with me somehow. I imagined that it knew me, and knew what I wanted, and took care of me. Maybe I just wanted a friend.

"At first," she continued, "I wouldn't step out of the room. I'd just sit inside, mouth open, gawking in awe at whatever world I'd landed on, peering around the doorway as far as I could. I was afraid. I didn't know whether I could get the portal to open up from the other side again, or if I'd be able to find it if I wandered off." She took another sip of her juice. "And, as you probably know, the vast majority of planets in the universes are uninhabited. I saw planet after planet but never any life, not even animals. Plants, occasionally, but even that is rare. Slowly, I grew a little more bold, taking a step or two out of the portal and gazing around me in astonished, disbelieving wonder. I'd take my notebook with me and write and write and write. Every new place sparked my imagination more than the last. And somehow, I was always gone for less time than I thought I'd been gone. If I wrote on other planets, I could get books done in half the time I usually did. I can't really explain it. Whether it was time travel or inspiration, I don't know, but it was incredible.

"But my curiosity overtook me the day we met," Gesil said. Emma's ears perked up. "I popped some coordinates into the panel, lay down on the floor to travel—I normally do, it's just more comfortable for me—and then waited for the door to open. When it did, this time, for the first time ever, I saw people. Chaos. People running by, screaming." She paused. "This is probably where I can't tell you much right now." She pursed her lips and sat thinking for a few moments, deciding what parts of her story to share. "Well, this is what I'll tell you. I stepped out of the portal. You weren't near, but you weren't far, either. You, and Ben, and some others."

"Me?" said Eve. "Was I there?"

"Or one of us?" asked Chuck, indicating himself and Charlie.

Gesil shook her head. "Like I said, you might have been there, but I didn't see you. It was pandemonium. Or it seemed so to me, anyway. I saw Emma and Ben, and later, Dr. Waldo, but none of the rest of you." She paused again, editing her tale in her head. "I stepped too far away from the portal, and … well, you had to save me, let's say that. The Great Battle of The Void, that's what you told me was happening."

"That's it!" Bek cried out. "Now I remember! That's where I've heard of The Void before! You wrote about it in your latest book, *The Layers of Time!*" He grinned from ear to ear, pleased with himself for solving the mystery.

The dark forest hue of Gesil's skin grew darker, a Ka'Jovo blush. "Hmm," she said. "Yes, you're right. It never occurred to me anyone would figure that out."

Bek continued to beam, doing a little dance in his chair, all his arms waving. "That's right, Bek, master investigator, figured it out. Who figured it out?" He pointed to Chuck and Charlie.

"Bek figured it out!" Charlie cheered.

"Bek's the man!" Chuck said, mimicking Bek's chair dance with his mere two arms.

"Settle, settle!" laughed Aly. "Our guest isn't finished!" But she flashed a special smile at her husband, shaking her head but clearly amused.

But Emma, having nearly been killed in her battle with The Void before, was less thrilled. "We were fighting The Void?"

Charlie suddenly remembered holding Emma in his arms on the steps of the lighthouse, not sure whether she would live or die. His demeanor quickly changed to concern. "Why were they fighting The Void? And why weren't we all helping them? And did they …" He didn't finish. He wanted to know how it ended, but, he thought, maybe he didn't.

"I can't say more," Gesil said. "Dr. Waldo warned me. But yes, a fight against The Void. And that's where Emma saved me. And," she said, pulling back one of her left sleeves, "where she gave me a bracelet of my own."

The bracelet Gesil revealed was similar to the ones all the space travelers were wearing, but Emma looked more closely. "There are more stones," she said with awe. "This is … is this one more advanced than ours?" Subconsciously, she rubbed the bracelet on her own wrist.

"It's from eleven years in the future," said Ben, "so it probably is much more advanced. Dr. Waldo is always fiddling with technology and gadgets. I can't imagine he wouldn't have made improvements to the bracelets in that time."

Gesil pulled her arm away from the inspection. "I'm not sure you should see it," she said. "I don't want to do harm to time. 'Time is tricky,' Dr. Waldo always said. Who knows what might happen if we tried to change things."

"Time is tricky," said Emma softly, repeating Gesil and repeating the words she, too, had heard so many times from the old scientist she'd started thinking of as a mentor.

"There's a dead universe," said Gesil, "somewhere. I don't know where. I haven't been there. Dr. Waldo knows of it though, or he knows of it in the future, at least. He has a hypothesis that it could have been created when someone tried to change time. He says the whole universe has collapsed in on itself, and the universe's time is inconsistent with anywhere else, and even within the universe itself time has no meaning. There's no reliable measure of time there, he says. He hasn't yet figured out a safe way to test his hypothesis, but that's what he thinks."

Kata's ears perked up. "A dead universe? I was in a dead universe recently, before I came here. I wonder ..." She trailed off, lost in thought.

"Anyway," said Gesil to Emma, "when we had a few moments, you gave me the bracelet—it was an extra you were carrying—and you told me a few things about how to use it and the elevator, how to get home. And you told me about the Hub," she said, a look of joy spreading over her face. "I know you use yours as a science lab, but I've created a writer's sanctuary in mine. It took me a while to learn how to build things just using my intention, not having anyone to show me, but I'm rather pleased with how it looks now," she said.

Gesil let out a deep sigh. "I can't tell you. I can't tell you what a relief it is to talk about these things. I never told a soul because I didn't want someone bad to discover the portal and use it for evil. I didn't want to be responsible for unleashing some great plague on our world. I can't say my motives were purely unselfish. Of course I liked having a portal to the multiverse all to myself." Her eyes welled up with tears. "But I believe keeping that secret has isolated me. I don't go anywhere because I'm afraid I might say something. I spill it all into my stories, and people rave, and I want to tell them, 'If you only knew.' But you all, you know." She sighed again, a sigh filled with both pain and deep relief.

"It's a big responsibility," said Emma. "It's hard to know what you can and can't say. It was hard at school for Charlie and me, not being able to say much about our summer."

Gesil nodded. "Well, then. Like I said, we didn't have much time to talk last time I met you. I don't actually know why you've brought me here today."

"I really want to see your Hub," said Ben. "And it might be what we need, anyway. We're stuck here and can't get home."

"Don't you have your—" Gesil started, then stopped herself mid-sentence.

"Our what?" asked Eve. "What were you going to say?"

"We lost our pigeons and Dark MATTER spheres," said Emma, watching Gesil's reaction carefully. "Is that what you mean?"

Gesil shook her head and smiled. "That is exactly what I was going to say."

But Emma wasn't convinced. "Do we have different ways of traveling in the future? What were you going to say, really?" she asked.

"All I'll say is this: knowing Dr. Waldo as you do, do you think he'd really not invent something new between now and then?"

Emma let out a throaty grunt. "Ugh!" she said. "Can't you just tell us?"

Gesil laughed. "Time is tricky, my new old friend. I, for one, am not going to be responsible for the collapse of another universe. But yes. We need to get you home, so you can fight The Void in the future and come save me in my past."

"To the Hub!" said Ben. "Let's go to the Hub!"

"But first, to the surface!" said Charlie. "Finally!"

chapter fifteen

Emma stood at the tall ocean windows in the living room, gazing out into the alien world unlike any she'd imagined, the bag Aly had given her to replace the one she'd lost slung over her shoulder. They'd all gathered up their few remaining belongings, and Kata and Aly were making a final check of the house to make sure nothing was left behind.

Seeing his sister lost in thought, Charlie came over and put an arm around her. "Water," he said.

"Water, magnet, dark galaxy," she replied, and smiled to herself. *What would I do without Charlie?* she thought. Then she frowned. Why had Charlie not been with her in the future battle against The Void?

"It's okay, Em," said Charlie, instinctively knowing what was on her mind. "I won't ever leave you intentionally." He gave her shoulder a squeeze and joined her in one last look at the strange underwater world of the oo'broo.

"That's just it, Charlie," said Emma, her brow furrowed. "You wouldn't. So why aren't you there in eleven years? What happened? Or, what happens?"

"Probably I was off chasing some intergalactic monster, saving the rest of you," said Charlie, humbly. "Or maybe I'm married in eleven years and my wife's about to have a baby, and I can't come fight The Void. Or maybe Dr. Waldo left me in charge of the Hub and I am conducting important Hub business." Emma laughed lightly at this last idea. Charlie continued. "Or maybe, Em, don't forget, Gesil wasn't sure I wasn't there. I might have been just around the next hill. One valley over. Hiding in a cave with Chuck." He squeezed Emma to his side. "Don't worry about it. We can't do anything about it now, anyway."

Emma sighed.

"Do you think we'll ever come back here?" she said, still staring out at the deep dark sea. "All these places we visit, and the people we're meeting now, it's worse than just having friends in another state. We may never see them again. And I really like Bek and Aly. And Gesil."

"Well, we know you'll see Gesil again, so there's that," said Charlie. He gently turned her away from the underwater view. "Come on. It's time to go." He led his sister to the hallway where the others were all waiting: Aly and Bek, Eve and Kata, Chuck, Ben, and Gesil.

"Ready?" said Aly, looking at Emma.

"I guess so," Emma said. She looked back over her shoulder at the place they'd called home for the past week. "I'll miss you guys," she said.

"This isn't goodbye, Emma!" laughed Bek. "Not even for now! We still have to see if we can get you home!"

"Yeah, it might not work!" said Chuck. "In which case, if we're stuck here forever, I'd like to request my own room? Charlie snores."

"So do you!" said Charlie. He and Chuck high-fived.

"Let's go!" said Eve. "I am ready to see the sun again!"

"You do have a sun, don't you?" asked Ben.

"We do have a sun," said Aly. "Just the one. All right, let's go."

She tapped a code into the panel by the door. It slid open with a mechanical whoosh, revealing the long hallway.

"What all is down here?" asked Ben as they walked down the hall. On either side of the hallway were various doors, all of them shut tight, containing potential mysteries they'd never discover.

Aly gestured toward the room she'd taken Eve and Emma to the day before. "That's the conference room over there, where we meet with the Klyvnini." She pointed at another door. "This one leads to our housekeeper's quarters. She's the one who kept you fed."

"We should thank her," said Emma, as they passed the door.

"She's a little shy," said Bek. "And a lot afraid of you all. We'll tell her for you, how's that?"

Emma nodded her agreement.

Aly continued the hallway tour. "Down there is a storage area. And off to the right, that's an emergency area, in case there's a threat."

"What kind of threat?" asked Chuck.

"Any kind of threat," said Aly. "The worst threats are the ones you can't predict, you know."

Like the future, thought Emma.

The group reached a larger doorway at the end of the hall. Aly stopped before it and turned to the group. "Ready to go up?"

"Seriously? Beyond ready!" said Charlie. "Let's go!"

Aly tapped yet more buttons on yet another panel. The door slipped open, this one revealing a spacious elevator room. "Everybody in!" she said.

The large group piled in, filling the room to capacity, and the door slid shut behind them. Bek punched the top button on the panel, and the elevator started to move.

"Odd," said Emma, "all these elevators, yet I haven't been in an actual elevator for a while."

"A lot less nauseating," said Charlie.

The elevator reached its destination and the door opened again into another hallway.

"More hallways!" moaned Chuck. "I'm starting to believe we'll never see daylight again!"

Bek laughed. "We are almost there, young Chuck!" he said. "Do you think we can't hear you snore, too? We are quite ready for you to go home!"

Momentarily taken aback, Chuck's jaw dropped open slightly before he realized Bek was joking. He punched Bek on the shoulder. "You've been good to us, old man. You're welcome on my Earth any time!"

This time, Bek led the way. They walked down another short, undecorated hallway, its white walls stretching up to high ceilings, and veered left. When they turned the corner, they saw before them their journey's end—or its beginning: glass doors, leading to the outside. Sunlight streamed through the thick window panes, throwing patterns of mottled light onto the floor.

"Sun!" cried Charlie, running forward to a sunbeam. "Beautiful sunlight!" He stood in the beam, eyes closed, soaking in its warmth.

"It's so bright!" said Eve, squinting. Having spent years traveling to distant worlds, she had developed a keen eye for subtle details. "I think maybe your sun is closer to your planet than ours. Or it's bigger."

As they stepped through the doors to the outside, Eve's theory seemed all the more valid. The sun beamed down on them, unforgiving in its glare. The heat of it was still bearable, but it was definitely warm. Those who had put on extra layers of clothes quickly peeled them off, and Dr. Waldo's WaldoWear was put to the test. To the wearers' delight, the WaldoWear cloth somehow adjusted to the heat, giving them a refreshing feeling of coolness.

"Careful not to get burned," said Emma, looking at her own pale skin.

"Make note to tell the committee, please, of the need to bring sunscreen next time," said Charlie.

"Noted," said Emma.

"Is your home far?" Eve asked Gesil. "Can we walk there?"

"We could," said Gesil, "but it's easier to drive. Do you have transportation like this on your planet?" She pointed around the building to an area where several car-like vehicles were parked.

"Cars!" said Charlie. "Yes, we have cars, automobiles, that's what we call them." He and Chuck raced over to inspect the vehicles. Like cars on Earth, they had four wheels, two at front and two at back. Most of the cars had four doors; a few had two, and fewer still had six.

"Who do all these cars belong to?" asked Emma. Surely Aly and Bek didn't need so many cars just for themselves?

"Some come with the job and the house," explained Aly. "One is our housekeeper's. And a few belong to other people who are downstairs working right now."

"There are more people in the house?" said Emma, remembering all the closed doors they'd passed in the hall. She wished and hoped once again they could come back here again one day.

Bek, meanwhile, led them to one of the vehicles with six doors. "There are so many of us, let's take this one," he said.

"I'll drive my own car," said Gesil, walking toward a small gray-green car with two doors. "Would someone like to ride with me?"

Five hands shot in the air. Gesil laughed. "Emma, why don't you come with me. Bek, do you know the way to my place?"

Bek nodded. "We'll meet you there."

Leaving the others behind, Emma followed Gesil to her car. Emma stood by the front right door. Gesil looked at her, amused.

"Are you going to drive?"

Looking into the window, Emma could see a driver's wheel on the right side of the car. She blushed. "Oh, sorry. In our country, the driver sits on the left." She walked around to the other side.

"Your country?" asked Gesil. "What is a country?"

"What is a country?" asked Emma with surprise. "Don't you have countries?"

"We have the land and the water," said Gesil. "Is that a country?"

Emma frowned. "Well, I mean, not really, no. Countries are … they're how we separate ourselves. How we define ourselves."

"How you separate yourselves? What do you mean?" asked Gesil. She pushed a button, and the doors unlocked. Gesil opened her door and got in, and Emma did the same on the other side of the car.

"It's like, it's where you live, where you belong. Different countries have different ways of doing things. Like, in our country, the United States, drivers sit on the left in the car. But in other countries they sit on the right," Emma said.

"So a country is about where you sit in the car?" said Gesil. She pulled a strap across her, something like a seat belt. Emma followed suit.

"No, it's like … well, it's the language you speak, and the food you eat, and … I don't know, the clothes you wear." As she spoke, Emma realized she'd never really thought about how odd the concept of a country might sound to someone who wasn't used to the idea.

The puzzled look on Gesil's face confirmed this. "Why would you speak different languages?" she said. "Do you mean that if I learned your language, I wouldn't know the language of everyone on Earth?" She started the car. A very quiet hum, so low it was almost nothing more than a vibration, was the only sign that the car was operating. Gesil backed out of her parking space, and headed down a wide, paved road.

"Well, no," said Emma. "I mean, Earth is bigger, I think, than Jovo. There's more land. More people. It just … I don't know, probably everyone used to speak the same language, a really long time ago when people first started talking, but then they moved apart, and different languages developed." As they drove, Emma tried to concentrate on the conversation while looking on at the landscape with wonder. She'd seen several planets by this time, and many of them had some variations on the same themes: plants, trees, rocks, dirt, hills and mountains, oceans and lakes. Still, she couldn't help but be amazed at the variety within those basic categories. Here, there were no tall pine trees like back at Dogwinkle Island. Instead, the tallest plants were maybe twenty feet high at most, with thick clusters of enormous teardrop-shaped leaves spreading out from the top of the tree to about two-thirds of the way down the trunk. Other trees looked almost like giant mushrooms, but with bristly caps of needles on top. Bushes of many varieties lay low along the ground. The paved road indicated civilization, but Emma saw no other buildings. Or, for that matter, people. She wondered if people on this planet also lived inside hills, like on Lero.

"Interesting," said Gesil. "It is fascinating to know how much alike planets can be, but yet how different. Every civilization finds its own way forward. Not always in the most pleasant or harmonious manner, either."

"No, definitely not," said Emma, thinking of the wars she'd learned about in history class. And, apparently, the wars she was yet to fight, herself.

Soon, Gesil pulled up to a gate blocking a wide opening in a long, tall wall that hid the property within. She looked behind her to see that Bek had caught up to them in his vehicle, then pushed a device on the car's dashboard that opened the gate. Gesil drove through, waited for Bek to do the same, and then closed the gate again behind them.

"Almost there!" Gesil said merrily to her passenger.

Gesil aimed the car down a long winding road, this one paved only with dirt and stones. Whether it was anticipation or an actual change in the air, Emma felt like she could feel a surge of energy as they grew closer to their destination. With relief, she allowed herself to believe they might have found a way home.

After maneuvering the car around a final curve, Gesil parked in front of a small, cozy-looking house. "It looks so much like our houses," Emma said. The home was built from giant stones ranging from white to gray to beige; the door appeared to be made of a kind of reddish-brown wood with a wavy, irregular grain. A thick stone chimney stack climbed up the left side of the house, topping out over the roof by just a few feet. Slabs of giant, flat stones, embedded into the ground, led from where they were parked to the front door.

"Sweet home," said Gesil, looking at her house. "It would have been easier if I could have built it out of intention, like in the Hub, but this will do," she said fondly.

"Is the elevator inside?" asked Emma, getting out of the car and following Gesil to the front door.

"It is. I didn't want anyone seeing me disappearing and reappearing. That would cause even more gossip than already surrounds me," said Gesil.

By this time, the rest of the group had caught up with them. "Shall we go in?" said Gesil, opening the door.

The inside of the house was snug and unassuming. A small living room and a pocket-sized kitchen filled the front of the house. "I don't have guests, so no need for a big dining room," said Gesil. "Back there are my bedroom and the bathroom," she continued, pointing to the back half of the house. "Upstairs is just one big open room, where I go to write or think." She walked to a door at the end of the dining room. "And here," she said, "is the portal."

Gesil opened the door and walked into the small closet. "Coming?" she said to the others, who quickly followed her into the small room. As they did, the door to the elevator slid open. "Everyone inside!" Gesil said. Once everyone was in, the portal door closed. Gesil waved her Key in front of the wall on the other side, and the door to Gesil's Hub slid open.

"Welcome to my sanctuary," Gesil said, stepping into the endless area.

"Oh, wow," said Emma, gaping in awe at the beauty of the expanse as they all exited the portal and spread out in the limitless space. Where Dr. Waldo had created the ultimate science lab in his Hub, complete with every kind of computer and scientific instrument he could think of, Gesil had intentioned into existence a calm, bucolic paradise. The sky spread out to infinity in a brilliant blue, with an occasional fluffy cloud floating by. The ground was covered with a thick carpet of soft grass. The space immediately before them was mostly flat, but off in the distance were rolling hills covered in wildflowers of all colors; a majestic snow-capped mountain rose from the horizon even farther away. A river meandered through the landscape, and various walking paths led to points of interest: benches, a gazebo, a hammock swinging idly between two short trees. One path led to the river, which it crossed with a short stone bridge. And another path led to a giant building that looked very much like Gesil's own home, but much larger.

"Dr. Waldo told me about his Experimental Building," explained Gesil. "That building is my own version of it."

"What's inside?" asked Chuck, eager to explore. He had not had much chance to create things in any hub yet, and was hoping now might be his time.

Gesil answered with a smile. "Do you want to see?" she asked.

"Obviously!" said Chuck.

"Yes!" said Eve.

"Totally!" said Charlie.

They walked the path to the building's massive front entrance. "Emma and Ben, you and Dr. Waldo taught me how to create things here in my Hub. At first it was really difficult," she said, "but I practiced a lot. I even learned to un-make my mistakes, which is good, or you'd see a massive hole in the ground where I meant to build that mountain. I somehow got 'up' and 'down' reversed. I was still learning." She smiled. "Eventually, I created this building. My writing retreat." She opened the front door and a gentle wind greeted them.

"A breeze from inside?" said Charlie. "I'd ask how that's possible, but in the Hub …"

"Everything is possible," said Emma and Ben simultaneously. Emma laughed.

The building was not as vast inside as Dr. Waldo's Experimental Building was, but the design was similar. Once inside, the lobby branched off to the left and right down wide hallways, with a grand, ornate staircase in the center leading to a second floor.

"Which way should we explore first?" said Gesil.

"Left," said Emma.

They followed the hallway to the left, passing doorways with plaques over them. "Beach house," said one. "Woods," said another. "Hot springs," read a third.

"Hot springs?" said Chuck. "What's in there?"

"Hmm," said Gesil, teasingly. "Might be hot springs?" She opened the door for them to peek inside. Sure enough, the scene opened up to an outside setting, a rocky landscape leading down a short path to a pool, its crystal-clear waters steaming into the fresh air.

"This is my kind of room!" said Charlie.

"Not now!" said Emma. "We don't have time."

Charlie turned to Ben. "We are totally going to have to make a room like this in the Experimental Building back home."

"Indeed," said Ben. "I think that's an imperative."

Gesil pulled the door shut and wandered farther down the hall. "This is one of my favorites," she said.

The plaque over the doorway where she'd stopped read "Tree-house." She opened the door and stepped inside.

"I didn't want to actually climb up a ladder into the treehouse," she explained. "Call me lazy. So I made it so the doorway opens up to the top level. There is a ladder that leads to the ground level, but mostly I stay up here and write."

As they all crowded into the rustic room, a cat-like creature greeted them, rubbing itself warmly around their legs. Seemingly appearing from out of nowhere, another cat-like creature joined the first. Their ears were slightly different from those of Earth cats, but they were of nearly the same size, with soft fur and loud happy purrs.

"You have cats on Jovo?" asked Emma, trying to decide if it would be safe to pick one up. They looked friendly enough, but one could never be sure.

"Not exactly," said Gesil. "I saw animals like these once in my travels. I liked them, so I came home and created some in my tree-house. They're not real ... or rather, they are real, but they disappear when I'm not here. I didn't want them to get lonely if I was gone for a while. But they have access to the ground level, too. I made them so they don't need food, as I didn't want them to starve, either. Creating live creatures is rather tricky, as it turns out." She picked up one of the purring animals and handed it to Emma, who hugged it to her chest, feeling the vibration of the creature's hum thrumming into her own chest.

"Awwww," said Emma, rubbing her face into the impossibly soft fur of the cat's head. The furry creature responded by purring even louder. "So sweet."

"This is where I do most of my writing," said Gesil. "I use the other rooms too, sometimes, but I like it here the most." She sat down at the desk and looked out a window before her. The view was magnificent, more mountains in the distance, a babbling river just below.

"Ben, we've got to make a room like this, too—" Charlie started to say, but then looked around. "Hey, where's Ben?"

"I think I saw him head back out," said Bek, "after we left the Hot Springs room. Wasn't paying much attention to him, to be honest, but now that I think of it, that's what my brain is telling me." He winked at Emma. "Good thing to have a brain that's paying attention even when I'm not! I need it!"

"I suppose that's a good trait for a doctor," said Emma. "Not the not paying attention part! The good brain part. But I also think we should find Ben. I don't like it when one of us gets separated from the rest of us." She remembered all too well when she once was left behind. "Let's find him."

She walked briskly back down the hall, not wanting to betray her sense of worry. "Ben?" she called out, peeking into doorways. "Oh, nice," she said, briefly distracted on seeing the Beach House scene, a warm wind carrying the scent of the ocean to her from across the white sand. She moved on.

"Ben? Where are you?" Emma called more urgently, picking up her pace and heading out the front door, the others running along behind her. "Ben? Ben? Ben!" A wave of relief rushed through her as she saw him, not too far away, seated on a bench. He cradled something small in his hands. On his face was a look of radiant joy and pride.

When Emma got near enough to hear him, Ben held up the object in his hands. "Dark MATTER," he said, as she sat down next to him on the bench. "We can go home."

chapter sixteen

Emma gently took the precious sphere from Ben's hands. "A Dark MATTER sphere? Where did you get this?"

Ben shrugged and blushed. "I made it. You know, the Hub. Everything is possible. I made one before, back at Dr. Waldo's Hub. Just to see if I could. It worked. So, you know, I thought I may as well try here, too."

"*Will* it work?" asked Emma, turning it over in her hands. She didn't want to doubt Ben, but she also didn't want to end up in pieces, spread across the galaxies, because Ben had made a faulty sphere. It looked like the others, but that didn't mean it would act like the others.

"It should," said Ben. "I mean, I don't want to brag. But it will work. Don't worry." He smiled at her. "I wouldn't hurt you."

"Dude," said Charlie. "Dude, you're great and all, and I trust you and whatnot, but I am not trusting that thing. I mean, you're like an apprentice scientist. I am not ready to be ripped apart just yet."

Chuck nodded his agreement. "My family would not want me to come home as a bag of plasma," he said.

"Guys, I appreciate that, but I really think it'll work," said Ben.

"Therein lies the problem, my good man," said Charlie. "You *think*. But you don't *know*."

"Do you have a better idea?" asked Emma, somewhat relieved they might not have to test out Ben's creation. She liked him, but perhaps not so much as to trust the second Dark MATTER he'd ever made.

"I have an idea," said Eve. "Gesil, do you think your elevator will connect with Emma and Charlie's Earth?"

"It might," said Gesil.

"I should be able to tell, if I look at the coordinates closely," said Ben. "I did a lot of planet mapping the last few months."

"Okay," said Eve. "Here's what I think. I think we collect all those coordinates and everything else we can use to pinpoint where we are now, and where we might end up on Earth. And then we write all that information down, tape it to the Dark MATTER, and send that back to our Hub. Let them know we're on our way. If it gets there, great. And if not, well, that's better than our not getting there." She looked at Chuck. She did not want to become a bag of plasma, either.

The rest of the group agreed to this plan. They trotted back to Gesil's elevator, where Ben and Eve studied the panel, muttering and comparing notes and opinions. Ben wrote down some information and a quick note to Dr. Waldo on a piece of paper Gesil supplied him with. "Best I can do," he said. "Based on what I can see, this elevator should take us to our Earth. I'm not sure where, but we should get there. And after that …"

"After that, we'll deal with wherever we end up," said Kata.

"Okay. Ready?" said Emma.

"Ready." Ben attached the paper securely to the Dark MATTER with a sticky substance Gesil gave him, then entered the coordinates of their own Hub into the device. He swiped the control panel and let go instantly.

It disappeared.

"Hopefully Dr. Waldo has it now," said Charlie.

"And now, our turn," said Emma. She looked at Aly, Bek, and Gesil. "Gesil, I know we'll meet again. Aly and Bek, I hope we do, too. You've been so great to us. Thank you for everything. I don't know what we'd have done without you."

"The pleasure was *all* ours," said Bek, his smile as bright as the Jovo sun. "You all had better visit us, or we will track you down!" He patted Chuck on the back warmly.

"We have a famous scientist on Jovo," said Aly, "who studies particles that have come together and then are separated. It's too complicated to explain quickly, but basically she says the particles are 'entangled.' She says once they have been entangled, or connected, they stay connected, even if they travel far apart. They become part of one another in some way." Aly smiled. "I think we are entangled now. We will see you again, I am certain."

Emma squinted. Had she heard something like that before in school? Science was science, wherever you might go, wasn't it? She shrugged and laughed. "Yes, I have a feeling, too, that we will see you again."

After hugs all around, Emma, Eve, Chuck, Charlie, Ben, and Kata piled into the elevator.

"Be safe," said Aly.

"Happy life," said Bek.

"Until we meet again," said Gesil.

As Emma and the others waved goodbye, the elevator door slid shut.

"Earth, here we come," said Eve. "I think." She typed in coordinates that she and Ben had agreed would get them to somewhere on Earth. They all held hands, and hoped.

The door slid open.

Dr. Waldo stood before them, jumping with excitement. Whatever effects had plagued him from his time at the ghost planet, he seemed fully recovered and his old self again.

"Oh my stars! Children! I cannot believe it! Ben, you are brilliant, sending that Dark MATTER sphere! Did you make that yourself, young man? You will have to tell me all about it. We had been so worried for you all. You've been gone for weeks! Where have you been? Wait, no, you'll have to tell me later, first we need to get back to the Hub and back in time six weeks, so much to take care of, then we'll talk, no time, no time! Kata? Kata, is that you? My stars, they found you! No time, no time, we must hurry!"

"Dr. Waldo!" cried Charlie. "Never happier to see you, my man!" He and the others poured out of the elevator. "Earth!" said Charlie. "Never happier to see you, Earth!"

"Six weeks!" said Emma, rushing out of the elevator to hug the old scientist. She vaguely noted their surroundings: an isolated lighthouse, somewhere where it was relatively warm and also daylight. Six weeks, that would be sometime in February? Her mind tried to put the pieces together.

"New Zealand," said Dr. Waldo, answering the unasked question. "Good thing your friend's lighthouse didn't end up in Greenland, so cold this time of year! Yes, yes, New Zealand, wish we could stay and visit, adding this lighthouse to my map of elevators, but for now we need to get you home."

Dr. Waldo handed Chuck a device. "You first, young man, this will send you back in time and over to your universe. Two for the price of one, yes, two for one!" he giggled and danced with pride.

"Are you sure, Dr. Waldo?" asked Chuck. "Maybe I should do one thing at a time?"

"Oh, no worries at all, young Charlie! This will work, certainly, get you home in a snap." He snapped, to demonstrate his point. He looked at their bags and his brow furrowed. "Do you not have all your backpacks anymore? What about your iPerts?"

"Sorry," said Ben. "I didn't have room to explain everything in the note. We lost them. We lost pretty much everything."

Dr. Waldo shook his head with a chuckle and reached into the bag he was carrying, pulling out another iPert and handed it to Chuck. "Here, good sir, take this. Call us when you get home. Eat your vegetables. Do your homework. Be a good boy!"

Chuck shook his head. "Good old Dr. Waldo! Don't change, my man!" He gave hugs all around, then activated the device Dr. Waldo had given him, and disappeared.

"I do hope that worked," said Dr. Waldo, under his breath.

"What?" said Charlie. "What was that?"

Dr. Waldo perked up. "Oh, my, did I say that out loud? Nothing, not a worry at all! Everything is fine, just fine! Chuck is probably home in the past as we speak. Now we need to get you home in the past too, to answer his call! Everyone ready? Of course I'll stay here, can't have two of me in one place, but I'll be there when you get there, just the old younger me, of course, perfect sense, yes, I'll see you there!"

"Dr. Waldo," said Eve, "if you don't mind, what's the rush? We're traveling back in time anyway. Does it really matter how fast we travel?"

"Good point, Eve!" Charlie said, and instinctively reached to high-five Chuck, forgetting for a moment that his parallel twin was gone. Emma reached up a hand to take Chuck's place. Charlie smiled at her. "Dork," he said.

"Dork," said Emma.

"Well, my, yes, I suppose you do have a good point. Still, I would think you all are quite ready to get home and tell us your tales?" said Dr. Waldo.

"We definitely, definitely are," said Emma. "Dr. Waldo, please send us home."

Moments later, they were back in the Hub, standing in the lounge they'd created themselves.

"Are we here on the right day?" asked Emma.

Ben looked at a small clock he'd created, which was sitting on an end table. "We're back. Same day we left, just a couple of hours later. As if nothing ever happened."

They all looked at each other. As if nothing ever happened? But so very, very much had happened.

"Kata? Kata, is that you?"

Eve's father, Milo, who had been briefing a scientist in the Hub on his latest travels, had seen the group reappear. At first his focus was on his daughter, but then he realized there was one more person in the group than when they had left.

"Hello, Milo," said Kata. "Yes, it's me." She walked to him, and together they went to find some space to talk.

Eve watched them go, mixed emotions wrestling on her face. "Well," she said. "We'll see." She sat down.

Rupert the two-dimensional elephant seemed somehow to realize they'd been gone longer than the clock indicated. He came over and raised his trunk in greeting.

"Hi, sweet Rupert," said Emma, slowly petting his side. She loved this giant two-dimensional elephant. She thought about Gesil's cats, how Gesil made them so they would disappear when she wasn't there, so they wouldn't get lonely. Emma stopped and looked at Rupert in his two-dimensional eye. "We're not meant to be alone, Rupert," she said. Then she stared into the space beside him, focusing and thinking very hard for several moments. Slowly, a new form shimmered into existence beside Rupert. Another elephant. A companion. "Rupert, meet Hermione," said Emma.

The elephants intertwined their paper-thin trunks and ambled off to get acquainted. Emma was sure she saw a bit of a smile on Rupert's mouth. She looked back at her own group and saw Charlie staring at her.

"What?" said Emma, defiant.

Charlie just laughed.

Just then, a phone on the table rang. Eve picked it up to answer it. "Hello?" she said. She paused to listen to the person on the other end of the line, then smiled. "Chuck is home safe," she said with a smile. "He says to tell you all hello." She hung up.

Dr. Waldo came jogging over with a tray of tea and scones. "Sent myself a note from the future, I did, so I'd be prepared for your return. Now then, children," he said. "Tell me everything."

So they did, everything from the dark galaxy stone and the magnets, to Kata's theory about interwoven universes, to an enthusiastic recounting of their new friends Aly and Bek and Gesil.

"We meet Gesil again in the future," said Emma. "You and me and Ben. When we're in a grand battle against The Void. About eleven years from now."

"We do?" said Dr. Waldo, his mind whirring. "My, my, my. Time is tricky! Time is tricky!"

"Gesil even wrote a book, *The Layers of Time*," said Emma. "I wish I'd remembered, I wanted to bring it back with me so I could read it."

"Hmm," said Dr. Waldo. "This is all very, very interesting." He started rapidly muttering to himself, but no one could make out any words. He ran off without warning.

"I don't know about the rest of you, but I, for one, could use a nap," said Charlie, watching Dr. Waldo race off to who knew where.

"And a nice, hot shower," said Emma.

"Speak for yourself," said Charlie.

"I was," said Emma. "If I never see these clothes again I'll be happy!"

They all raced off to the cabins where Eve and Milo and some of the others stayed when they were in the Hub. Showers were taken, then everyone quickly reconvened in the lounge.

"Now then, now then!" said Dr. Waldo, running back once they were all gathered together again.

He was not alone. With him was a tall woman with four arms, skin the color of a night forest, and a firm but kind and confident manner.

"Aly!" cried Emma, jumping up. "What? How?"

Aly beamed, spreading all her arms to embrace Emma in a big hug. "Your Dr. Waldo!"

Dr. Waldo blushed. "I, well, may have just done some time traveling just there. And distance. Yes, time and distance traveling. I went to visit Gesil and see her Hub, and she took me to meet Aly and Bek, and, well, Aly is interested in learning about the work we do in the Hub, and so, yes, yes, well, time travel and distance travel, you see. And Aly and I took a little side trip to hear the physicist Dr. Brian Greene speak at a lecture on your Earth, yes, we had a bit of a giggle, fascinating man, he's on the right track, on the right track! And layers of time! We have been studying it and you are correct, I think, I believe you are correct, there are layers of time!"

"You just studied all that? Just now? While we showered?" said Emma with disbelief. She laughed. "Dr. Waldo, I have missed you. It is good to be home."

Dr. Waldo waved a hand. "Well, you children go home and get

rested, visit with your parents, read some books, do what you do. In the meantime, Dr. Aly and I will do more research. Oh, and Emma, as to that matter we were concerned about, I've been studying, I don't think we need worry as much as we thought we might. I shall fill you in soon. And then when you're ready, we'll travel through time. If you'd like to, that is."

Suddenly, all the exhaustion Emma had felt was gone. "Travel through the layers of time?" She looked at the others.

"Yes," said Dr. Waldo. "Are you ready?"

Emma, Eve, and Ben and Charlie all spoke at once. "Ready!" they cheered.

"But maybe a nap first," said Charlie.

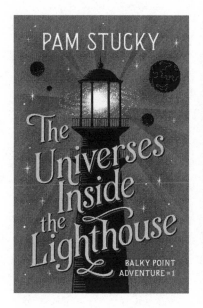

The adventure continues...

More aliens, more universes, more planets, more adventures!

Don't miss all the thrilling adventures of Emma, Charlie, Ben, Eve, Dr. Waldo, and all the rest! Start with Balky Point Adventures #1, *The Universes Inside the Lighthouse*, and continue with #3, *The Planet of the Memory Thieves*! Available in print and ebook now!

connect

The Secret of the Dark Galaxy Stone is the second book in the Balky Point Adventures young adult science fiction/science fantasy series. If you loved this book, tell your friends and let Pam know! Leave a review online, send a tweet to @pamstucky, and/or drop Pam a note at facebook.com/pamstuckyauthor. Thank you!

Stay tuned for more Balky Point Adventures! Be among the first to know when a new story is coming out by signing up for Pam's mailing list at pamstucky.com!

Visit pamstucky.com to find out more about Pam and her other fiction and non-fiction books.

acknowledgments

I visited Lightning Ridge, Australia, once, but that was a *very* long time ago. Thank you to the people at Lightning Ridge Tourism, who sent me information that helped me envision the town in my mind and, hopefully, describe it in a way that made it come alive for my readers. My apologies for the liberties I took in bringing a real town to a story of fiction. Visit Lightning Ridge on Earth in Australia, or online at www.lightningridgeinfo.com.au. I hope to stop by again myself one day soon and visit the labyrinth!

I was delighted to find a cover artist who captured my vision and made it a reality in both *The Universes Inside the Lighthouse* and now *The Secret of the Dark Galaxy Stone*. Thank you, Jim Tierney, for your time and talent. Visit Jim at www.jimtierneyart.com.

My early readers are priceless, both in their comments on a book as it starts to take shape, and in the support and encouragement they offer me along the way. I am eternally and infinitely grateful to Beth Stucky and Paula Hostick for their input and wisdom, and for cheering me on through the rough patches.

As always, to all my family, friends, and supporters, thank you for your kindness, thoughtfulness and never-ending encouragement. With people like you by my side, I know for sure that everything is possible.

24157502R00156

Made in the USA
San Bernardino, CA
03 February 2019